Doorway to Eden

by

K. D. McCrite

Doorway to Eden

Contact Information: info@thewildrosepress.com

Cover Art by *Debbie Taylor*

The Wild Rose Press, Inc.
PO Box 708
Adams Basin, NY 14410-0708
Visit us at www.thewildrosepress.com

Publishing History
First Edition, 2023
Trade Paperback ISBN 978-1-5092-5120-9
Digital ISBN 978-1-5092-5121-6
Previously Published: Oghma Creative Media, 2019

Published in the United States of America

A light, muted, as if from a small candle, burned in the farthest corner of the room. A strange, soft radiance, it beckoned her like a love call. She approached the corner with ambivalence, as though the light might be a warning, or maybe it was a promise unborn.

The light diminished as she approached, and by the time she got there, only shadows lingered. Squinting, searching for the lost source of brightness, she found nothing. A trick of her fear and imagination? Maybe her eyes, straining to see in the dark room, had conjured a ghost light to trick her brain.

Her gaze fell on the nearest pile of junk. She saw the corner of a blackened picture frame jutting above everything else. How long did she stand there, waiting...for what? She started to turn away but found herself held in place by unseen hands.

A shiver raced up her spine, and inevitability bore into her, as solid and undeniable as her own existence. She looked again at the corner of the picture frame, all that was visible from where she stood.

That was what she'd been looking for.

Praise for K. D. McCrite

"Lost in love and lost in time, Abbie and Andrew held me hostage in this riveting story of a passion challenged to bridge the bondage of another time." --Parris Afton Bonds

Dedication

Dedicated to Betty Cleland, my sister-dear, who introduced me early to stories with unusual twists and turns.

Prologue

August, One hundred years ago

Hester Kyle shook out the money she had stashed in the toe of an old stocking. She could count it all in a glance.

Clutching the money in one fist, she slipped from her room and through the house then darted out the back door. It wouldn't do for any of her family to know she had cash. Pa would demand it, Ma would cry for it, or one of the brats would steal it.

No sirree, nobody was taking what she'd scrubbed floors to earn. She had planned to buy herself a new dress, a fancy one with ruffles and lace in which to marry Andrew Wade, but all that had changed. Now she had something else she needed to do with her earnings, and Mr. High-and-Mighty Wade would rue the day he had turned away Hester Kyle's love.

The air smelled of baked earth and dry, sunburned grass. The early afternoon sun seemed to broil her in her skin, and there was not a whisper of a breeze. Hester hurried on her errand. It was too hot to be rushing like this, but she wanted to get to Granny Hodge right away. The old woman could cure all manner of ailments and disease with her herbs and suchlike, but everyone knew she also could cast monstrous dark spells.

Hester entered the woods. It was cooler there, and

shady. She toyed with the notion of stopping for a moment in the dim shadows, just to catch her breath, but the memory of rejection goaded her onward in search of Granny, in search of revenge.

Two days ago, she'd followed Andrew into these very woods, her heart racing and her body aching. He'd been at his Uncle Cy's house, spending a few hours with the old man, likely helping with repairs or a bit of farm work. He was like that, helping folks.

She'd surprised him by stepping out of the bushes near the creek. The day had been another scorcher and she'd left the top buttons of her red gingham dress open.

"What are you doing here?" he asked with a curious smile.

She flung back her rich, dark hair and met his eyes boldly. "I hear you're leavin' the Ridge again right soon."

He nodded. "I am."

"Comin' back?"

"Of course."

She took a step closer. "Whyn't you just stay?"

"I need to finish my training."

"You're a good enough doc, just like you are." She tossed back her hair again and moved another step toward him. "Folks come to you all the time for ailments and such when you're at home."

"But I'm not a doctor yet."

She closed the short distance between them. "You been going away to that school for a long time." He remained silent. She ran a bold finger down the line of buttons on his shirt. "Reckon I could make you stay."

He shook his head. "I'm going back day after tomorrow."

Hester linked her arms around his neck. She smelled her own musk, and it excited her. "I could make you stay." She kissed his throat and chin, sought to kiss his lips.

He turned his face away, gently unclasped her arms and pushed her away. "I'm sorry, Hester."

She took a deep breath, her generous bosom swelling, and started pulling down her bodice.

He grabbed her hands before she could bare her breasts. "Please, don't do this."

"Why not? They ain't a man on the Ridge that don't want me."

He said nothing.

"You ain't no different. You got all the parts, I reckon." She smiled knowingly. "You like women, don't you?" She grabbed one of his hands and pressed it against her breast. "You like me, don't you?"

He yanked free and stepped back. If he'd only give her a chance to prove what she could do, how much pleasure she could give him. Why did he resist what other men clambered to possess?

"It has nothing to do with whether I like you. My studies and my training come first. There's no time or place in my life for a girl. Any girl."

"Huh!" She stared hard at him. "Would you want me if you wasn't going back to the university?"

He frowned and looked away for a moment. "Hester, I—"

"Andrew Wade, you know I've been loving you ever since I was knee high. Ain't no man on this Ridge as fine actin' and good-lookin' as you. I'd make you a good wife, and you know it. Let me prove it to you." She began to unfasten more buttons, and when he tried to

3

stop her, she fought against him and freed herself. "Look!" she shouted as she tore open her dress. "Look what I got!"

He turned away, as if she was some kind of dirty, trashy thing that repulsed him. "For God's sake, cover yourself, Hester."

She wanted to smack him, to wake him up from his high-and-mighty dreams. "What kind of man are you, anyway?"

He began to walk away, not looking at her.

"Come back to me!" she screamed.

"I'm going."

She caught up to him and grabbed his arm, fingers biting hard into muscle. "You can't leave me, Andrew Wade."

He stopped walking and drew in a long breath. He turned, clasped her upper arm with a gentle but firm grip. He looked straight into her eyes. His eyes, so beautiful, so brown.

"Hester, I've been working for years on my medical degree. I will not abandon my—"

A wild hum rang in her ears. "I don't care what you want! I want to be your woman! Now!"

He shook his head but kept looking at her as if she were a child. "There are a lot of men on this Ridge who'd be honored to have you for a wife." His voice was as kind and quiet as always. "You're beautiful and passionate. It won't be hard for you to find a man to love you. I'm flattered that you want me, but you must understand – I'm not going to take you as my sweetheart, my lover, or my wife. Not now, not ever."

Why did he refuse when she ached so bad it hurt? She stared at him, breathing hard, while he simply gazed

4

at her. The pity in his eyes broke her, and she lost all sense. She lashed out, fingernails clawing the skin of his face and neck. He grabbed her wrists, but she was strong and fought like a trapped cat, struggling, screeching, cursing, trying to kick and claw, trying to destroy him and his stupid dreams.

"Stop it, Hester," he shouted. "I'm not changing my mind."

She kept fighting and screaming until she exhausted herself. With one last futile attempt to launch her knee into his crotch, she quit. Her face felt scorched and sweat poured from every part of her body.

"Let go of me," she said through clenched teeth.

He tightened his grip. "Are you finished with your fit?"

She bared her teeth, hissing at him. "Mister High-and-Mighty. You think you're too good for a Ridge girl like me. Reckon you think you're gonna get you some uppity rich girl somewhere, don't you? Some snotty gal with silk dresses and fancy hats with feathers who'll look down her nose at us Ridge girls." She tried to pull her arms free of his iron-hard clasp, and growled, "Let go of me!"

Watching her closely, he loosened his grip bit by bit. Hester yanked free and stepped back, rubbing her wrists.

"You just wait," she said. "You're gonna get what's coming to you, and when you do, I'm gonna laugh 'til the day I die. Just you wait and see."

She spat on the ground near his feet, turned and ran through the trees, away from him, back toward the scrappy, fallow farm where she lived.

****

These memories stoked her rage anew as she neared

Granny Hodge's cabin. She broke out of the trees and into a small clearing where the sun bore down like the wrath of God. Shading her eyes with one hand, she looked at the cabin on the other side of a meadow. The woman she sought was in front of the cabin, hoeing her garden patch.

Hester hurried toward the bent figure in the faded blue dress and sunbonnet. By the time she reached Granny, the woman had stopped her work. She clutched the wooden hoe handle in one gnarled hand and stared at Hester.

Hester shoved down her sudden fear, hid it beneath her hatred and fury. "I need your help, Granny."

The woman spat a stream of tobacco juice in the dirt near Hester's bare feet. She did not move her rheumy gaze from the younger woman, and for a long time she did not speak.

"It's a man what's brung you here," she said at last.

"Yes. Andrew Wade. Do you know him?"

"Reckon ever'body hereabouts knows him or knows of him."

Hester winced. Of course, everyone knew him. Everyone liked him, respected him. That's why she had wanted him. In her dreams, she wouldn't be the drunkard Etcyl Kyle's daughter, she would be Doctor Andrew Wade's wife. She would live in a big, fine house with servants and everybody bowing to her like she was somebody. But she had a new dream now, and it was fearsome, even to think about.

Still watching Hester, Granny worked the tobacco in her mouth and spat again.

"You ain't wantin' no love potion, but it'd sure be a heap better than what you got in mind."

6

"It's too late for love potions!" Hester flung back her hair. "I tried everything I could think of to make him want me, but he ain't got no heart. Nor anything else, I reckon, 'cause I couldn't even get him to lay with me." She pulled herself up straight and shook back her hair again. "Look at me, Granny. Ain't I enough for a man?"

Hester had a high, full bosom, a small waist, and round hips. Her dark hair hung, rich and full, to her waist. Her arms and legs were long and supple, her skin dusky and smooth. Thick, black lashes framed deep brown eyes. Her full lips were as red as fresh berries.

"You're right pretty," Granny said finally, "but you'd best forget that man. He's never made it a secret that he's gonna be the Ridge's first doctor. He don't want to be tied down with no woman and young 'uns, not for a long time. You'd best set your cap for somebody else."

Hester's renewed fury rang in her ears. She stomped one bare foot on the hot earth.

"I don't want no one else, and I ain't gonna wait for him to get done at that university. Look here." She dug the money out of her skirt pocket and opened her hand. "This here is all I got, and you can have it, every bit, if you'll put a spell on him."

The old woman's eyes brightened at the sight of the coins and crumpled bills. Granny's greed was almost as legendary as her healing skills.

She shifted her eyes up a moment. "Sounds to me like you ain't wantin' a spell. You're wantin' a curse."

"Call it what you will. I just want him punished for what he done to me!"

Granny Hodge looked at the money again. "That all you got?"

"I done told you. I been saving for months to buy me

7

a wedding gown, but I ain't gonna be getting that. So here it is. All I got."

The woman did not hesitate again. She scraped the money from Hester's sweaty palm. Hester stared at the dark, crescent-shaped birthmark on the woman's left hand. Everybody said it was the devil's mark, and that it was the devil himself who gave Granny her powers. Hester feared the devil, but he didn't scare her enough to keep her from using him when she thought he'd help. She watched Granny tuck the money into the deep apron pocket.

Once the old woman took the money, a change came over her. She became more misshapen and peculiar, even menacing.

"Come with me." She leaned the hoe against the side of her cabin and went inside without looking back.

Hester followed, but at a distance. She paused just outside the door then gathered her courage and stepped across the threshold.

The odor of herbs and stale wood smoke met her immediately. Every available space was filled with jars and vials. Drying herbs hung from the low ceiling. There was barely room for the bed, table and chair, cookstove and two rocking chairs. Ugly paintings, mostly trees and rocks, without much color or light hung on the walls. Hester liked paintings of big houses and people dressed in jewels and fancy clothes. Granny's dark pictures made her feel strange inside her skin. She looked away.

Granny Hodge removed her sunbonnet, revealing flattened, sweat-damp gray hair caught in a wispy knot on the crown of her head. She spat her wad of tobacco into a rusty can then drank a dipperful of water from the bucket on the table.

Settling into one of the cane-backed rockers, she fixed her eyes on Hester who stood unmoving in the doorway.

"It's right hot today. Git yourself a drink of water. Then set down." She pointed at the other rocker.

Hester declined the water but sat on the edge of her chair, tipping it forward. She twisted her fingers while Granny rocked back and forth, staring straight ahead.

After a bit, Hester said, "Well, ain't you gonna do anything?"

The silent old woman continued to rock, her chair thumping a slow, hypnotic rhythm. Hester jumped up. She prowled the room like a restless cat, but she kept glancing at Granny who seemed to have forgotten all about her.

"Look, if you ain't gonna do anything, I want my money back."

The rheumy old eyes shifted to her. "Set down."

Hester returned to her chair, again perched on the edge like a hungry bird.

"Set back."

"But—"

"I said set back."

Hester squirmed but did as she was told. Granny Hodge continued to rock and to stare at her. She didn't like being watched that way, like the old woman was crawling around inside her mind, digging out secret places and private thoughts. She tried to look away, but Granny's gaze trapped her like prey.

Soon, her body grew heavy, her joints liquid. No matter how hard she tried, she could not force her eyelids to stay open. The thump-thump of Granny's rocker was like a heartbeat.

K. D. McCrite

"Tell me what you want, girl."

Hester heard the question from a great distance. Her fury no longer burned like a wildfire. In fact, nothing within her had the power to stir. She tried to open her eyes but failed.

She struggled to push out the words. "Punish him."

Granny Hodge grunted. "So what's that mean? He didn't do nothin' wrong."

"Make him pay for what he did to me." The words came more easily that time, as though her tongue and lips were waking up while the rest of her body napped.

Granny heaved a deep sigh. "You want him to be ugly? Poor? Sick or mangled or blind? You want him…dead?"

The word hung heavily between them, like a dense black curtain. Hester felt a tiny shiver of fear, but in her relaxed state, it quickly retreated.

"I want him to feel how I been feelin' for so long. He oughta yearn for somethin' so bad it's all he thinks about, even when he sleeps. He should try to get what he wants 'til it's like his heart's gonna bust, like he's sure he's done gone crazy, locked up with his wantin' and achin'. And then, after a long, long time, he can die."

The request seemed to linger in the air like a smothering cloud. She struggled to breathe, could not move, could not speak. There was no sound or movement around her. She labored to come out of the fog, or dream, or whatever it was.

From far away but growing closer, came the quiet rhythm of Granny's rocking chair. The sound suddenly ceased.

"You go home now."

Granny's voice drew Hester into full wakefulness,

but she was overcome by panic and confusion. Her fingers dug into the arm of the chair, fearing she'd fly out of it if she let go. Little by little she was able to open her eyes and her mind began to clear. The day seemed far advanced although she had been unaware of its passing.

Granny Hodge stood at the small table and stirred something in a pot.

"Did I sleep?" Granny said nothing. Hester reared up in the chair, trying to see what was in the pot. "Are you making a potion for Andrew?"

The old woman did not look at her. "I'm fixin' my supper. You go now."

"Oh, but you have to—"

"You go now." The undertone running through Granny's voice caused chills to rise on Hester's skin.

She stood and remained unmoving for a short space of time. When her rubbery legs found strength, she edged toward the door of the tiny cabin, wondering if Granny would say more.

She licked her dry lips and cleared her throat. "When…when will he get what's coming to him?"

Granny turned slightly and looked at her from rheumy eyes.

"Everybody gets their reward or punishment – in due time."

"But…"

The old woman carried her pot to the stove. Hester knew that even if she stood in the doorway all night, Granny would not say another word.

Daylight was just an orange smear along the western edge of the woods when she left the cabin. Darkness greeted her as she entered the trees, and it grew denser the farther she plunged into the forest. But Hester had been born and raised on Sumac Ridge; neither the black shadows which leaped and shivered, nor the shrill night sounds frightened her.

The strange weakness she'd felt at Granny's lifted completely. Andrew Wade would get his comeuppance, sure enough. Joy welled within her, and she grinned in anticipation. Him and his highfalutin plans to be the first doctor on the Ridge. She'd soon be avenged, just wait and see. He'd be needing a doctor himself before Granny's spell was finished with him, yes sirree—

She fell headlong over a tree root and crashed hard against the earth. Unable to breathe, sure her heart had exploded, she lay without moving. Then air rushed back into her lungs, and she remained on the ground, giving herself a moment to recover.

She started to stand but paused as a weird, prickly feeling brushed across the back of her neck. Was somebody spying on her? She turned her head slowly, sensing danger but seeing no one.

"Who's there?"

She peered into the last of the dying light, straining to hear above the thunder of her pounding heart.

"That you, Granny? I done told you, I ain't got no more money."

What she saw froze her blood. A few feet away, its long sleek body coiled and poised to strike, a huge snake had fixed its unrelenting stare on her.

The creature began to inch forward. She screamed, tried to scramble away, but fear turned her clumsy and she sprawled on the ground again. She got to her feet and began running, dodging trees and undergrowth.

The serpent played with her, chasing her deeper into

the woods. Her legs grew heavy and awkward, each fleeing step more difficult than the last one. She fell again.

Heaving and terrified, Hester tried to stand, tried to catch her breath. The night around her was black and unknown. Where was she? Where was the snake? Maybe she'd outrun the evil thing. But, no. She could feel its gaze, sense its intelligence and its intent.

Fangs, sharp and burning, sunk into the soft, pulsing vein in her throat.

Venom poured into her blood like a river of fire. She grabbed the thick, lashing body and tried to yank it free, but the more she tugged and fought, the more deeply the fangs settled.

She screamed again and did not stop screaming until her throat swelled shut, and she collapsed, her rapidly bloating body turning blue. When her heartbeat ceased, the snake released itself and slithered away into the night.

****

Granny Hodge, enjoying her pipe on the front porch, stared across the darkened meadow toward the woods. Hester's cries were far away, but the night air had carried them clearly. When the screaming stopped, Granny heaved herself out of the porch chair and knocked her pipe against the rough-hewn support post.

She gazed toward the woods again.

People did not realize the force of Granny's curses. Sometimes, if there was enough hatred in the one who had come begging for a curse, the power spilled over on them, and they got caught in their own black deed. She could tell them, of course, but most folks wouldn't pay for a spell or a curse if they thought something bad might happen to them. She could tell folks, of course, but she never would.

Once in a while, some good would come along to break a curse. It happened only rarely, more's the pity, because Andrew was a good man. He did not deserve what was going to happen to him, and Granny regretted what she had to do. But a pact was a pact, and she had to keep her part of the bargain. If she failed, she'd suffer a worse fate than that selfish young woman who now lay dead in the woods.

The ancient woman took the money from her pocket and looked at it. The amount was pitiful, but it was more than she had this morning. She stumped into the cabin and pulled out the intricately carved ebony chest from beneath her bed. She took a key from her pocket, unlocked the chest, and pushed back the lid.

Gold and silver shone in the lamp light while bright jewels winked and sparkled. Granny added Hester's pittance to the store then locked the trunk and hid it once more. Maybe someday, if she saved enough, she could buy back what she had lost so long ago.

Until then, there was nothing to prevent her from making a way out for Andrew, if the right person came along…and if that person came in time.

The old woman went out into her yard a few steps and looked up at the sliver of moon, a crescent-shape like the one on her hand. She began to chant:

"Passion spurned;
hatred burned.
A curse of thirteen hundred moons must pass.
Then death will come,
unless love breaks the curse
and sets the prisoner free."

The dark night shivered around her as Granny heaved a sigh of sorrow. She turned and went back into her cabin to prepare her canvas and sort her paints.

Chapter 1

Andrew carefully arranged his two new shirts in his valise and looked around the small, sunny bedroom to see if he had forgotten anything. This was his final year, and the last time he'd leave for the university. At the age of thirty, most medical students had finished their studies and were already practicing. He had worked and saved his money to pay for that education long after others of his age were in their final years of study.

"Don't forget to take your dinner, son." Ruby Jean Wade came into the room. In her plump, work-worn hands she carried a small, brown-wrapped parcel containing fried chicken and thick slices of buttered bread. "It's a long train ride back to your school."

He stopped adjusting the straps on his valise to turn to her.

"Thanks, Mama," he said, accepting the food. "I'll think of you when I eat this."

Looking away, she nodded and blinked hard. Her lower lip trembled. He put his arms around her, hugged her and stood back.

"Now, Mama, how many times have I left? Don't I always come back? This will be the last time. Next summer, when I return, I won't have to leave the Ridge again."

Ruby Jean crimped her lips into a hard, straight line as she looked up at her son.

"I know that. Don't never think I doubt it for a minute." She reached up and laid one calloused palm against his cheek. "But I'm gonna miss you just the same. Can't a-one of you kids leave home without leaving an empty place in the house."

"Mama, you got seven young 'uns to take care of. Here I am, over thirty. It's time I'm out of your house."

The hand that lay against his face gently pinched his cheek.

"Don't matter if you're three or thirty-three. Ever' last one of you kids is still my baby and will be 'til I'm moldering in my grave."

"I know that, Mama." He smiled at her. "We all know that."

"See that you remember it, too. When you bring some fancy young wife from the city, see that she understands it, and we'll get along just fine."

He laughed as he packed up the books he had not sent ahead to the university. He closed and strapped the case and set it on the bed next to his valise.

"Mama, how many times do I have to tell you, there is no young woman, fancy from the city or otherwise?"

Ruby Jean, ever the vigilant housekeeper, squinted at his dresser top then wiped her hand across the invisible film of dust.

"Hester Kyle seems to think there is. Seems to think *she* is, the way she's been hanging all over you lately. Disgraceful how she acted at the church supper last week. I hope you don't take up any notions about her."

He touched a long scratch on his jaw and silently recalled his last encounter with the woman.

Now, two days later, in the warm, sunny bedroom of his home and with the wound on his face healing and

Hester an ugly, fading memory, he said, "Mama, don't you worry about me having any notions about Hester Kyle. I think she finally understands how it is."

"Hmm." Ruby Jean eyed him. "Stick by your guns, son. You've worked too hard to let any piece of skirt ruin your life."

"I know."

"'Course I ain't sayin' you shouldn't ever have a wife. You're gonna need one someday."

He smiled at her as he picked up his valise and the case with his books and the food she had prepared for the trip. "Let someday take care of itself, Mama. Today has its own concerns."

At the gate of the clean, shady front yard, his young twin sisters ran to him. From the nearest field one of the brothers strode toward them. His father and other two brothers were in the meadows on the far side of the farm, and his other sister was in town, working as a seamstress at Miss Betsy's. They had said their goodbyes at breakfast that morning.

"You comin' back at Christmas?" Karol and Maggie, the twins, asked in unison.

He put down his cases and gathered both girls to him for a long, hard bear hug.

"I am." He let them go. "The two of you help Mama around the house without fussing and complaining."

"We will," they chorused.

Matthew-Levi, Andrew's younger brother, approached them. "Don't reckon you'll ever take up a winnowing hook again."

Andrew grinned. "Maybe not, but I can stitch you up when you get too rambunctious at the Harvest Dance."

Matthew-Levi grinned back. "Shucks," he muttered. Matthew-Levi was too bashful even to go to the dance.

Andrew bent to pick up his cases again, and as he straightened, he ran his gaze over his home once more. When he was away from home, he always kept in his mind the cheering remembrance of this rambling, gray-boarded house, comfortable in the cooling shade of the towering oak and maple trees. This image always sustained him. Today, however, as he took in the sight and breathed deeply the scent of warm earth and Mama's summer flowers, it comforted him to know this was his final leave-taking. Next year, he'd be living on Sumac Ridge for good, and he'd see this home and his family every day.

He kissed his mother and little sisters goodbye and nodded to Matthew Levi. "I'll be home for a few days at Christmas. Keep the home fires burning for me."

Ruby Jean futilely sniffed back a sob. Karol and Maggie began to wail. Matthew-Levi shifted his feet and rubbed his jaw. Andrew gave them all a smile and went out the front gate.

****

The day was hot and still and dry. Heat waves danced ahead of him on the scorched, shadeless stretches of dusty road as he walked to the small town of Smith. It wasn't much of a town, just the train station, general store, post office, lumber mill and Miss Betsy's Sewing Parlor where she made clothes for a big store in St. Louis. Trains stopped in Smith only twice a week. He wondered if the little settlement would ever grow into a real town. Most folks in the area were farmers or worked in the timber. He planned to build his home and office in town so folks could find him easily, and he had the perfect location picked out across the street from Miss Betsy's and the general store.

The rattling wheels of an approaching wagon interrupted his thoughts. The big man on the seat took off his slouch-hat and waved it over his head.

"Howdy, Andrew!" he hollered as he got closer. "On yer way back to the big city?"

"Hello, Earl. I'm on my way back. I start my training with Doctor Lowell this year. You've been to the mill this morning?"

"Yep. Goin' home fer dinner. You might just as well come along. Lottie and the kids'd relish seeing you."

Andrew shook his head and set his luggage on the ground. In this heat it seemed to get heavier with every step.

"Got to catch the train if I want to make it back by Monday. How's Lottie feeling today?"

Earl pulled out a ragged, limp red bandana and wiped his face and neck. "Oh, tolerable, I reckon. She says this weather is right hard on her, says this is the last young 'un she wants to have. Said as how she wished you was back fer good 'cause she knows you'd take care of her if things get…well, you know how it was with the last 'un. Granny Hodge did her best, but…"

"I don't think I could have done anything more, Earl. Babies sometimes just don't grow right in the womb. Not the fault of anyone, it's just the way of things."

Earl shook his head and stared in the distance at nothing. "Reckon you're right. Still, I can't help but believe having an educated doc will make a big difference in these parts." His gaze rested on Andrew. "You took right good care of me last Christmas when I broke my leg."

Andrew smiled. "It was Granny who taught me how to set a broken bone, Earl. Trust her to take care of you. I'm hoping that when I set up practice, she'll assist me. She's too old to be way out there in the woods by herself. Assisting me would give her a good reason to move closer to folks."

The man squinted at him. "Son, don't you know Granny has been old since I was kid? Pop said she was old when he was a youngster." He mopped the back of his neck again. "I've always thought they was something peculiar about that old woman, with all her potions and tonics and the way she can look at you outta her eyes. And that mark on her hand? Folks say it's the devil's mark."

"Granny's got a reputation, but she's got a good heart."

Earl scratched a whiskery jaw. "She learn you how to cast spells and whatnot?"

Andrew laughed and picked up his suitcases. "No. She keeps all that to herself. Earl, it was good to see you. I need to get going. Tell Lottie to rest every day and eat a good diet. Get those kids to take on more of the chores. She's not as young as she used to be."

"No, she ain't. I wish she wasn't havin' to go through this again."

"Well, it takes two, Earl."

The man looked down, his face red. "I know it. I get ashamed sometimes."

"No help comes from being ashamed. Just remember what we talked about, and the time of the month when conception is most likely to happen."

"I'll do that."

"I need to get to the station now. Don't want to miss my train."

The other man looked up. "Want me to take you into town? Be glad to do it, Andrew."

He shook his head and started to move away. "Thanks, anyway. You just get on home to Lottie and the kids. She's probably got dinner already waiting for you."

The wagon resumed its clattering way down the road, and he continued his walk in the opposite direction. The last stand of woods before reaching town was just ahead. Eager to leave the hot glare of the August sun for cooling shade, he quickened his step.

He heard a distant moan and stopped. Had he really heard someone in pain?

"Hello? Is someone there? Do you need help?"

When no one answered, he continued walking. At the edge of the woods he heard the sound again, louder this time. Definitely a groan of illness or pain.

He put down his cases again, pulled his watch from his pocket. If he missed the train today, Matthew Levi or his father would have to take him in the wagon to the next train station, a day's ride from where he stood. Otherwise, he would have to wait until next week. Arriving late at the university and missing the first round of study was a bad idea, but he refused to ask his father to miss two days of work.

The groan came again, more intense, more desperate. Miss the train or not, he would not go away if someone needed help.

Settling his burdens under a scraggly blackjack tree just off the road, he followed the sound into the woods, seeking the one who needed him. He saw nobody but called out again.

"Here," a weak voice spoke from a dense thicket nearby. "Please, please help me."

He crashed through the woods. "I'm coming. Help is on the way."

Then, as he neared his destination, an unexpected cool, almost cold wind blew over him. He pushed aside a thick, tangled branch full of thorns. The next step he took seemed endless as he fell into a cold darkness.

Chapter 2

August, one century later

The shop smelled of dankness and neglect. It was unlike the stores Abigail Matthews preferred. She usually limited her shopping to high-end designer boutiques. For the next two weeks, though, she planned to step out of the routine and look for a missing piece of herself. She sought something that would restore her trust and banish the self-doubt that seemed to have taken over. Four years of criminal law practice without a break was more than enough. And after what had happened a week earlier, she might very well be making a major life change soon.

So there she stood on the threshold of the open doorway into the dismal little junkorama, feeling fidgety and more than a little out of place. In the back of her mind, she acknowledged that something had drawn her there, tugging mentally at her skirt like a persistent child. She'd pulled into the rut-filled, unpaved parking lot of the Lost Treasures Shop a few minutes earlier with a nagging sense of anticipation—or was it a sense of foreboding? The parking lot was deserted except for her pearl-white luxury sedan and an old gray van with its rusty grill nuzzled up to the shop's peeling paint. Scraggly weeds grew around rotted tires.

Abbie stopped just inside the door and curled her nose at the moldy odor. Maybe she should turn around right now. Or maybe she should at least take a look around the place. So many wrong decisions lately made her ambivalent about everything. She stood, clenching and relaxing her fingers, trying to rid herself of this anxiety.

No one moved. No one made a sound. The place was deserted and deservedly so. Who could stand to shop there, let alone work in such a morbid little establishment?

"You'll find what you seek below."

Startled, she glanced around, searching through the dim interior with straining eyes.

"Hello?"

She nearly jumped out of her skin when a gnome-like figure in a dark, shapeless garb stepped from behind a shelf and into the aisle few feet away.

"You'll find what you seek below."

"Oh, but I'm not really—"

"Below." It was almost a command.

The person turned, drifted away into the murky shadows. The silence was complete—no shuffling steps, no whisper of clothing to mark passage. It was as though the creature had never been.

Abbie took a few steps toward the back of the store, pretty sure the person had gone that way.

"I'm not really looking for anything," she called. "Actually, I don't know why I even…" She let the words evaporate into the musty, empty air.

I don't even know why I stopped here, she finished in her head.

She should leave right then. There was something weird and spooky about this whole situation. Her friend, Linda Richardson, dubbed "Lefty" because of her powerful left-handed softball pitching, lived at least another hundred miles down the road. Abbie had promised to be there before dark.

Instead of leaving, she walked toward the back of the store, toward a small open doorway. The narrow steps led down into a cellar so dark it looked endless. What lurked in that darkness? Trolls with long, gnarled fingers reaching for her? Demons with grotesque red eyes and fiendish grins? If she went down, would she be able to return to the world of sunlight and air? Abbie rarely gave in to such foolish imaginings. She wanted to turn away, but the temptation of the unknown abyss pulled her without mercy.

Ridiculous. She was being utterly ridiculous. The only menace down there likely was spiders—she shuddered at the mere thought—and maybe rats.

Abbie stood on the third step down, unaware that she had gone that far. More than ever she wanted to turn and flee. Instead, she followed the urge to continue downward. Slowly, with fingertips barely touching the filthy railing, she descended, one foot, pause, the other foot, pause, until she reached the final step.

She waited until her eyes grew accustomed to the darkness. One small window on the back wall allowed a bit of daylight to seep through its dirt. A single dim bulb, suspended from a filthy cord, offered the only other source of illumination. The odor of mildew and decay nearly made her retch.

She jumped as something small and furry scurried past her feet. How many more small, furry "somethings" might she encounter? To a city girl accustomed to living in a spacious high rise and working in another tall, gleaming building, the cramped cellar was as foreign to her as a meal of dirt.

She wanted to ignore her bizarre need to be in that awful place, and escape. She turned and looked up the stairway. Her heart stopped. The grotesque body was etched against the gloomy light behind it, every detail outlined, from the misshapen head and humped shoulders to the stumpy legs. The unblinking eyes, riveted on her, glittered eerily although no light shone to reflect from them.

Abbie choked, trying to swallow the dryness in her throat. A coughing fit brought tears to her eyes, and by the time her vision cleared, no one stood at the head of the stairs. Maybe the figure was some part of a weird hallucination brought on by last week's horror and her subsequent sleepless nights.

She stood frozen, hardly breathing, wary of going forward into the cellar, terrified of returning upstairs until she realized facing the shadowed unknown terrified her less than encountering the dwarfed, menacing figure above.

A shudder ran through her, a sudden chill that did not come from the dank air but rather from deep inside her. Unless she moved, the icy tremors creeping through her body would render her immobile, unable to do anything but stand in place like a ninny. She would die, quaking like a dry leaf on a dead limb, in that black hole. Through sheer willpower, she turned and walked one deliberate step after another until she was out of sight if the creature upstairs returned to stare down at her.

She lost her anxiety for a few moments as she took in the collection the basement held: a pile—waist high and six feet wide—held plastic flowers in assorted faded colors, two rusty bicycle frames without wheels or seats, a huge three-legged metal desk with one side smashed in, several boxes of moldy books and magazines, and heap after heap of old clothes congested with mildew.

How could anyone find anything down there? Surely no lost treasures existed in that nasty junk. And she wasn't looking for anything, anyway, no matter what that odd person had said.

She took a deep breath, exhaled through her mouth, hating the odor that surrounded her. That stink would likely stay with her long after she left the shop.

"I'm getting out of here," she muttered.

Gathering courage which seemed to have ebbed in the last few minutes, she drew in another breath of foul air and turned. Her teeth were clamped, her fingers clenched into tight knots around her purse. She would have scurried from that place, but stopped, her attention captured like a wild bird in a trap.

A light, muted, as if from a small candle, burned in the farthest corner of the room. A strange, soft radiance, it beckoned her like a love call. She approached the corner with ambivalence, as though the light might be a warning, or maybe it was a promise unborn.

The light diminished as she approached, and by the time she got there, only shadows lingered. Squinting, searching for the lost source of brightness, she found nothing. A trick of her fear and imagination? Maybe her eyes, straining to see in the dark room, had conjured a ghost light to trick her brain.

Her gaze fell on the nearest pile of junk. She saw the corner of a blackened picture frame jutting above everything else. How long did she stand there, waiting…for what? She started to turn away but found herself held in place by unseen hands.

A shiver raced up her spine, and inevitability bore into her, as solid and undeniable as her own existence. She looked again at the corner of the picture frame, all that was visible from where she stood.

That was what she'd been looking for.

But her rational mind told her she sought nothing. So why did she feel as though a long search neared its end? Rather than hash the notion in her mind, she gingerly plucked away the debris of dank cardboard boxes and ragged books mottled with mildew. She stifled a cry when a bloated spider ran across a brittle plastic raincoat the color of a rotten orange. It scuttled into a crevice in the rubble. Shoving aside her antipathy for eight-legged creatures, she continued to clear away junk surrounding her target. Her heartbeat accelerated. What was she about to find?

Her gaze rested on the corner of the painting. Holding her purse strap between her teeth, she reached in and lifted the painting from its miserable corner, ignoring the cobwebs that came with it. Dust caked the canvas so thickly she could barely discern the large house with its mansard roof and arched windows. It was surrounded by trees and thickets, all under a sky so ominous her skin nearly prickled from the approaching storm.

The painting embodied how she'd been feeling lately, lost in desolation of mind and spirit, alone and in need of something fine to restore her. As primitive and disturbing as the image of the house and storm was, she had to have it.

Releasing her fear of the peculiar creature upstairs, Abbie carried her find to the cluttered, shadowy room above. The sound of shuffling footsteps preceded the appearance of the gnome-like person.

"I see you found it." A smile creased the misshapen face, revealing stubby yellow teeth.

The person went behind the counter at the front window and stepped into a full shaft of dusty sunlight. In the brightness, Abbie realized the little figure was an elderly woman, crippled by advanced arthritis. The deep creases and folds of time had settled into her face, and wisdom lay in her dim eyes. Abbie felt like a fool with a runaway imagination. Since when had she become so uncharitable without cause?

"Did it call to you?" the old woman asked. "This painting?"

"Yes. In fact, it..." Abbie looked at her closely, trying to read the expression in the old eyes. "How did you know I'd find something I wanted...something I had to have?"

The woman smiled an odd smile. "I only directed you downstairs. You found it on your own."

Abbie leaned the painting against the counter and opened her purse. "How much do I owe you?"

The old woman eyed her from head to toe. Abbie's ash blonde hair in its neatly coiled chignon, the wheat-colored linen sheath dress, designer leather purse, and manicured nails suggested wealth. Abbie braced herself for an astronomical figure.

"Since you need it," the woman said, "maybe you oughta just take it."

"Take it? I couldn't do that. Here." She handed over her credit card.

The woman ignored the card and stared past her, into the shadows of the shop.

"Greed is right costly," she muttered. Looking at

Abbie again, she said, "One dollar for every minute you were down there looking for that painting."

Abbie blinked.

"I have no idea how long, but surely it's worth more than the short time I was in the basement."

The woman rubbed a deformed thumb across the crescent-shaped mark on the back of her thick hand.

"Time's a funny thing," she said. "Sometimes hours seem like minutes and minutes seem like years. Years can feel like eternity, like forever."

"Yes, but I still don't know—"

"Time is very important."

Maybe the woman was senile. Maybe she was just eccentric. Either way, Abbie wanted to pay her something. She put the credit card back in her wallet and pulled out a checkbook. She filled out an amount she thought was fair.

"Will you accept this?" She tore out a check and handed it over.

"Yes."

The shopkeeper did not even look at it. Finally, Abbie laid the check on the counter near the cash register.

"Remember what I said. For some folks, time can be *a matter of life and death.*" Here she peered straight into Abbie's eyes. "Others must find what they come to the earth to do or die trying."

The old woman seemed to pluck statements out of the air, or maybe out of Abbie's thoughts. She shivered.

"I'll remember."

She got as far as the door when the woman's voice stopped her:

"*Passion spurned;*

31

hatred burned.
A curse of thirteen hundred moons must pass.
Then death will come,
unless love breaks the curse
to set the prisoner free."

Abbie stared at the woman who moved from the sunlit corner and blended into the shadows.

"Hurry. Time grows short."

Granny Hodge watched the young woman drive away. Would it work, this undoing she'd slipped in? Andrew Wade's days were almost at an end. If he was unable to fulfill his own destiny because of the curse, it would be one more wicked deed committed by an ancient woman who only wanted to be released from her dark power.

Granny closed her eyes. Behind the lids she saw the old chest, full of coins and jewelry, ancient currency as well as new. The uncounted years of saving—what had it all brought her? She could never buy her freedom from the unholy ability. Of what use was riches to the one who had endowed her with that power? He had her, and others like her, to do his awful work. They would do anything he asked them to do just to receive the desires of their hearts.

For Granny, the desire had been immortality, life without end. But foolishly, she had neglected to request that youth and health accompany her immortality. She had continued to grow older and more infirm, and by now she had passed centuries in this crippled, pain-filled body.

Having exhausted every bargaining notion she could imagine, Granny wondered if doing good deeds were the antidote for the black actions of her past. The problem with good works is that the recipients always had questions for which Granny had no reply. The deeds must be accepted with blind faith.

Turning from the window, the old woman wondered how many people had the courage of blind faith. Not many. But maybe this time, it would be different.

Chapter 3

Abbie called Lefty, who answered on the first ring.

"This better be you, Abigail Jane Matthews."

"It's me. And I'm late."

"No kidding. Is everything all right?"

Abbie hesitated. She had driven these last three hours of her trip, contemplating the daunting knowledge that her life would never be the same. Not that change was a bad thing, but the unknown yawned before her.

"Of course. Everything is…it's fine."

Lefty never let anything get past her. "It doesn't sound fine, Abbie. *You* don't sound fine."

The glaring late afternoon sun broiled her through the windshield.

"Let's save this conversation until later. I'm in Tomville, sitting in front of Shelby's Shop 'N Go where you told me to stop and call you. Are you sure my GPS won't get me there?"

"It will. But in the most round-about way possible and will take you twice as long."

"Sounds crazy to me, but I'll take your word for it. So, tell me how to get to your house from here, and give me good directions, please. I do *not* want to get lost out here in the sticks."

"I wish you could forget about being lost in the Appalachians that time."

Abbie had tried and failed to shove aside the

memory that continued to haunt her two decades later.

"You weren't there. Lost, alone, while the sky and the woods got darker and darker. I was a scared little kid, Lefty. I still have nightmares and wake up terrified."

"I understand," the other woman said softly. "I really do. But I promise today *you will not get lost*."

"Hmm. Maybe. This is my first time in the Ozarks, you know." She glanced at the landscape. "I didn't realize there were so many steep hills and big trees."

Lefty laughed. "You are in one of the oldest mountain ranges in the world, hon, and you're going to find thick forests and rugged hills. Millions of years have worn away the sharp edges of the Ozarks, but they're mountains nonetheless."

"Oh, goodness. What have I got myself into?"

"Tell you what. If you're not here in fifteen minutes, I'll come looking for you, so don't worry. Okay?"

"Promise?"

"Absolutely."

The knots of tension between Abbie's shoulder blades lessened a little.

"Lefty, you're the best friend in the world."

"Aw, shucks, ma'am," her friend drawled like a cowboy in an old television show. "Just do me a big favor, all right?"

"What's that?"

"Do not, repeat, *do not* call me Lefty in front of anyone else. I'm a respected recovery room nurse. It wouldn't do for a slew of patients, not to mention doctors and co-workers, to start calling me 'Lefty'. It might damage my credibility or something. Would you want someone named Lefty taking *your* blood?"

Abbie laughed with her, although she thought her

35

friend was only half-joking.

"I will not spill your deep, dark secret."

"Great! Now, listen, girl, hurry yourself along now, because I have supper cooking."

Ten minutes later, following Lefty's detailed directions, Abbie pulled into the driveway of the shadiest yard she had ever seen. Lefty emerged from a deep front porch.

Abbie jumped out of her car almost before she turned off the engine. She ran to Lefty and flung her arms around the woman. They had been best friends since second grade. As college roommates, they'd been inseparable until a law office and a hospital took them in different directions. Abbie offered the comfort of her home when Lefty's Aunt Sally, her only living relative, passed away, and Lefty never ceased to cheer on Abbie's upwardly mobile climb.

There was very little they did not know about each other. Although nine hundred miles and three years had separated them when Lefty moved from Ohio to Arkansas, the women kept in close touch through text messages, phone calls, and email. It was Lefty to whom Abbie had turned this past Monday when she realized she could not return to life as she knew it.

"I need to get away from here, from everything," she had said on the telephone to her friend that night. "I need time to think. And I really need to talk to you."

"By all means, get yourself down here. But there's a little conflict. I'm scheduled to speak at a conference in Savannah next week. I'll be gone for several days. I'd try to get out of it, but this has been scheduled for months. And, of course, I'll be driving, not flying. You know me and my need to be firmly grounded to the good earth. You said you're leaving Dayton in the morning? That'll give us a few days to visit before I must leave."

Abbie had been bitterly disappointed, of course. Lefty was the only person she knew and trusted well enough to listen to her story without making judgments. And the woman had a remarkable knack for being objective in spite of their close friendship.

"I'd be more than happy for you to go with me, Abbie. You know I'd be gone all day, but we could run around Atlanta in the evenings. See the sights, do the town. You know."

Abbie took a deep breath and let it out slowly.

"I need to get away from the city. I need peace and quiet, and plenty of time to think. That's why I thought…"

"At the risk of repeating myself: come down here. It's quiet and bucolic. You can tell me what's going on, and we'll talk about it. While I'm gone, you can have the place to yourself with time and solitude for thinking."

It was not the ideal situation, but it would do. And maybe having time to herself, away from everything familiar was exactly what Abbie needed.

"You're the best friend ever."

Now, two days later, the friends were laughing and hugging after their lengthy separation.

"Three years is too long!" Abbie said.

"*Much* too long. Let's not let it happen again." Lefty linked her arm with Abbie's. "I've missed you! Come into the house. You must be starved."

"Yes, I am." They walked across the shady lawn toward the house. "And tired. And travel stained." She stopped when they reached the steps and looked around Lefty's home. "This is absolutely beautiful."

"Thank you." Lefty squeezed her arm. "Knowing how you like glass and steel and busy sidewalks, I hope this spot in the back of beyond won't be a disappointment to you. It's very quiet here. Not much excitement, I'm afraid."

"I need to do some serious soul-searching. I *need* the quiet and the peace."

"Here's the place to do it." Lefty gestured to the front porch, the roses, and the towering trees. The lowering sunlight gilded everything they looked at. "I've prepared a room upstairs for you, and it has a beautiful view over the back yard and the pond. Perfect for deep thinking. It was my room years ago when I came to visit Aunt Sally in the summer. One year I pretended I was Emily Dickinson."

"Oh, I remember that!" Abbie laughed. "You wrote bad poetry."

"Bad, nothing. It was *terrible*."

"Well, at least you gave it up for softball."

"Thank God for small favors."

They giggled like schoolgirls as they went inside. Waning daylight streamed through sparkling windows. Abbie eyed the blue and white décor, the collection of patchwork quilts, the antique porcelain knickknack collection. Braided rugs in shades of blue adorned gleaming hardwood floors. The décor was a far cry from the sleek stainless and white leather of her apartment, but she liked what she saw.

"This is lovely. So welcoming."

"Thanks. I find my tastes are turning more toward the simple and homey these days. Remember how we decorated our dorm room in red and black?"

Abbie laughed. "*Tres chic.*"

Lefty nodded, grinning. "Very *tres chic*. Well, thank goodness those days are over! No more posters, no more tragic poetry. We've grown up."

"Haven't we just."

Lefty patted her hand. "Sounds like we definitely need to talk. But for now, why don't you freshen up then come into the dining room for dinner?"

A few minutes later, Abbie entered the cozy, fragrant dining room. The aroma of warm bread, roasted meat, and cinnamon enticed her appetite.

"Bearing in mind your picky palate," Lefty called from the kitchen, "I cooked what I hoped you'd eat. Baked chicken all right?"

"Wonderful." Abbie sat down at the table with its snowy linen cloth and blue willow patterned china. A tall cobalt blue goblet of iced tea sat near her plate, its sides beaded with moisture.

Lefty emerged from the kitchen with a feast on a tea cart: baked chicken, cinnamon apple rings, fluffy mashed potatoes, fresh garden salad, several ears of corn drizzled with melted butter, thick slices of fresh tomatoes and cucumbers, and a basket piled high with soft, warm yeast rolls. Abbie, for whom all food had tasted like cardboard for so long, stared at dinner and felt the welcome pangs of her appetite return full force.

As they ate, their conversations ranged from differences in their lifestyles to people they knew who had been married or divorced, had children, or moved to exotic locations.

"You haven't mentioned Michael in a while," Lefty said.

Abbie grimaced. "We broke up several months ago. I've put off telling you because I'm such a miserable failure at relationships."

"You just haven't met the right guy, that's all."

"And not likely to. I mean, look at my record. David, who entered the priesthood after we'd been together nearly three years. There's Robert, who preferred to spend his time with a telescope looking for signs of life 'out there' rather than living the life he had here. And let's not forget dear sweet Michael, who decided an eighteen-year-old college girl was more his kind of woman."

Lefty patted her hand. "I repeat, you just haven't met the right guy. Don't give up."

"I've come to the hard-won conclusion that there is no right guy." She smiled sadly then brightened. "So let's talk about your love life, pal. You met anyone?"

"Not likely when the only men I meet are either going under sedation or coming out of it." She shrugged. "Besides, I rather like my life the way it is. If I meet someone, then fine. If I don't, that's fine, too."

"Well, I can tell you right now, it'll be a cold day in August before I meet the man of my dreams."

A bit later Lefty said, "Shall we sit on the porch swing?"

Abbie's stomach knotted as she thought of the darkening woods surrounding the house. She had never liked dark, shadowy places. Lefty must have read and recognized the expression, but like the good friend she was, she said nothing of Abbie's fear.

"Let's sit in the front room instead."

Abbie settled into a blue-checked armchair so big and soft it almost swallowed her. The light from a table lamp gave the room a soft glow as they sipped brandy. For a while they sat quietly, listening to tree frogs and crickets. Abbie cast a look toward the darkness outside the window. If the country night and all its creatures stayed outside, Abbie could tolerate the sound. In the city, the lights and movement of human life fed her comfort and security. She wondered if she had made another foolish decision by coming to this isolated place.

Lefty's voice interrupted her uneasy thoughts.

"So tell me what's going on. What terrible thing has brought you to my doorstep, looking thin, worn, and exhausted?"

Unexpected tears pricked Abbie's eyelids. It had to be a combination of exhaustion, alcohol, good food and a good friend, because she rarely cried.

"One of my clients murdered a child last week."

"Oh no! What happened?"

"I defended him a month ago on a charge of felony child endangerment. I did such a good job, he was able to walk right out of the courtroom as free as you and me." Her voice broke, and she cleared her throat. "That little girl would be alive today if it hadn't been for me."

Lefty sat forward, hands clasped around her brandy snifter. She rested her elbows on her thighs and gazed intently at Abbie.

"Don't say that. It's not your fault if some creep—"

"Yes, it is!" Abbie snapped. "Yes, it most certainly is my fault. From the minute I saw him, I knew what he was. I've learned to distinguish truth from lies, the good from the corrupt. I knew he was as bad as they come, but I defended him. He walked right back into the world a free man. Then he beat his girlfriend's five-year-old daughter to death. It never would have happened if I followed my heart's urging, if I had stood for truth instead of profit and status."

Lefty stared hard at her, as if trying to see past the misery and into the deeper parts of her mind. She set her empty brandy snifter on the end table next to her chair. She said nothing.

"Well?" Abbie prompted. "Tell me what you're thinking. Tell me I'm not responsible or that I'm irresponsible. Tell me I'm a good soul, or that I'm a total jerk. Tell me *something*!"

Her friend sucked in a deep breath and let it out noisily.

"Truthfully, right at this moment, I don't know what to tell you." Her voice trailed and she looked away for a time before speaking again. "I've never been faced with a decision like that, but to be perfectly honest, don't believe I could have done what you did." She turned her gaze to Abbie. "I'm not condemning you, please understand. I realize you must have had a reason, but I just don't know how, or why, you defended someone you *knew* in your heart had hurt someone–a child–and could do it again." She shook her head. "*Why?*"

Abbie leaned her head back against the chair and closed her eyes. She hated hearing these words from her friend, but she understood them. Hadn't she been asking herself the same thing the past week?

"I don't know." She paused. "No, that's wrong. I *do* know. It's my job. It's what I do." She raised her head, looked at Lefty, trying not to see the reproach on her friend's face. "I'm a criminal lawyer. I defend people charged with crimes." She shuddered, listening to her own words. "How awful does that sound? I defend robbers and thieves and rapists and murderers and guys who evade the IRS. It's what I *chose* to do." Her voice grew thick and labored. "I don't want to do it anymore."

Her friend remained silent, waiting for her to continue.

"I got into law practice because I thought I wanted help to make a difference in the world. And you know, at first, that's exactly what I did. I got all the cases that no one else wanted, like the jilted wife who needed maintenance from a philandering husband, or a tenant who desperately needed hot water and an exterminator in his apartment. Good things. Right and just things."

"I remember when you were working on those kinds of cases. You had a good start So what happened to change all that?"

"I'm not sure. An accumulation of situations, I suppose. I moved into a more expensive apartment, then into a bigger one in a better part of town. I bought a new car, then a bigger and better one. Clothes, friends, entertainment. I guess I climbed the ladder of success and fell into a trap."

"Or more likely, you walked into one. No one forced you to go up that ladder."

Abbie nodded. "You're right."

"Well, do you like it? That apartment, that car, those friends, the latest fashions? The entertainment? Are they worth the price you're paying now?"

"I don't know. I thought I did. I mean it's what my folks always wanted for me. Bigger. Better. But the way it is now…" She shook her head, miserable. "It all feels so wrong. I'm *sure* this is not the way my life is supposed to be going. Something has to change. That's why I'm here, in a place foreign and a little frightening to me. I need to sort this out, but I'm pretty sure I don't want to continue practicing criminal law. At least, I'm through defending scumbags so they can walk the streets. But the rest of it?" She shook her head. "I don't know."

Lefty leaned forward, her expression serious, very earnest. "It's long been my belief that anything is possible if you want it badly enough. But it takes commitment." She paused. "Think about it, then make the decision you feel is best."

Abbie let her friend's wisdom and counsel soak into her mind. Yes, this is what she needed. To ponder, to decide, to commit. But whatever she chose to do, she must be sure it was the right decision.

Again, as neither woman spoke, the night sounds took over the room. She became aware of the soft ticking of the old clock somewhere in the house. It struck ten times, deep and melodious, a gentle comforting sound.

Lefty stirred in her chair. "You've had a big day. You have traveled far and eaten much. You have a lot of things to think about. But right now you need to get some rest. Leave your worries down here tonight." She stood. "Come on, and I'll show you to your room."

Chapter 4

During the next few days the two women caught up on the years that had separated them. With her friend's undying love and support, Abbie embraced a measure of relief which she hoped would comfort her in the upcoming days of self-imposed isolation.

"Plenty of food in the fridge." Lefty got into her red SUV Saturday morning. "And town isn't that far away, if you need anything." She turned the key in the ignition, and the motor purred to life. "I'll call you every day to see how you're getting along."

Abbie hesitated only a moment. "That's sweet of you, but I'd rather you not call, if you don't mind. Solitude is what I need. Maybe by the time you get back, I'll have had an epiphany, or something."

Lefty searched Abbie's expression, as though seeking a truth that might be hiding.

"Well, maybe you will have solved your own dilemma. Being alone opens your mind if you'll let it happen." She put the SUV in gear. "If you don't want me to call you, at least promise you'll get in touch if you need to talk."

"I will. I have you on speed dial, and I saw that you've posted the hotel number on the fridge. I saw it right next to the number for the fire department, the sheriff's office, and the pizza delivery place."

It was nice someone was concerned for her. In spite

of her many friends back in Dayton, Abbie never felt the level of true friendship from them that she and Lefty had always shared.

Her friend drove a few yards along the circular driveway then stopped to peer at Abbie through the dim light of early morning.

"I feel awful, leaving after you've driven so far. Are you *sure* you don't want to come with me?"

How easy it would have been to say yes, to go with Lefty and not stay here, alone in the backwoods with only herself to fight this odious stranger she was becoming, but Abbie knew it was something she had to do. She would never have resolution in her life if she did not face her fears or change the state of her existence.

"I'll be fine." She spoke with more assurance than she felt. "Everything will be fine, I promise."

Lefty studied her face a moment longer. Doubt and concern oozed from her eyes, but she nodded. "All right then. I'll see you in about ten days."

When the crunching sound of tires on gravel faded, a silence descended that quickly sent Abbie into the house. She switched on the television to erase the unfamiliar and uncomfortable quiet, then turned up the sound as she showered. She dressed in a pair of khaki shorts and a soft white T-shirt and pulled her long, blonde hair back in a free-swinging ponytail.

Gazing in the mirror while she opened her make-up bag, Abbie laughed aloud.

"Why do I need this stuff when the only person who'll see me is *you*?" She pointed at her reflection. "And I know what you look like beneath the paint."

In fact, she knew what she looked like beneath herself, and these days, she wasn't as pretty as she appeared. She tossed the bag into the dresser drawer and planned to leave it untouched for the next two weeks. Maybe she wouldn't even look in a mirror.

By mid-afternoon, she had turned off the television and was lounging on the porch swing. Birds flitted from branch to branch, and two gray squirrels chased each other up and down every tree in the yard. Filled with the variety of bird songs, the world around her was not as quiet as she thought. With a shove of her bare foot, set the swing in motion and settled back even more against the soft cushions. The next thing she knew, she was waking up from a long nap and the sun was almost down.

That evening, she soaked in a lavender-scented bubble bath until the water turned tepid. She dressed for bed in a short, silk nightie with spaghetti straps. Abbie loved the feel of the cool, soft fabric against her skin, like a lover's sweet touch. The midnight blue silk shimmered in the lamplight as she dried and braided her hair.

A few minutes later, in the ultimate quiet of that Ozark summer night, she turned on the small table fan, plumped her pillow, then stretched between the soft, clean-smelling sheets and snuggled down for a good night's sleep. The soft hypnotic drone of the fan's motor muffled cricket chirps and frog songs. Sleep should overtake her with no effort.

It should have, but it did not. In the darkness, her mind wrestled with an uneasy thought: *Something is out there.*

Not "out there," like a prowler or hungry wild animal. Nothing as tangible as that. That "something" was a feeling. A need like the one she had experienced earlier when she had given in to the urge to stop and enter that dismal little junk shop.

The "something" hovered in the air, whispered in her mind's ear, shivered across her skin, and skittered into her bloodstream. It refused to let her sleep.

She needed to see the painting.

In fact, that urge gripped her so tightly, she feared she might not reach her car quickly enough. She sat up and snapped on the bedside lamp.

She slid out of bed, thrust her feet into thin house slippers, got the car keys from her purse and went downstairs. She switched on the porch light, but the bulb flared and died. Abbie tamped down her fear and stepped out the front door.

With no traffic lights or streetlights, the outdoors was blacker than she had seen that horrendous long ago night when she got lost in the forest. She nearly returned to the bright safety of the house, but the painting called her. Compelled her. She had to see it.

She opened the trunk and yanked out the painting by its grimy frame. In the house she leaned it against the banister on the lower stairs. She fetched some soft cloths from the tiny broom closet, found yesterday's newspaper in the recycling box, and carried everything up to her bedroom. She spread the paper across the floor and placed the painting on it. A hard, flat piece of wood with canvas stretched across it had been nailed to the frame.

She wiped away some of the dust from the intricate carving. The frame might be valuable, but it was the painting that intrigued her.

Cross-legged on the bedroom floor, she propped her elbows on her knees and rested her head on the interlaced fingers of both hands.

What was it about this dismal, primitive portrayal that beckoned her? Was it the desolation of that house as it sat strong but helpless beneath an approaching storm? Did she equate her dreary state of mind to a long-neglected house? Hadn't she forsaken pleasure and peace to continue a vocation for which her interest and passion had died? Was her heart as dark and sorrowful as that house?

With gentle fingertips, she touched the dusty image. A tear stung her eye. Yes, this house resembled life, built with hopes and dreams to enfold her into its welcoming embrace. Somehow, she had allowed the outside world to tangle about her vitality, to choke its beauty and purpose with snarled overgrowth. And now the storm of an unknown future approached. That storm could destroy, or it could cleanse and offer her a fresh start.

She reached for one of the soft cleaning cloths and gently began to wipe away years of accumulated dust. The cloth gathered the dirt, but the painting remained bleak.

She snatched back her hand and blinked hard. Had those clouds just moved across the glowering sky?

That light in the upstairs window. Had it been there before? She did not remember any spot of light on the dark surface of this painting when she'd looked at it earlier.

Abbie swallowed hard.

Of course it had been. It must have been.

She stared hard at the upstairs light and at the clouds, then blinked her eyes. Her afternoon nap must not have been long enough. She really needed to get more sleep.

But she refused to abandon this task just yet. The paint in the lower left-hand corner was cracked and chipped. Unlovely as the painting was, she did not want to cause damage beyond what time and neglect had done.

With the cloth she gently wiped cobwebs and grime from the edges. She bent closer and dabbed the tip of the cloth against the damaged corner. To her dismay, a tiny piece of paint, wedged near the frame, flicked off. She moistened her fingertip with her tongue and retrieved the tiny bit from the floor.

Leaning closer, her face mere inches from the picture, she hoped to fit the minute chip in place, like a piece from a jigsaw puzzle.

What was that sound?

She did not move, but her body tensed as she listened hard. The sound was as compelling as a whisper but as relentless as a roar. She straightened her spine, turned her head to look at the night outside her open window. She saw nothing but blackness. The curtain barely stirred.

Seeing things. Hearing things. She *was* tired.

Again she bent over the painting, saw exactly where the fragment belonged. Straining to see that small gap made her dizzy. The point on the canvas seemed to swirl, a rapid whirlpool of crystalline blue. She blinked hard.

The sound returned.

She reached out quickly to cover the spot but the moment her finger touched the marred canvas she felt her breath dragged from her lungs. All thought and reason slipped away, and she no longer had weight or substance.

Then there was nothing but a cold darkness.

Chapter 5

The cold awakened her. The kind of cold unlike a winter's chill had crept stealthily, deeply, into her skin, penetrating muscles and organs. It settled into the marrow of her bones. Abbie tried to move. She felt as if she had been battered without mercy then folded and crammed into cold storage.

And the wind. It pounded against her without ceasing.

With an effort she did not know she could muster, she struggled to her knees. She grabbed a nearby tree and hauled herself up, inch by inch. The chill wind whipped against her, wrapping and molding the silk nightie to her skin.

Abbie sent a panicked look at her unfamiliar surroundings. Where was she?

The bit of dark sky revealed through the encircling forest glowered ominously. Tree branches swayed and bowed; leaves thrashed like something caught in a trap. But it was not the impending storm that shoved the fear into her frozen bones and shifted it to full-blown terror. It was absolute silence. No howling, no roaring, not even a rustle. The only sound was her own rapid breathing.

Again she shot a horrified glance around her, all haziness gone from her vision. She was not deaf, but she most assuredly was lost. Not only lost, but lost in a thrusting, violent storm as the alien world around her remained totally and freakishly soundless.

She gripped both sides of her head while hysteria raged to free itself and run wild in her mind. She refused to panic. She closed her eyes, gathering her wits and focused her thoughts. What was the last thing she remembered doing?

It took a moment for the memory to release itself. A bath at Lefty's. Dressed for bed. And after that...after that, everything was blank.

She opened her eyes and studied the forest surrounding her. Lefty's home was tucked into the woods. Had Abbie taken a walk, fallen, and knocked herself out? The painful lump she touched near the top of her head testified that she may have done just that. But no. Taking a stroll at night was a foolish notion. She would never have done such a thing. The memory of being lost in the wilderness had always been enough to deter her from roaming freely and unaccompanied in the countryside, especially at night.

She never went anywhere without her phone, but if it was there, it lay buried within the thickly tangled vegetation around her, completely hidden, lost. Besides, she was wearing her nightie. Maybe she had sleepwalked.

But there was another thing that did not add up. The weather. When she had arrived at Lefty's, the afternoon's temperature had reached ninety-five degrees. It had been hot and dry and still. Lefty had told her no rain had fallen for five weeks and none was predicted soon. Yet here she stood while the day around her was cold and dismal, like a day in November.

Only it wasn't November. It *couldn't* be November, because in November no green leaves remained on trees.

So it had to be August, because if it wasn't, where had the time gone? And where had she been as it passed?

Her knees gave way. She slid to the ground, slumped and freezing, her mind as dull as the grayness of the day around her. Where was she? How did she get to this place? How was she going to get out?

And why did the wind blow without ceasing? If it stopped, just for a minute or two, maybe she could think. But the soundless buffeting had invaded her brain and was now blowing away her sanity.

She wrapped her arms around her knees, head tucked into the protection of her arms, trying to get warm, trying not to lose her mind.

"I have to think," she whispered. "I have to think!"

She marshalled her willpower to focus on one point rather than let her thoughts run amok. Through sheer strength of mind, her heartbeat settled, and her brain slipped into a semblance of normal, calm functioning.

Perhaps she was asleep. This was one of those dreams she sometimes had where she knew she was sleeping but had felt awake.

Gulping in a deep breath, she stood quickly, hoping the sudden movement and the shock of the cold wind against her entire body would do the trick. But it did not. She tried the old cliché of pinching herself. She even slapped her cheek. It sounded like a gunshot in that silent world, and the sting nearly brought tears to her eyes, but it did not bring her into wakefulness.

If she truly was lost, then she was lost in the woods. The wilderness, with all that it embodied and promised, horrified her.

But terror would not help her to leave that place, and she fought against it.

Looking at the sky, or as much of it as she could see through the upper branches of the trees, she noted that it remained leaden, glowering, threatening her with storms and with darkness. She did not want to be in these woods when night fell; she refused to think of bears, wildcats, and snakes.

She stepped away from the tree. She turned full circle, searching for a break in the woods, a path, anything that might lead to civilization. But everywhere she looked, she saw only tangled undergrowth and huge trees with low, heavy branches bending in the wind. She saw no road, no trail, no path. Any course she chose might be right or could be wrong. She had to take a chance because standing like a frozen ninny in the forest was about as stupid a thing as she could conceive. Glancing around once more, she chose a direction and plunged into it.

Although she struggled like a mad woman in chains, she made little progress. The vines and briars beneath her feet shredded her slippers. They grabbed and clung to her as if they had a sentient mind. She refused even a moment's thought of whatever crawling, slithering life might exist beneath the brambles.

How long she fought the wild vegetation, the chill wind, and her terror, she had no idea. She simply kept moving, stomping down brush with each step, forcing herself to stay calm.

At one point she looked back to view her progress. Seeing no sign of her passage renewed her fear. The frightful undergrowth had swallowed everything. She had the strangest feeling that the forest knew her, had trapped her and was never going to let her go.

She stood still, staring behind her, chafing her icy

arms, fighting tears. She forced herself to face forward once more. She stomped down more bushes, advancing a few steps.

"I can do this," became her mantra, keeping her focused on the words and not on what might be lurking, watching and waiting in that terrible forest.

Hours seemed to have passed before she finally broke into a clearing of sorts, unseen until that moment because of the monstrous trees and brush growing around it. A few yards away, across what may have been, at one time, a full, lush lawn sat the monstrosity of a house. The dark, hulking Gothic structure stirred a chord of memory. Perhaps she had seen something similar in Hitchcock's *Psycho*, or maybe the Munster residence at 1313 Mockingbird Lane.

The house did not exude the malevolence of the forest and the lowering sky. Instead, it seemed to reek of loneliness. It looked sturdy, well able to face down the encroaching vegetation, but it seemed to be closing in on itself, preparing to die.

She shook her head, clearing her thoughts. Right then she did not care whether she had seen the old house before. All she wanted was to find shelter from the silent cold wind, get to a telephone and find her way home.

She stumbled and scrambled toward the house. No trees or overgrown bushes blocked her way through the clearing, but the groundcover was just as snarled and treacherous as that through which she had already passed. It seemed an eternity before she reached the porch steps and labored up them on weak, trembling legs.

Her body was stiff, aching with cold. Although the thin soles of her delicate house slippers had protected the bottom of her feet somewhat, they had not held up well throughout her trek. At that moment they clung to her icy feet with a few scraps of tattered fabric. She yearned for her boots and thick, soft socks, craved her comfy down jacket and jeans, longed for the warmth and comfort of a fire. Once she was on the porch, she nearly cried with relief.

"Please, someone, be home."

She grasped the tarnished brass doorknocker—a ring held in the mouth of an ugly gargoyle—and pounded it against the dark panels.

Not content with that, she pummeled the door with both fists.

"Please, please, open the door! Someone, please be home."

Chapter 6

Andrew's treacherous mind was playing tricks on him again. Long ago, when he first came to this place, sounds had haunted him. Talking, laughter, music, odd roars, and strange rumblings. Back then he had sought maniacally for the owners of the voices and the source of the sounds until he exhausted himself only to find nothing.

Back then, he had yearned to hear a voice, any voice, other than his own, just so he could know that a world apart from this place existed. For a long time now, the only noises he heard were of his own doing. His spoon against a bowl, his footsteps as he walked from one room to another, the click of a latch when he opened or closed the door. Over the course of time, these quiet sounds proved that he still lived and breathed yet remained inexplicably and utterly alone. To save his sanity, he long ago had ceased to listen, or even hope, for a voice not his own or any noise not of his own making.

He had no idea how long he had been in this God-forsaken place, but the only face he'd seen was his image reflected in the window glass or in the dripping well bucket when he fetched water. His was not a bad face. In fact, it was quite a good face, with dark eyes and strong regular features framed by dark, unruly hair. The amount of time that had passed seemed an eternity to him. He knew he should look and feel old by now, but he did not.

He had never known one hour of illness or disease. His appearance was neither wasted by years nor dissipated by the pain of his isolated existence. He still had the same strapping, healthy body of a strong thirty-year-old man.

So when he heard a relentless pounding on the front door and a woman's voice pleading for entrance, he knew his mind played tricks on him once again.

He listened for a moment, then turned his attention to his meal of beef stew and bread. His food never varied, neither in amount nor flavor. Tea, potatoes, carrots, onions, apples, beef, and bread were what he had available; tea, potatoes, carrots, onions, apples, beef, and bread were what he consumed. No vermin had ever invaded his larder, and like the Biblical story of the widow whose flour and oil never ran out, whatever he removed and used at one meal would be on the shelf by the next meal. Long ago, he had stopped questioning how this happened and accepted the phenomenon that nourished his body.

He had almost forgotten the taste of pork or fish, the bite of fresh, hot coffee, the singular burn in his gullet from a shot of whiskey. Those sensations were a dim memory, as was nearly everything else that had once been familiar. For sanity's sake, he had learned to live only from moment to moment.

The shouting voice and door-thumping ceased at last. He cocked his head slightly, listening for any remnant of sound. Hearing nothing but silence, he cleared the table. It took only a moment to wash and dry his spoon and plate and put them in the cupboard. He stared at the collection: one spoon, one fork, one knife, a single cup and plate. They had been in this kitchen when he arrived, and he had never needed more. He took a deep breath, let it out slowly, turned and went into the parlor across the hall.

In that room, the walls were lined with books. The books, also in the house when he arrived, had been his only friends. They had been his salvation, and he loved them with pure devotion. How they had come to be in this desolate place mystified him as much as his own presence or how his food supply never dwindled or why he never sickened or aged. Over the course of time, he had learned to thank whatever good fortune had granted the books to him. Without the company of these beloved volumes, he surely would have gone mad.

The latch clicked and his front door opened.

He froze. It was a trick of the mind. It had to be. With his senses sharpened and skin prickling, he ignored the sensation of another presence in the house as he picked up his book from the small table next to his favorite chair. It would not do for him to acknowledge, even for the length of a heartbeat, that someone else might be with him. Insanity would result from that way of thinking. It had almost happened before, long ago, when he believed he could depart this limbo and pick up his life.

"Sir? Please, sir. I knocked, but you didn't hear me. Can you help me?" The voice, frantic and breathless, was also as sweet and fresh as an April morning.

His breath stopped. What madness was this?

Those voices from long ago had never spoken to him. One thing he valued as highly as his books was a sound mind. He clung to it fiercely, for if he lost his reason, then he lost everything.

He closed his eyes, forced himself not to look, not to hear, not to sense the sweet soft, gentle presence of a woman in his world.

After a bit, he allowed his eyes to open. He gazed down at the printed pages of the book he held. Ah, *they* were real enough beneath his gaze and his touch. He leafed through them, settled himself into his much used armchair.

"Sir!" Her voice became louder as she approached. If she was real at all. "I need help. I seem to be lost. Something's wrong, and..."

He fought the urge. He curled his hands into fists, tightened his jaws, clenched shut his eyes. He sensed her increasing nearness and clenched the book so hard his knuckles whitened.

Not there. Not real, not real, not real.

"Sir!" she shouted, grabbing his arm.

He leaped inside his skin at her touch; his heart nearly burst from his body. She gripped his arm, the coldness of her fingers reaching through the fabric of his shirt.

"Sir, can you hear me? I need help!"

With her touch, his resistance broke. He turned his head suddenly sharply to view the apparition.

What was this cruel fever in his brain that conjured a beautiful woman in her chemise – a clinging, revealing chemise? His stupefied gaze began at the top of her head and traveled downward. She had hair the color of ripe wheat, eyes as blue as a sky he hadn't seen for an eternity, and a face, delicate enough to be porcelain, framed by curling wisps escaping a thick braid that hung down her back. Her large blue eyes blinked at him, and he paused his perusal long enough to look into them. Those eyes met his straight on, without fear, speaking silently of strength and passion. His gaze traveled over a nose that was short and straight, lips that were generous to a fault. Her shoulders and arms were bare, smooth and firm. The dark blue chemise she wore clearly outlined her slender form.

She was a fantasy although her touch was as real as the voices from long ago. He could not stop himself from staring at her the way Adam must have gaped at Eve the first time in Eden.

The book he had clutched so desperately fell from his slack fingers. Andrew, who had been an eternity without a woman, stared at her so long that she folded her arms and leaned toward him angrily. He dug his fingers into the armrests of his chair, swearing he smelled her perfume.

"Excuse me!" Her voice was loud, her anger unhidden behind a mask of decorum. "Someone needs your help and all you do is act like you've lost your senses! What's wrong with you?"

He blinked, moved his gaze back to her flushed face and angry eyes.

"Good. Now that I have your attention, will you please let me use your telephone? I seem to have lost my cell phone out there. " Her voice cracked, and she shot a fearful look out the window. "I don't know where I am or how I got here." She turned back to him, her eyes full of fear. "Please. Won't you help me?"

He swallowed noisily, barely hearing her voice above the anthem singing in his blood. He reached down to retrieve his fallen book, shifted in his chair so that she was not easily in his line of sight. He tried to read, but the words on the page were only lines and dots to his vision.

One slender pale hand grabbed the book and yanked

it from his grasp.

"If you are mad at the world and want to shut yourself off from everyone, that's fine. I'm not here to change that. I just need your help, and then I'll be on my way."

He gaped at her. How could an apparition pluck a book from his hands?

"Please let me use your phone. Or if you don't want to do that, at least tell me where I can find the nearest one."

He listened to her words, then realized that the very act of listening trapped him more deeply in this flight of fancy. Perhaps she would vanish if he commanded it.

"Leave me." His voice, a commodity he no longer needed, was rusty from disuse.

Color rose in her cheeks. Her eyes glittered. "I will be happy to leave you. In fact, I *want* to leave you. But I don't know where I am, or how to return to where I came from."

She was the most beautiful thing he had ever seen.

How wonderful it would be if she were real, if she were to stay there with him. Someone as beautiful as this flower to look upon, to talk to, perhaps one day to touch and hold and share life. Could it happen? After all this time, was it possible?

Then he came to himself, awakening as if he'd been lost in a dream.

He felt he was about to lose control, and he must preserve his strength of mind. Trapped in an isolated world where there was neither sunlight nor night, no variation of time or season, no challenge to meet—these were out of his control. And so was being consumed by this hallucination.

He would banish the vision. He had tried ignoring her. He had tried commanding her. Maybe his analytical brain needed to hear logic to dispel this intrusive and unacceptable situation. He stood up, paced the room, felt her gaze fixed intently upon him.

He turned to face her and looked straight into those blue eyes.

"Here's the situation. You come to me in this—" he gestured to her clinging attire—"looking like that," running his eyes over her length, "so it is obvious that you are the invention of a brain-fever I didn't know I had. An invention beautiful enough to bring me to my knees, *if* I was a weaker man, but you are a mere creation just the same."

Her eyes grew larger and rounder as he spoke.

"You see," he continued, "it all stems from this extended exile of mine, and after the battles I've fought to maintain my sanity, I refuse to let a seductive little piece of baggage like you destroy me. In short, my dear young woman," he concluded like a great orator, "you do not exist!"

He clasped his hands behind him and waited for her to evaporate, melt, fade away, or whatever visions did when they were banished.

The woman before him was blinking rapidly, as though someone had kicked sand in her eyes, as if she were about to burst into tears.

No, no, no! He mustn't be moved by a phantom that sheds a woman's tears. Manipulative little wiles like that had failed to work on him in the past, and they would not work on him now.

"How dare you!" she spat at him instead of shriveling away into nothing.

Her hands were clenched at her side, her body shaking. He realized then she was neither about to burst into tears nor evaporate. She was furious and ready to spend her rage on him. The last young woman he had dealt with and who had not gone away when he encouraged her to leave had bared her fangs and unsheathed her claws. He braced himself for the same reaction, although he doubted ghostly claws would do much damage.

She stood a hair's breadth away from him before he even knew she had moved. She stood so near that he felt heat coming from her trembling body and smelled the sweet, womanly smell of her. These sensations were real, uncomfortably real.

"How dare you say such things to me when I only asked for your help! I'm lost and confused, and right now I'm angry that anyone can be so callous."

"You are not real." He backed away, not because she intimidated him, but because her nearness nearly drove him mad.

She advanced as he retreated until he backed into a bookshelf. She stood on the tips of her toes, leaning toward him, so near he could feel her breath.

Do visions breathe?

"Maybe it's *you* who is not real. I must have fallen and knocked myself out. I'm probably unconscious right now, and that's why I'm in the middle of this strange house in the middle of these spooky woods, talking to Howard Hughes the Second on *a cold day in August!*" Her voice rose in pitch until the last five words became a shriek.

He looked down at the face a mere six inches from his. The heat of anger radiated from her, and he could feel it all over his body.

In that moment, he lost the fight, the struggle with willpower, the battle for control. He yanked her soft female body against the length of his lonely, aching one. He kissed her full on the mouth, but the kiss was neither gentle nor seeking in the plundering of her lips. He was hot and starved, devouring a sweetness he had not known in a time untold.

In his arms, she struggled like a mountain cat, digging her fingernails into his shoulders, then she shoved him so hard he staggered and had to grab the arm of his chair to steady himself.

Her eyes glittered, and he kept his distance, appalled by his own actions.

Chapter 7

The man standing in front of Abbie looked as if he had just been pole-axed. Unfortunately, she felt none too steady herself. For all she knew, she might have stumbled across a serial bomber with a passion for his own company.

But she had seen killers face to face. She recognized soullessness in their eyes or glimpsed an inner coldness that no amount of smooth talking or confident posturing could disguise. None of them had charmed or weaseled their way into her trust. Without a doubt, she knew this man was no menace, except perhaps to himself, shutting himself away from the world as he had done. At least he had released her the moment she protested. And looking at him now, he was obviously contrite, embarrassed, even ashamed.

He closed his eyes as though taking his inner bearings, opened them again, and gazed at her. For a moment, he appeared totally lost, then he drew in a deep breath and let it out slowly, silently between his lips. With one shaking hand, he wiped his face.

"Haven't I lived through enough hell without you?" His voice was almost a whisper. "Why have you done this? Why don't you leave me?" The words perplexed her no less than everything else he had said.

He turned away, as if the sight of her tortured him. He went from the bookcase to the window, staring out at the dark sky and tangled vegetation which threatened to swallow the house and its occupants. With his back to her, he stood without moving for so long he could have been carved in stone.

She watched him, willing her breath and heartbeat to return to their normal, quiet pursuit of keeping her alive. Broad-shouldered and tall, he stood straight and proud, his head unbowed, hands clasped behind him in an attitude of waiting or perhaps resignation. It bothered her no little bit that she found herself attracted to him. Yes, he was to a man gorgeous enough to inhabit her wildest dreams, so perhaps that attraction was normal. Beyond her physical reaction, though, something else awakened and stirred. Deeper, more complex, even tender, her empathy grew for this person who seemed a bit off-center, a lost soul needing to find a home. He seemed so alone.

She crossed the room to stand beside him, looking at the gloomy aspect beyond the window. It was a desolate scene, unbearably depressing.

"Where are we? What is this place?"

He did not answer, and after a time she tried a different question.

"Who are you?" She paused. "Why are you here?"

She waited for him to speak as she gazed through the glass and watched the wind whip leaves and branches.

His reply was slow in coming. "I would ask you the same thing, but I know who you are and why you are here."

The words perplexed her. His expression was as bleak as the world beyond the window. She touched his forearm lightly.

"Why don't you tell me who you think I am?"

He met her eyes, and though his gaze smoldered with desire, something else lay within his eyes. Hopelessness, maybe.

"When you beat on my door and called out, I knew your voice was nothing but my imagination. And when you walked into my parlor, I believed you were an hallucination. But I see I'm wrong."

She smiled. "Well, that's a good thing."

He took in and held a deep breath then let it out slowly.

"No. It is not a good thing. I have no other choice than to believe you are a demon from hell in the guise of every vision I've ever had the courage to dream. You've been sent here to torture and tempt me beyond the brink of madness." He shifted his gaze to her fingers resting on his arm. "Your touch burns me. Please remove your hand and step away."

The agony on his face was almost unbearable to witness. What had brought this man to such a tortured existence? She dropped her hand and took a couple steps back.

"You're wrong about me," she told him softly.

He rubbed his forehead as though in pain and turned to the window again.

"I think not. You are a witch, a sorceress."

She chafed her arms and moved closer to the fireplace. She held her hands toward its warmth.

"You seem to believe that I have many personalities. You have labeled me as a delusion, a demon, a witch, and a sorceress." She looked over her shoulder at him. "None of which is flattering, by the way." She smiled slightly when he slid a sideways gaze at her. "In reality, though, what I am is cold, confused, tired, and very lost."

"And nearly unclothed," he added, flicking a glance from head to foot.

She straightened her spine even more and lifted her chin.

"The last thing I remember is preparing for bed. I'm sorry if my choice of sleeping attire offends you."

He laughed, a small sound that rasped in his throat and sent him into a fit of coughing. He tossed her a second detailed appraisal.

"Oh, I'm not offended. Quite the contrary, as you well know. After all, that's why you're here, isn't it, to make my body burn to have you, to lie with you?"

She bristled, but then the words sank in. From his perspective, her presence could certainly mean something other than why she was there.

"If you'll just let me use your telephone, I'll get out of here." She paused briefly. "You *do* have a phone, don't you?"

"No."

"Oh. Well, could you drive me to the nearest one so I can call for help? You *do* have an automobile, don't you?"

A small frown flickered across his brow.

"No, sorry."

She bit her lower lip. This man really was isolated. And now, unfortunately, so was she.

"I assume it's too much to hope for a motorcycle?"

He shook his head.

"A bicycle?"

"No."

"Roller blades, skateboard…?" Her feeble attempt at humor failed to amuse her and seemed to confuse him as his frown deepened and she sighed. "If I had known I was going to get lost, I'd have brought my cell phone."

He regarded her with a look that was both puzzled and impatient.

"Do you realize you're talking gibberish?"

Annoyance edged into her tone. "I most certainly am not, and if you fail to understand what I'm asking then it seems to me that you have shut yourself away from the real world for far too long. Forgive me for stating the obvious, but I think you've lost touch with what's out there."

He arched one heavy dark eyebrow and said nothing.

She swallowed her frustration and paced the room. Perhaps it was her training that had taught her to pace. She usually found her best resolutions in that tiny pathway of walking back and forth, her mind centered, totally focused. This time, however, no solution seemed forthcoming. She was stuck in this situation and was going to have to deal with it. She stopped pacing and faced him.

He had not moved except to fold his arms across his chest, a universal and subconscious signal of self-protection. He had put on an expression of patience worn thin, though she sensed a deep wariness. Was he really that apprehensive of her?

"Listen, it's not my intention to disturb you, distract you, or drive you to the brink of madness, but you really are going to have to lead me out of these woods. Either take me to your nearest neighbor or to the highway. And I would appreciate the loan of a coat or a jacket or a robe or something."

"I can't do that."

A bright spot of temper reignited in her belly.

"For heaven's sake, I'll pay—"

"I will give you something to wear," he interrupted hastily. "God knows we'd both be better off. But I cannot lead you out of here."

She stared at him then flung her arms wide in an overload of frustration.

"You want me to leave. I want to go. Why won't you help me?" When he said nothing, she sighed heavily. "At least tell me how to get out of these woods."

He shook his head. "I'm sorry, but I can't do that."

"What do you mean you can't?" Her voice hit a shrill note. "You live here!"

He winced. "Kindly refrain from shouting."

"*Shouting?* You've only just begun to hear shouting unless you tell me how to get out of this place and back to the main road."

He finally moved, walked to one of the bookshelves. He appeared to peruse the titles as though she were no longer in the room with him. She yearned to throw something at him, but a display of temper, no matter how well-deserved, would not benefit her. She took a deep, slow breath.

"If you won't help me out of here, what do you suggest I do?"

He pulled a volume off the shelf and looked at it as though he had never seen a book before today.

"I suggest you leave the same way you came."

She glared at him.

"Have you not heard one word I've said? I don't know how—" A wave of dizziness crashed into her, breaking off the words. She swayed, grabbed for something to break her fall.

He crossed the room and caught her in the time it takes the heart to beat once. He helped her into the armchair.

"You're ill."

"No, not ill," she murmured, swimming up out of the wooziness that gripped her. "Injured, I think." She touched the tender place on the side of her head. "I blacked out, or fainted, or something, and when I came to, I was in the woods."

He was silent a moment, regarding her. "You don't know how you got here?"

"Haven't you been listening?" she replied with some heat. "I'm…" Just thinking the words made her shudder. "*I'm lost.*" She clenched and unclenched her hands, trying to squelch a rise of panic. "I got lost in those woods. I don't even know how I got there. " Her head pounded, and she could not continue.

He hunkered beside her chair and peered into her eyes. "And the last thing you remember?"

Trying to remember increased the pain in her head. "I told you before. Getting ready to go to bed." She closed her eyes, opened them again. "I took a shower and dressed, but there was something else, something I was doing, but I can't recall." She shook her head slightly, winced at the throbbing.

His eyes narrowed. Although he stared at her, she knew he did not really see her. A form of recognition, an awakening, stole across his face.

He rubbed his trembling hand over his chin and jaw. "It is possible? Can it be?"

"Excuse me?"

He stared at her a moment longer then shook his head as if to clear it.

"You said you were injured?"

At last, he seemed to be listening, as if she were an actual person, not some foolish scrap of his imagination.

"Yes. But a bump on the head seems minor when compared to the fact that I have no idea where I am or how I arrived here."

"Where's this bump?"

She touched the throbbing spot on her head, the place where all pain seemed to center and expand. He gingerly probed the area with his fingertips.

"A good-sized knot with a cut." He examined her right arm and both her legs. "And you have considerable scratches to the skin as well. None of these are deep enough to cause you a serious problem." He stood. "Come into the kitchen with me so I can attend to your injuries."

He was solicitous in manner and voice. Had she finally reached through his peculiar notions and awakened him to reality? She got to her feet and followed him out of the cozy parlor.

In the small kitchen the woodburning stove radiated a warmth that wrapped its comfort around her like a welcoming embrace. A stew pot steamed fragrantly on top of the stove, beckoning her with a promise of nourishment. A small table and cupboard flanked the only window in the room. A larger cabinet had been built along the back wall, and its worn-smooth wooden top appeared to have received many scrubbings. One door led to the outside, and another smaller door was tucked into the far corner of the room. The kitchen, for all its rustic appointments, exuded efficiency and spotless attention to cleanliness.

"Sit there, please." He dipped his head toward a

chair at the table. "I'll be back in a moment."

He left the room, and she heard his footsteps going up the stairs. A short time later, he returned, a colorful rag quilt over his arm.

"Here. Stand up and let me put this around you."

She stood, and he wrapped the warm coverlet around her then moved the chair closer to the stove and indicated for her to sit.

She remained where she was, luxuriating in the warmth of the thick, soft quilt around her. She watched as he opened the larger cupboard and removed two stone jars and a mortar and pestle. He measured dried leaves from each jar into the mortar, and with the pestle ground them to a fine powder. His hands looked strong, with long fingers and clean, blunt nails. His face was a study of concentration.

He said nothing as he worked, and that lapse into silence bothered her. She did not want him to start pondering again on whether she was real or some dark spirit sent to wreak havoc. She needed him as an ally in this strange place.

She broke the silence. "You've not told me your name."

He glanced at her. "And you haven't told me yours."

He dribbled hot water from a kettle on the stove into the powder, a few drops at a time. With his forefinger, he tested the consistency of the paste he was making until he seemed satisfied.

"I'm Abigail Matthews. Abbie." When he said nothing, she prompted, "And you are …?"

He looked up from the greenish-gray glob in the mortar bowl.

"Andrew Wade. Sit, please. Abbie." He offered her

a smile, a tentative and rather endearing one. "Please call me Andrew."

She took the chair near the stove, glanced in the mortar he put on the table near her. It looked vile.

"I'm not supposed to eat that, am I, because I positively refu—"

He laughed. "No. This is a paste for that lump on your head. It will help numb the pain and take down the swelling."

"Oh."

"I wouldn't expect you to eat it."

"Nor would I."

"The taste would be off-putting, I should imagine." He smiled at her.

"The *appearance* is off-putting. Sort of like pea soup and cement."

He laughed again. He brought more hot water and poured it into a small, galvanized basin.

"I ought to tell you, I don't have much faith in home remedies. If you'll just give me some aspirin, I'll be all right until I can get to a doctor."

He gave her a quick, sharp look then turned back to the cupboard.

"You had a bit of dizzy spell a minute ago." He reached for another jar. This time he measured leaves into a cup, poured hot water over them and covered the cup with a saucer.

"Well, that's probably because I haven't eaten anything for a while."

His brow creased. "You haven't?"

"I don't think so. I don't remember."

His frown deepened as he returned to her. He tipped her head sideways, parted her hair, and once more examined the tender site.

Dipping a small, clean cloth in the water, he said, "I think you'll find a combination of this plaster and the tea will be sufficient for the pain." He peered into her eyes and added quietly, comfortingly, "Now, I'm just going to clean this wound. It may hurt a little."

His touch was incredibly light and gentle, but pain shot from the cut as he dabbed it with the cloth. Abbie drew in a sharp, sudden breath and flinched.

He stopped. "I'm sorry." His voice was as soft as a butterfly's breath, an apology in his eyes.

"That's okay. I'm not usually such a baby about these things."

"These things?"

"You know, cuts and scrapes, bruises. Shots."

"Shots."

"I don't mind needles. I even give blood without cringing." She met his eyes. "Why are you looking at me like that?"

He blinked and shook his head, then began tending the cut once more. "Your words…sometimes they are strange to me. I apologize." He cleared his throat. "Where is your husband while you've been getting lost? He should be looking out for you."

She frowned. "I'm not married, and I can watch out for myself."

He paused. "And yet you're hurt, and you're lost. You obviously haven't eaten for a while."

"Yes, but…well, a husband would hardly change that."

He lifted one eyebrow but said nothing until he put aside the cloth.

"I'm sorry cleaning that wound took so long, but I'm

convinced the cleaner it is, the less likelihood of infection. One thing we absolutely do not want is infection to set it. Now, I'll just apply this plaster, and I'll do my best not to hurt you this time."

Abbie hardly felt it as he daubed the mixture onto her scalp.

"You have lovely bedside manners. You would be a good doctor."

His hands stilled their task a moment, fingertips a hair's breadth from her scalp. She ventured a sideways glance at his face. The expression in his eyes was those of a man haunted. But what was it that tormented him enough that he chose to shut himself away from the world? He caught her gaze, smiled so briefly it was merely a flicker.

"Thank you for saying so. I rather fancied the notion of medical practice at one time."

"It's not too late, you know. To be a doctor, I mean. You're still young."

He said nothing but tipped her head again and finished applying the paste. "That will help with the pain and swelling in short order."

He stepped outside with the pan of water and a moment later returned with it empty. She watched as he silently scrubbed his hands in fresh hot water and dried them on another clean cloth.

He brought the cup to her, removed the saucer, and indicated the contents with a dip of his head. "Drink that. It will ease the pain and your light-headedness."

Abbie picked up the cup, held it between her hands, and looked at the reddish liquid.

She gave it a suspicious sniff. It smelled bitter. "What is it?"

"Bloodberry and barley-thorn."

She wrinkled her nose. "That sounds toxic."

A scowl, darker than the menacing sky outside, settled on his face. "It's not poison! I cure, I do not harm."

She widened her eyes. "So you *are* a doctor!"

He said nothing, but she pursued the subject. "Why?"

"Why what?"

"Why are you here instead of someplace where you can heal people and save lives? Don't you realize how badly good doctors are needed? What advantage is your healing talent if you don't use it?"

He stared at her for a space of time, then his scowl faded, and his shoulders drooped. He turned away, but not before she saw the lost expression in his eyes.

"Ah!" he said, half a sigh, half a groan. He went to the cupboard and put away the jars. "Drink your tea." From the other cupboard he got a bowl, filled it with stew, set it before her with a spoon, a plate, and two pieces of crusty bread. "Eat that. Every bite of it. I'll draw us some fresh water."

He picked up a large bucket near the backdoor. His problems, whatever they were, lay deep inside him. She ached for him and the depth of his despair. Maybe she could get him to open up, at least a little.

"Forgive me if I'm out of line by asking this, but is there a chance…that is, is it possible…well, what I mean is, do you suffer from agoraphobia?"

"I beg your pardon?" He paused with his hand on the doorknob.

"Agoraphobia. It's when someone—"

"I know what it is." He stared hard at the floor then

lifted his gaze to her. "I'm not agoraphobic, but please believe me when I tell you I cannot leave this place."

His circumstance and reasoning completely dumbfounded her. And it was obvious he was disinclined to enlighten her. Even so, her compassion stirred once more. She crossed the room to him.

"I'll find my way out somehow. When I get back to town, I'll bring someone out here to help you."

She half-expected another explosive protest. Instead he offered half a smile, one that did not reach his eyes.

"Someone to help me leave, you say? Dear lady. Don't you realize that if I could leave, I would have done long before now? There is no one who can help me. This I know."

Abbie laid her hand on his arm. His muscles tensed at the touch.

"I will bring help," she promised softly, giving his forearm a gentle, reassuring squeeze before letting go.

He looked into her eyes for a long moment then turned away.

"I'll get the water now." He glanced at her over his shoulder as he opened the door. "Eat your food and drink your tea while the plaster dries. You'll feel better soon."

Chapter 8

Sitting snug in the quilt, a fire burning in the stove nearby, and her stomach full of good food while the pain in her head faded minute by minute, she assessed her situation. Alone in a strange wood, with a peculiar but gentle man, she couldn't help but compare what she'd found to her familiar world. He possessed compassion, a trait she rarely found in her clients, and even less in her co-workers. She was often struck by the callousness of her friends whose lives were blessed with prosperity and abundance, yet their natures seemed unable to reach beyond their own needs and desires.

She studied him as he moved about the room. It was obvious to her that his kind heart and generous spirit overshadowed his eccentricities. He was nothing like the people she knew back home. So why, when he had so much to offer others, had he sequestered himself into such a lonely existence?

He left the room again, and when he returned, he placed a tan shirt and a coffee-colored pair of trousers on the table next to her.

"Whether you undertake to leave or whether you choose to stay, you'll need to wear something other than…well, other than what you have on beneath that quilt."

His words bothered her a little, as if he believed she might prefer to stay in the middle of nowhere. Maybe he hoped she shared his partiality to isolation. Yes, she wanted to be away from the city for a while, but not here in this dreary old house in the middle of the woods.

She started to say so but caught his gaze and read something in his eyes. Was it hope? In any case, she shifted her attention to the clothes and smiled as she picked them up. While the big shirt was no problem, the pants were miles too long and too large around the waist. Certainly, she would be warmer in them. Anything would be warmer than her blue silk nightie.

She glanced at him. He gazed at the clothing in her hands as if he shared her doubts. Their eyes met. He smiled, and she laughed.

"Not to worry. I'll find something to cinch them." He left her, returning with a length of cloth. "An extra sheet, but we can make it work."

He tore three long, narrow strips and knotted the ends together. He braided them tightly and tied the other end, making a belt for her.

"You'll be much warmer once you're dressed. Go into the parlor, next to the fire. I'll bring you a cup of tea when you're finished."

She wrinkled her nose. "I don't think I want another—"

His lips twitched. "Regular black tea, hot and comforting."

She returned his smile. "Thank you. That would be nice."

In the book-lined parlor, the fire burned cheerfully, brightening the room. She held the shirt and the pants near the fireplace, letting the sturdy fabric soak in the heat before she slipped into the garments. She sighed as the delicious warmth caressed her skin. She tied the rag belt snugly around her narrow waist, adjusted the excess fabric, and rolled up the pants legs and shirtsleeves.

She folded the quilt and laid it across the back of an armchair. The quilt brought a splash of red, blue, and yellow florals to a room of brown chairs, brown book covers, and dark wood floors.

"I'm dressed now."

She stood near the fireplace. The flames' warmth trickled through the thin fabric of her slippers, but she wondered if her feet would ever feel anything other than chilled. She studied what was left of her ridiculously thin slippers. They had been fine in Lefty's house. But here? She might as well be wearing Kleenex on her feet. Her host's shoes would never fit.

As if he had read her thoughts, Andrew walked in with a pair of socks.

"These will be too large, but they're wool. Maybe we can shrink them in some hot water."

"Wonderful! Thank you. My *feet* thank you."

"You and your feet are welcome."

She sat on the raised hearth, peeled off the slippers and pulled on the heavy socks. "Oh, that is heavenly. Thank you so much." She stretched out her legs and wriggled toes numb from cold. "Food, clothes, warm fire."

He pulled the overstuffed chair from the corner and placed it in front of the fireplace.

"Why don't you sit here? You'll be more comfortable." When she moved, he went to the hearth and rearranged the burning wood with a heavy poker. "Are you warm enough now?"

"Yes, I'm getting there." She cocked her head to one side, studying him. Her confidence that he was a decent, kindhearted soul grew moment by moment. He was obviously skilled, his manner empathetic once he realized she was real, not an illusion or product of what he called "brain fever."

"Some hot tea will warm you on the inside."

"I'm sure it will. But will you please give some thought to returning to—"

"I'll get your tea." He walked out of the room, leaving her to stare at the empty room.

Was his withdrawal from society as abrupt as his withdrawal from the room? Of course, his life was none of her business. Who was she to judge him, anyway? Hadn't she given in to the pressure of a world gone mad for wealth, power, and possessions? Hadn't she assumed the role of a high-profile attorney to earn money and prestige? Hadn't she squelched that inner voice so she could follow what appeared to be the most profitable path?

Up to this point in her life, she had not served the highest good. She had served the highest pay. In many ways, she'd shut herself off from doing the right thing, just as Andrew had. The only difference being, for whatever reason, he helped no one, while she, for the sake of gain, helped the wrong people. Who was she to lecture him?

He returned with a cup of steaming, fragrant tea and handed it to her. She bent her head to inhale the warmth.

"Thank you." She smiled. "And I'm sorry. I should mind my own business."

"There is no need for apologies. I understand why you're curious." He settled in a matching armchair. "And please know that it was my life's dream to heal the injured and the sick." She waited, but he shook his head.

83

She let the subject drop and sipped the tea.

"No one has ever shown up at my door until now." He spoke haltingly, as if he was unsure he should say anything at all. "How did you find me?"

His eyes shone with hope, but his expression was guarded.

She held the cup between both hands and met his gaze.

"Honestly, I don't know. As I told you before, the last thing I remember was getting ready for bed. When I try to recall anything beyond that, it's like a blank spot on a recording." She shook her head and sipped her tea. Its heat trailed through her system, coaxing relief.

"What does that mean?"

"I mean, there is no memory there. Nothing. I know, without a doubt, something happened to me, but I have no idea what it was. And then I woke up" —she shot a fearful look at the window, saw the trees shivering and bending in the wind. "—in that awful forest." She shuddered and looked away.

His intense gaze seared her face. "But you did not know this place was here before you arrived?"

She shook her head. "I'm a city girl who prefers skyscrapers to tall trees and the sounds of traffic to the sounds of crickets. There is no way I would have purposely gone into the forest."

"I see." He hesitated, then asked, "Did you see anyone else in the woods?"

"No one." She shuddered again. "I simply can't understand how I came to be there. It's as if...as if someone slipped a roofie in my drink."

"Roofie?"

She nodded. "Or a drug like it. But the thing is, I was

completely alone. I needed that time by myself so stayed at Lefty's place. I didn't go anywhere, no bars or restaurants." She swallowed hard, trying to tamp down the anxiety which threatened to rise again. "Do you think someone broke into my friend's house and drugged me?"

"I…I…perhaps that's what happened."

"Or maybe I ate something I shouldn't have. But it was leftovers, and it was fine the first time around." Panic began creeping out of its hiding place and slinked into her bloodstream. She sat straight up. "I should go back, look for signs of a break-in. She's my oldest friend, and she let me stay there while she was gone. If I had my cell, I'd call or text her, or call the cops."

She buried her face in her hands, hating the idea of returning to a place where she'd be alone if someone meant to harm her. At least here, in this gloomy old house with Andrew, her isolation was shared. But she owed something to the friend who had generously taken her in. She needed to make sure Lefty's beautiful home was untouched.

She lifted her head. "You're staring at me again."

"I think the knot on your head has affected your sensibilities again. Maybe you should lie down."

"No, no. I'm just fine, but when the storm is over, Andrew, I must get out of here."

"The storm?"

She looked toward the window. He followed her gaze.

"The storm will not pass."

"Of course it will. All storms pass."

"Not this one."

A shiver slid down her backbone. "You say that with such resignation, such assurance."

"That's because it's the truth. I'm sorry if that frightens you."

In spite of her fear, disbelief reared its head. "I'm sure it's too much to hope that you have the internet out here?" She glanced around, looking for some sign of Wi-Fi connection.

He looked completely baffled by the question, and she knew the answer.

"Do you at least have a radio? Maybe we could hear a forecast."

"I have no, um, radio. Really, I think you—"

"Of course you have no radio." Her endurance reached its end. "You don't even have electricity."

She stood, and he got to his feet.

"I really must leave," she said.

"It's impossible to leave this place." He spoke with such earnestness, leaning toward her as though to instill this notion as fact.

"Anything is possible."

He shook his head. "You don't understand! I've tried, time and again. *There is no leaving this place.*"

"And I'm telling you, I do not have the luxury of thinking that way. I *must* return to my friend's house and see if it's all right. I *must* let the authorities know there might be a dangerous person driving the highways and backroads, sneaking into houses, drugging women, harming them… " She let her voice trail.

If she'd been abducted, how had she escaped? She was extremely fortunate not to have been injured or killed.

He grabbed her shoulders, shook her gently. "Listen to me. It's impossible—"

"*Anything is possible!*"

"If that's true, then it is possible that storm is unending, and your exile in these woods will be endless."

She went cold all over and jerked free of his hold.

"That's crazy talk. I refuse to accept anything so preposterous. Why would you say something like that unless you're trying to trick me into staying here longer? Which I have no intention of doing."

He shrugged and turned away.

"If you want to go, do so. I will not try to stop you."

She blinked. "Really."

"Really." He met her eyes. "Go."

She'd never seen someone look quite as miserable as he did at that moment unless it was her own reflection in the last few weeks. Her fear and anger withered.

"Listen. You've taken good care of me, and I thank you for that. I appreciate the food, drink, loan of your clothes, and you treating my wounds. But I must leave."

He made an impatient gesture and leaned toward her.

"I'm not making up lies to keep you here. I wish I *could* take you out of here, but I can't. It's foolish for you to go looking for a way back to your friend's—"

"*No!* What's foolish is to sit here and waste your life instead of..." She broke off, hearing the strident sound of her own voice lashing out. That's not what she intended to do at all. "Forgive me. I'm the last person who should be talking about wasting a life." She raked her hands over her hair, fingers catching in the tangles. She sought his dark eyes, reading in their depths his loneliness, his hopelessness. "Are you *sure* you don't want to come with me?"

"It's my heart's desire to go back with you, even to lead you out, but believe me *there is no way out*. I can't make it any plainer than that."

A lengthy silence fell between them. His inability to leave this awful old house in the heart of the forest was far beyond her understanding. Her heart ached for him, but she would not stay, not another hour.

She laid one hand on his arm. "I'm going. But I'll come back with someone to help you. Soon. I swear it."

Resignation settled over his features. "As you wish."

"Can you give me something to help me mark my trail so I can find you again?"

He shook his head. "Marking your trail like Hansel and Gretel is useless. The forest will protect itself."

"That makes no sense."

"Nevertheless, it's true."

Biting her tongue to keep from snapping at him, she went into the kitchen, located a large knife, and returned with it. "I'll take this with me and cut a path like Indiana Jones."

His face registered a stoic acceptance, as she opened the door.

"Are you sure you won't come?"

"I'm sure."

She paused just a moment longer, waiting for him to change his mind. When he did not, she stood on her tiptoes, and kissed his cheek.

"Thank you for taking care of me. I'll be back soon."

He nodded, touched her shoulder, and said nothing.

She closed the door behind her, crossed the porch, and descended the steps. The cold, relentless wind immediately tore into her. She looked over her shoulder. He stood at the entry hall window near the front door. He lifted his hand briefly then stepped from view. A hard knot settled in her throat, and she fought back tears.

Foolish to feel so tender toward a man she'd just met, a man whose eccentric secretive natured belied his compassion and tenderness.

She turned from the grim old house and faced the forest that seemed more malevolent than it had earlier. The wind assaulted her as if she had no more substance than a withered leaf. She bore into it, thinking more about the man she'd left behind than finding her way back to civilization. What awful thing had happened to cause him to choose this kind of life? Had he ever tried to face his fears and conquer his pain, or had he simply backed away, resigning himself to isolation?

He was man of intelligence and heart. He could start over if he wanted to. Cut off from the world and all social interaction, he was out of touch with the times. But that could be easily remedied, because she would be more than happy to reintegrate him into society. Whatever had crippled him was something larger than a mere obstacle. She would return for him, even if it meant she must face this awful forest again.

She plunged deeper into the forest, slashing the knife into thick vegetation, marking her passage, and praying she was on her way to rescue. A vine, heavily stitched with tiny thorns, resisted the knife. It caught her clothes, thorns sinking into fabric, tearing open her skin. While the wind blew her hair around her face and into her eyes, she struggled to pluck the barbs from her flesh. She pulled back the shirtsleeves and trouser legs. Blood striped her skin. Odd that the fabric failed to rip or even snag. It was as if the vine was sentient and hungry.

She couldn't think about that. She had to keep going.

Pushing on, she hacked at the bark of a tree, but the wood resisted. With both hands, she wielded the knife and tried again to mark her passage. The knife slipped from her cold fingers into the brambles, but just as her fingers touched the handle, it slid deeper into the undergrowth, completely out of sight. She hesitated for only a moment, envisioning life forms that surely inhabited the dense thickets around and beneath her.

She shuddered, drew in a deep breath, and plunged her hands into the vegetation. She sought the cold metal with her fingers but found only stems, vines, and thorns. Her search became frantic, and she tried to tear away the plants. Everything resisted her touch.

Terrified the forest floor would draw her in and feast on her battered body, she scrambled to her feet and clumsily moved away a few steps. He had been right about the futility of marking her path. Had he also been right about the storm not breaking? She pushed her hair out of her eyes and glanced toward the stormy sky. It looked the same, with a sign of neither clearing nor worsening.

She gathered her courage, embraced determination, and pressed forward. If she could not find her way out of this forest, how would anyone be able to find her? Not that anyone would be looking yet. Lefty had gone to that conference in Savannah. No one from the firm back in Dayton would be second-guessing her whereabouts. Her parents, somewhere in Switzerland these many months, were unaware she was anywhere but home. They were likely too absorbed in their own pursuits to call her.

She continued to struggle forward. Breathless with effort, she looked behind and saw no sign of her passage. The forest was a separate world unto itself, closing around her even as she watched, and it terrified her anew. Had these the malevolent woods prevented him from going farther than the few steps it took to get to the well? As foolish as the notion was, the very experience of being caught within it, witnessing as it healed and protected itself, was enough to stop a heart from beating.

She shivered in the cold, silent wind and slowly faced forward again. Surely, there was a path somewhere. A fence or a creek, something she could follow. Something other than trees and bushes, and briars and thorns. She fought tears and she fought the wind. She fought her rising fears. Frightened or not, there was nothing she could do now but keep going.

A movement, not born of the wind, caught the corner of her eye. She turned, looking hard for whatever it was that had moved. For a moment, all she saw was thorny, scrubby brush and thick undergrowth. Another slight movement, and this time she saw it.

Bigger than any serpent she had ever seen in a zoo or television documentary, a snake lay curled, sleek and black, around the lowest branch of a small tree near her. Glittering eyes looked straight into hers as though reading her every thought. The red tongue lashed out, more as a taunt than a reptilian sensory instinct. The snake seemed to be the very embodiment of evil. Although Abbie knew the notion was foolish, she thought she detected an expression of malicious amusement on the narrow face.

She stepped back against a wind that tried to shove her nearer the awful serpent.

The muscles of the huge body rippled as the snake relaxed its grip and slid without sound from the branch to the ground. With deliberate slowness, it glided forward.

Watching the snake's approach, she became lost in

the gaze of those slitted eyes. Abbie turned numb, unable to move. The tongue flicked and her blood froze.

Run! she screamed silently. *Go now!*

She struggled, fighting an invisible web that bound her in place, helpless, waiting to be the prey of such a terrifying predator.

Plumbing depths of willpower beyond any she'd ever reached before, she broke free of that hypnotizing stare. Her scream burned the soft tissue of her throat as it erupted.

The snake coiled, prepared to strike. Without direction or plan, she fled. Legs pumping, arms flailing, she dared not turn her head to look, but she knew the snake was pursuing her. She knew if it reached her, it would kill her. She ran, screaming and stumbling, heedless of the whipping wind and mindless of the briars and thorns. Branches slapped her head and body. The obstacles in her way multiplied, thickened, and grew more tangled.

Did she drive herself deeper into the forest, or was she nearing a place of safety? At that moment, being lost seemed a minor complication. She ran until her breath heaved in and out in hard, ragged gasps. The stitch in her side stabbed like a knife.

When she spotted the house ahead, relief almost brought her to her knees. Ignoring her raw throat, she screamed like a banshee as she forced her legs to carry her onward.

"Andrew! Andrew!"

As she neared the porch, she dared a backward glance. The snake's jaws opened, baring huge fangs as it struck. She leaped to the porch floor, scaling the side without the aid of the steps.

The front door flew open.

She shrieked as she crashed into him. "Don't let it in the house!"

She shoved him back through the doorway and kicked the door closed behind them.

Chapter 9

When she had left him, Andrew watched for only a moment before turning away. How could it be that her presence, which had been a mere flicker in time, had given him such hope, such deep, brief fulfillment? To see her walk away from him tore his heart so brutally he felt his soul bleed.

At one point, he had reached for the door to call her back but stopped himself. Perhaps, if God existed and heard prayers, she would be able to leave even though he could not. Perhaps this exile was his alone. He hoped so. Although having her with him would fill him with a joy unknown, he could never wish for her to live isolated in a cold, dark place with no hope of liberation.

But if she could not find her way out of that awful forest, and she returned to him…

"No!" he growled. It was wrong to allow even a glimmer of hope for her to come back, because her return would mean her exile.

He returned to the parlor and tamped down the urge to look out the. Deliberately, he crossed to the bookshelf. He removed *Great Expectations* then replaced it, and did likewise with *House of Seven Gables*, *Jane Eyre* and *The Innocents Abroad*.

Escaping into the familiar pages of his books offered no release from mental torment this time. Nor would scrubbing the already immaculate house, or physical exercise, or working with his herbs. He could not stop thinking about her. She was all he ever desired in a companion. She fulfilled his concept of fantasy. Her touch, her voice, her kiss and her strength made him feel alive again. He was a fool for letting her go, and a fool for not going with her. He wanted her. He needed her. He thought he would surely die now in the desolate prison without her.

Maybe she had been a hallucination after all.

"Better for her if she is not real." He settled into his chair. "This existence is not life."

A second chance, he prayed desperately to the God he was no longer sure existed. *Give me a second chance, and I will not toss it aside.*

He heard something and lifted his head, listening hard. Abbie was screaming.

He leaped from his chair, rushed to the door, and flung it open. She hurled herself against him and kicked the door shut. Heart thundering, he stared down at her. He had wanted her back and here she was. Had wishing for her somehow brought her back?

She clung to him, her fingers digging into his arms, her face buried in his shirt. Great racking sobs tore through her body. He felt the repercussions of her violent trembling in his limbs and chest. He enfolded her in his arms, holding her close. He absorbed her shuddering movements and felt the wild flight of her heartbeat against him. Slowly, the trembling quieted. Her heartbeat slowed, and her sobs ebbed.

"Abbie." He rested his head resting gently against hers. "What is it? What has frightened you so?"

She took in a deep, ragged breath and let it out unevenly. "It came after me," she said brokenly. "It would have killed me if I hadn't reached you when I did."

She pressed closer, wrapped both arms around him, fingers clamping his back muscles, her eyes squeezed shut as though shutting out some awful vision. She clung to him as if she feared being torn from his clasp. He tightened his hold.

"There is nothing in this house, or outside it, to hurt you. Not a living thing."

She lifted her head, her eyes wide. "Yes, there is! A snake." She shuddered violently. "I saw it. It's out there, and it's evil."

"No, dear one," he murmured, rocking her tenderly in his arms. "There are no snakes here, nothing to hurt you."

"I saw it! *I saw it!*"

He pulled back a few inches to look into her eyes again. They were swollen with tears and dark with terror. Welts and bloody lesions marred her lovely face.

He disentangled himself from her tight grip and looked at her more closely. Drying rivulets of blood streaked her face, neck, and hands. He yanked back the shirtsleeves and saw more. Bending, he tugged up the baggy legs of the trousers. Her calves were bloody, as well.

"Turn." When she did so, he pulled up the shirt to see that her back had been scraped raw. "Come into the kitchen with me."

He took her abused hand in a gentle grasp and hustled her toward the kitchen.

"I saw it!" She pointed toward the outdoors. "The biggest, most hideous snake ever!" She stared at him from eyes that begged for his belief. "I know it sounds ridiculous," she continued as they entered the kitchen, "but I swear it was laughing, mocking me." She halted in the center of the room, shivering, and drew her arms close to her body as if protecting herself. She rocked back and forward on the balls of her feet.

He smoothed tangled blonde strands from her face and led her to a chair. Brushing his fingertips across her face, he studied the length and depths of cuts on her skin.

"Abbie." He spoke softly. "Look at me and know that you're safe now. Calm and quiet. Safe. Nice deep breaths, slow and steady."

He waited as she did as he suggested, her gaze pinned on his. Her expression eased, and her body relaxed bit by bit, softening, losing the tension that had wrapped around her like an iron band. At last she stopped shaking.

"Better?"

She nodded. "A little."

"Just keep breathing, slow and deep."

"Okay."

"There is a shrub called the dementia rose. It produces tiny aromatic blooms, but it's covered with small thorns that contain a poison which can cause hallucinations. I believe you've been scratched by it."

She shook her head violently. "No, no, no! I saw that snake as plainly as I see you right this minute. Huge. Black. Horrible. Bigger than any snake I've ever seen. And it chased me."

He chaffed her cold hand between both of his. "I know it seems real, but I swear to you, nothing lives except you and me and the vegetation outside. I've been here a long, long time. I promise you, there are no other creatures."

She looked into his eyes as though searching for deceit. A violent shudder ran through her again.

"*But I saw it!*"

"I know." Again, he brushed her cheek with his fingertips. "But it only seems real."

He held her gaze, giving himself to her, wanting to reassure her fearful mind and wipe away the terror.

"I want to show you something."

"Don't leave me!" she shrieked, reaching for him, grabbing his hand with all the strength she had.

"I'm not leaving you. I'm just going to get a book from the shelf. Come with me, if you want to."

With her trembling hand in his, she shadowed him into the parlor. He retrieved the volume and they returned to the kitchen.

"Sit down again, will you, please? Shall I fetch the quilt for you?"

She shook her head and settled in the chair once more. He knelt beside her, opened the book, and found the page he sought.

"Look here." He handed her the book. With his fingertip, he tapped the illustrations of a small, tangled shrub with tiny white blooms. Below the picture, the caption read *Rosa Dementia*. "Look at it closely. The actual bloom would be smaller than this drawing of it, and the shrub itself would be about this high." He measured a couple of feet from the floor. "Did you see this while you were out there?"

She studied the illustration. "I'm not sure. Maybe. It looks like everything else that grows in that awful forest." She stared at it a moment longer, then handed the book back to him. "I don't know."

He put the book on the table. "I tried to eradicate

that particular species from around the place, but everything here has a way of renewing itself as if it's never been touched."

She frowned, then shuddered, reaching for his hand again. Her grip was strong.

"I'm sure you've come into contact with that plant, and that is what caused this hallucination of a snake." He paused. "I want you to believe me, because it's the truth."

He waited for her answer as she searched his eyes, probing for whatever it was she needed to find.

"I don't know." She looked away for a time, then turned back to him. "Tell me this. If it was all just imaginary, wouldn't I see other things that don't exist? For instance, maybe *you* aren't real. Maybe this house is just a figment of the poison."

He blinked. "I'm real. I'm flesh and blood."

"Seems like I've heard someone else say that recently." She held his gaze steadily.

"I know. I'm sorry I doubted you."

"You're still doubting me. I saw something fearsome, and you don't believe me."

"I believe you saw something. I believe it chased you and terrified you. But I know that what you saw is not real. The vision was caused by a hallucinogenic. As to why you've not had other visions, the effects of the dementia rose are power but short-lived. A few minutes only." He opened the book again and put it in her hands. "Read what it says right here. I am telling you the true facts."

She read a short paragraph which verified what he'd just told her.

"So there is no monstrous, anthropomorphic

snake?"

"None. And now, do you believe me?"

Her smile was small and forced, but she nodded. "I believe you."

"Good. Now, these wounds need to be cleaned and bound, and kept free of infection."

He examined the scratches on her body again. He studied her arms for so long that she stirred restlessly.

"Is something wrong?" she asked.

He deepened his frown as he once more looked at the abrasions. "You wore these clothes out there with the sleeves rolled to your wrists and the trouser legs rolled to your ankles."

"Yes. And the socks with my slippers. Have I been exposed to something worse than that bush?"

He looked up quickly. Apprehension had rekindled on her face.

"No. You're going to be all right. It's just that, well…" He ran one hand through his hair and frowned at the shirtsleeve as he plucked it between his thumb and forefinger. "Your skin is torn and bloody, almost raw in many places. But this shirt is whole. Not a thread broken." He flicked the edge of her trouser leg. "And no harm to these trousers."

She extended her arms and legs. She raised her eyes to his. "The clothes should be in tatters."

"Yes," he said slowly. "This is what I've been telling you. Nothing diminishes or deteriorates here."

"I don't understand."

"Neither do I. I know that the sun never rises or sets. My garden produces with no lull in harvest. The oil level in the lamps remains the same. Wood burning in the stove and fireplace never needs to be replenished. You'll see these phenomena for yourself."

Chapter 10

"This place frightens me," she said as Andrew cleaned her wounds.

"I know it does." He worked in silence for a few moments, then looked up and met her eyes. "You aren't afraid of me, are you?"

She pondered the question, and perhaps she was right to do so. The place where they found themselves offered little more than shelter and food, certainly no cheer.

"I should be, shouldn't I? I tell myself I should be very afraid. After all, you're a stranger to me."

"Yes, I am."

She flourished one hand to indicate their surroundings. "Here you are, living this perplexing, isolated existence in what must be the one of the creepiest places on earth. We met each other a few hours ago, but..." Her voice trailed, and she looked away, losing herself in thought.

"But?"

Slowly, she turned her gaze and attention back to him. "It feels as though I've known you a long time."

A smile crept into his eyes. "Yes, it does."

"I wonder why that is."

"There's no wonder to it. It's this place. Time has no meaning or relevance here."

She shook her head. "That makes no sense."

"It makes no sense to me, either, but it's the way of things."

She looked beyond him, out the window at the gloomy day. "I don't doubt you, but I don't understand it."

"All we can do is accept that it is what it is."

His statement bothered her, pricked against her mind like an unwanted memory or dark thought. "I have never liked the idea of simply accepting what is. Without change, life would be dreary. Mind-numbing."

"You like a challenge." He met her eyes and gave her a quizzical smile. "Am I right?"

"You're right. I do."

He took her other arm, turned it over, and began treating the cuts.

"So, you didn't really answer my question. Are you afraid of me?"

She watched as he gently tended to her injuries. He stopped and glanced up.

"Are you?"

She hesitated, then shook her head. "The truth is, I'm *not*—which is bothers me considerably." She looked hard into his eyes. "You see, there was a time when I believed in goodness of people. I believed in honorable intentions and in the grace of second chances."

He lifted on eyebrow. "And you no longer believe in these things?"

"I'm not sure. In what little personal life I've had, I've entrusted my heart to the wrong men. Three times. In my work, I help give second chances that are trampled by repeat offenders far too often. What's sad is that I once believed I was helping to redeem society by giving a helping hand to those in need. Things rarely work out the way I hope they will, and yet I keep doing it because…well, because it's what I do." She caught her lower lip between her teeth and thought about what she'd just said. "Or what I did. Bit by bit, I've changed these last several months. Maybe it's because I've looked into the eyes of bad people too much lately. I know evil when I see it. The thing is…" She reached out, touched his hand with cold fingertips. "The thing is, when I look into *your* eyes, I see more decency and character than I've ever seen before."

He stirred, smiled a bit. "I'd like to think I have a good heart."

"Unfortunately, I don't trust my judgment anymore." She shrugged. "I think you're a truly decent man, and that scares me."

He frowned. "A decent man scares you?"

"No. My assessment scares me. As I said, I don't trust my own judgement. Here you are, a recluse from society who refuses to tell me why you have chosen to hide yourself away. Logic tells me there is a reason you're living like this, and it can't be good. And yet I know you are a good man."

"So you trust neither your instinct nor judgment."

"Exactly."

A long pause lay between them. The silence was broken only by the soft splashes of water as he cleaned the last of her wounds.

"When I was in the forest, trying to get out, before I saw the snake, I remembered you saying that leaving was impossible." She looked at him expectantly, hoping he could explain that fearsome forest beyond the house. "I think I understand why you said it. I'm a city girl. I'm not into nature, so pretty much the woods are all creepy to me." She gave him a little smile and looked at him closely. "But you don't really believe it's impossible to leave here, do you? Not really."

His brow creased and for a moment, his hands stilled. He drew in a breath as if about to reply, but then he rinsed the cloth in warm water, wrung out the excess, and put it in her hand.

"Please clean the cuts and scratches on your front while I make a poultice." He turned away and worked in silence while she did as he said.

"You aren't going to answer me, are you?"

"I have no answer."

When she finished washing the abrasions on her chest and stomach, she asked, "Did something happen to you?"

He mixed a fresh batch of the poultice and brought the bowl of it to the table.

"Please tell me."

"There's nothing to tell. Here, let me put this on your cuts." He quickly applied the salve to her back and extremities and set the remainder on the table beside her. "Put this on your front scrapes. Be generous with it. I can make more if you run out. In the meantime, I'll make you tea from the leaves of the tealround bush. It will help fight infection. It will also ease any lasting effects of the dementia rose."

Fear leaped into her throat. "I thought you said the toxic effects are short-lived."

"They are, but there could be a few after-effects that aren't pleasant. Nausea and headache for instance. If you drink your tea, I don't think there'll be anything to worry about. It will make you drowsy. Extremely sleepy, in fact, but rest will be good for you."

She turned her gaze to the window as he measured a small amount of coarse dark powder into a cup and poured hot water over it. The sky was still light, but the hour felt late. She was ready for sleep.

"What time is it?"

"I don't know."

She frowned and blew out a deep breath. "This is a guess, but I suppose you don't have a watch or a clock."

"You guess correctly."

"Seems like I've been here quite a while. Seems like it should be nearly night by now." She sighed again, softly, and brought her eyes back to him. "But you know what? If I'm honest with myself and with you, wouldn't mind staying a while longer."

He lifted his head and looked at her, sure his heart shone from his eyes. Soft light shimmered briefly through the kitchen window, almost like a bright shadow passing through. Andrew caught his breath and turned his head sharply toward the window. What was that? Had he imagined it? He rushed to the window and looked toward the sky. The clouds moved and roiled, the same as always but…There! He saw it: a small break where sunlight seeped through, and then it was gone.

"Oh, maybe the storm is breaking up." She joined him at the window.

"You saw it, too?" He looked at her over his shoulder.

"A bit of sunlight? Yes."

"Excuse me a moment. Please don't move."

He went outside, out into the soundless wind and cold. He scoured the sky with his gaze, searching for beautiful golden sunlight that he had not seen in time untold. He plunged into the forest and looked beyond the treetops, but nowhere did he see a brightening of the clouds again. He turned to retrace his steps and saw her at the kitchen window, worriedly watching him. She opened the door when he reached it.

"What's wrong?" She was clearly alarmed.

"Nothing. Not a thing. Please, sit down. You shouldn't move about so much." He guided her back to the chair and settled her in it.

"But—"

He touched his fingertips to her lips. "Not to worry. Everything is all right. Here. Have your tea."

He put the cup in front of her, then sat down and took one of her hands in both of his.

"You said earlier that you aren't afraid of me. I'm glad because I would never hurt you. And, please, don't be afraid of this place, because nothing here can hurt you, except the dementia rose. You mustn't go back into the woods until I've found that hateful bush and hacked it out."

"But what about Lefty's house? What about whoever it was that attacked me? I need to get in touch with the police."

"There's nothing that can be done about that right now. We'll talk about it later. After you've rested and recovered."

"You give me your word?" She met his eyes straight on.

"Absolutely. I swear it."

She studied him, as though probing the secret places in his heart and mind. His heart brimmed with the need to love and care for her. He touched the soft skin beneath her eyes.

"There are dark circles here. You're tired, and

you've been through a lot. So, I repeat, you need to rest."

He pushed the cup toward her and sat back, releasing her hand. She looked at the tea, then at him.

"If I drink this concoction and do as you say, will you help me leave?"

She seemed determined to go away, didn't she? Despair dragged on his heart and banished the lightness he'd felt moments earlier. He sighed and wiped his hand down his face. How could he help her do what he could not do himself? Yet how could he tell her gently there was no way to go home? He must find the words to cause her as little pain and fear and hopelessness as possible.

"If it's a deal you want," he said at last, "here's what I propose: drink the tea, then have a good long sleep. When you wake up, I'll answer your questions to the best of my ability and do everything I can to help you. *If* you drink this tea—" he tapped her cup "—*and* get some rest."

She searched his face thoughtfully. He watched her struggle and finally give in.

"I am awfully tired," she admitted slowly, picking up the cup. She pinned a no-nonsense look on him over the rim. "And I'm holding you to your end of the bargain."

Andrew nodded. He hoped the right words would come to him when he needed them. He hoped he could make her understand.

She stared down into the cup she held. She had not yet tasted it.

"This tea is dark red, like that other creation you had me drink earlier."

"The leaves of the mature tealround are red."

"Does it taste as nasty as that first tea?"

He chuckled at the enchanting way she curled her nose. "Not at all. In fact, it has a pleasing, rather sweet flavor."

She cautiously sniffed it. "It smells nice, a little like raspberries."

"Then drink it. You'll feel better when you wake up, I promise."

"I feel better already. That first stuff you gave me was disgusting, but I admit it relieved the pain quite effectively." She tipped her head to one side, her eyes studying his face. She smiled, and he felt his heart heave in his chest. "I appreciate your help. Thank you so, so much for everything you've done."

"It has been my pleasure to help you."

She took a small, wary sip of the tea then eagerly finished it.

"Wonderful!" She gave him a smile. "I hope there's more where that came from."

He took the empty cup. "Sorry. It's a strong sedative. A second cup would be too much."

"Ah, well." She sighed wistfully. "You would probably have given me a second cup of the bitter stuff, wouldn't you?"

He laughed at her and watched as she fought back a yawn.

"Where may I lie down?"

He led her up a steep, narrow flight of stairs and into the bedroom. His bed was a large four-poster, snug and comfortable. There was no doubt in his mind she would sleep deeply and sleep well.

"I'll draw these draperies to darken the room more for you."

"Surely, it'll be dark soon, anyway."

She did not yet realize there was never any night here, never any true daylight, only a gloomy, eternal grayness. She would find that out soon enough. Let her sleep first.

She sat on the edge of the bed and watched as he closed the draperies. He turned and saw the shadowy outline of her body. She looked small and fragile, very much in need of comfort. He ached to go to her, take her in his arms, hold and kiss her as he laid her back on his warm bed. But he would not do so. He most certainly would be overcome with desire. Indeed, he was overcome with desire for her at that very moment. To touch her, to kiss her when she was in this vulnerable state, might banish the trust she had invested in him. He would sleep downstairs in the parlor.

He picked up the extra quilt from the foot of the bed for himself. "Have a good sleep."

He was in the hallway when she called him back. He stood in the doorway, saw she had not moved from the edge of the bed, a slender figure in the gloom.

"Where do you sleep? I mean, what if…" She tried to keep her voice steady. "What if that snake, somehow…that is, I mean where will you be if I need you?"

She was strong, and her courage was beyond question, but he wanted so badly to hold her, to take away her fear. He smiled tenderly into the darkness.

"I'll be in the front room downstairs. All you must do is call. I'll hear you."

She sat silent a moment then said, "Thank you."

"You're welcome. Sleep well."

****

In the kitchen, he washed the dishes and set

everything to rights. He wanted to take his mattock into the woods right then and completely destroy the *rosa dementia*. It was a noxious and stubborn shrub. Although he thought he had taken every bit of the root from the ground long ago, it had returned. Things had a way of surviving in his dark world. He hacked weeds and thickets only when he felt the need of hard work, not because he desired an environment of manicured lawns and bright flowerbeds. He would never have those here.

Although he was certain the tealround would help her sleep several hours, he chose to remain nearby. Working in the forest, he would be unable to hear if she called him. He hoped when she awakened, her pain would be gone, her fears relieved, and her mind at ease.

The kitchen work finished, he went upstairs to check on her. His eyes adjusted quickly to the darker room, and he saw her curled under the cover, quilt pulled to her chin as though hunkering against the cold. Downstairs, fetched the quilt he had taken for himself and returned to spread it over her, tucking it snugly about her body. She did not stir. He made sure her breathing was quiet and even, then he returned to the parlor.

He idly stirred the fire in the grate then sat staring into the flames. He picked up a collection of short stories by Mark Twain that had never grown stale or failed to entertain him and settled into his chair before the fire. He opened the book to the first story and read a few lines. He read them again. When he had read them the third time, he set the book aside. His mind was totally on Abbie Matthews and her unexpected advent into his life.

What did the momentous events of this day mean? After his eternity of solitude, would she now be his companion? If his solitary existence at last had come to an end, was it possible the constant wind, the cold, the grayness, and the monotony of this existence would drive her to the brink of madness as it had done him? Would she be strong enough to withstand life with him as her only friend? Was there anything more he could do or give to her?

He told himself he must step outside his own dismal self and become sharper, more social, a brighter cohort. He needed to shore up his resources and offer them all to her.

What were his resources, anyway? He was still an intelligent man. Though the lack of stimulus had the power to weaken his mind, he had never allowed it to dull. He honed his brain by reading his books, by writing alternative chapters and endings, by pondering science and experimenting with his herbs.

At one time, an eternity ago, he had possessed a fine sense of humor. Hadn't he loved playing with his brothers and sisters, joking with his folks? Hadn't he and Matthew Levi played innumerable, good-natured pranks? Surely, that drollness, that sense of fun and adventure could be renewed. Couldn't he offer humor and intelligence to his new friend? Would she accept his offering, maybe reciprocate in a like manner?

Maybe she would share her life story with him. He longed to learn all about her, where she came from, and where she belonged. Recalling his own abrupt, inexplicable entrance into this world, he wondered how she had made her arrival, and from where. She spoke of preparing for bed and suddenly waking up in the forest. Clearly, she did not know her path of arrival any more than he had known his. They were simply here. Was it by accident, or by design? If by design, why? Who was the author of their fate? Were they in a dream? A fantasy? Someone's novel? If they existed only in someone's dream or fantasy, what would happen upon the dreamer's awakening? If in a book, what would happen when the writer penned, "The End"?

He scowled at such foolish imaginings and shoved their clutter from his mind.

When it was time for her to wake up and want the answers he had promised, how was he going to explain anything?

Dear God, what am I going to do?

He fixed his gaze on the ceiling as though fixed on the Almighty himself, but no answer came to him as he waited. He wished he could relax, but his mind remained on the woman upstairs. Did she continue to sleep peacefully? Was she warm enough? Hesitating only a moment, he went back upstairs to her bedside. Her hand and her cheek were warm to his touch, her breath as soft and regular as before.

He stood unmoving, looking down at her for a long time. Despite the deep, angry cuts and bruises on her face, she was beautiful. Her skin was neither dusky nor pallid, but a soft cream that invited his touch. Her blonde lashes were long and dense, her lips full without being thick. A part of him clung to a desperate hope that this lovely, slumbering angel could escape the life he could not. But another part of him, a deeper, more hidden section of his soul yearned for her to stay, to share with him her warmth, her words and smile, her heart and body. Could he admit, in the deepest part of his being, where his heart beat steadfastly, that her exile was his salvation?

She had the power to awaken passion in him. He

dared allow himself to believe he had done the same for her. But he had been in a desolate existence long enough to realize that life must be more than longing and desire to appease one's urges. Real life should be full of living and doing and purpose, of making some sense of one's place in the world.

Mere existence was worse than death.

"I wish had met you before this place!" he whispered to her, touching a strand of her pale hair. "I would have given you my whole self, my whole heart."

She slept on, oblivious to his words, his touch, and his presence.

He stepped away, preparing to return downstairs, but found he could not leave her. Instead, he settled on the floor on the far side of the bedroom, rested his back against the wall, and watched her sleep. She did not move and neither did he. He had no idea how long he sat there before finally rising and going back downstairs to sleep near the fire that never burned out.

Chapter 11

Although the room was dim and unfamiliar, Abbie knew exactly where she was when she awakened. Recent events rushed back to her in vivid detail: the cold and silent wind, the dark woods, the hideous snake, and her panicked flight from it. Those memories seemed more like the remains of a nightmare.

She pondered, just for the space of a breath or two, that maybe it had all been a bad dream, something created by her need to break free of a life that seemed to bind her spirit. But she knew better. Her dreams were not this detailed and focused. They were choppy, disconnected bits and pieces events that had no substance to them, sometimes even cartoon-like.

She thought of Andrew, his dark eyes and sensuous mouth. She remembered the pent-up passion with which he had kissed her, how she had felt in his arms—as if she could not get close enough to him. An enigmatic man with a wounded soul who seemed bound by his own desolate heart to a solitary existence. Dismissing for the moment his eccentric choices, she asked herself if she was ready to step into another relationship. Could she tamp down the pain old scars brought or ignore directives from her inner voice never to trust or love again? For that matter, did she even want to try?

And why am I even thinking about this? she asked herself and forced the thoughts from her mind.

She had been through a lot in a very short time. Was she prepared to renew her search for the way back to civilization again? Did she have the grit to face that menacing forest once more? Was her heart ready for her to leave the enigmatic Andrew Wade? Oh, there she went again, thinking about him!

She pulled the blanket up over her head, wishing she understood everything that had transpired in the last twenty-four hours and wondering why she didn't feel the same urgent need to get away that she'd felt the night before.

She stirred restlessly and turned over on her back. She stared through the dull light toward the ceiling. Obviously, she was unable to keep him out of her thoughts and finally gave herself over to them.

Although she barely knew him, he attracted her, tempted her. More than any other man she had ever known, he stirred something in her both gentle and eager. No one else had ever had the ability to stir her blood the way he did. Right now, today, a window of opportunity opened itself to her. She recognized it and embraced the prospect. Was this gloomy house his childhood home, or had he come from some other place, seeking solitude? What drove him to seek and maintain this private existence? Did she really need to know?

She should simply accept him as she found him, and maybe she could do just that if it weren't for the fact that he seemed utterly unhappy. Something, somewhere, sometime, had happened to him, and now he shut himself off from the world.

She thought of how kindly he had taken care of her. He was the only man she had ever known who demanded nothing from her, neither attention nor service, or even a touch, though touching had been done as he treated her wounds. She longed to kiss him, to touch him in other ways. Something inside her swelled, then melted with a rush of warmth. She longed to be with him.

Stretching a few inches at a time, she felt the ache in her muscles, the lingering pain in her bruised and scratched body. The knot on her head had diminished, but her fingertips told her it was still tender and swollen. She pushed back the blanket, and chill air rushed to greet her. Her toes curled as she got out of bed and stood on the cold floor. She grabbed the quilt and wrapped it around her as she shuffled across the room and opened the draperies.

The gray light outside was unchanged from the time she last saw it leaking through the glass. The sky continued to glower with the threat of a storm. It was as if no time had passed, though she felt completely rested. He had told her that the tea she drank before she went to bed had a sedative effect. Add that to her exhaustion and injuries, and she supposed she might have slept completely through the remainder of yesterday and all last night.

On the back of the small chair lay the clothes he had given her the day before. Hadn't she left them in a limp little puddle by the side of the bed just before she climbed between the covers? As she pulled on the clothes, she noticed everything was clean. He had no electricity, no modern appliances, but he had washed and dried her clothes. No other man in the world had ever done anything like that for her. Rather, they expected her to do it for them. She looped the belt around herself and tightened it. More and more she realized the depth of his kindness.

Combing her sleep-tangled hair with her fingers, she looked around in a futile attempt to find a mirror. She realized there wasn't a whole lot she could do about her appearance at this point.

The bathroom was an outdoor privy, offering only the essential hole—no mirror, no vanity, no shower. Her host looked a bit shaggy around the edges, but otherwise clean, so she knew there had to be some way to bathe.

Right then, though, she was ravenous, hungrier than she had ever been in her life. She hurried from the room and went downstairs. The scent of cooking food led her to the warm kitchen. On the stove, a large slab of steak sizzled in a skillet, and potatoes and onions fried fragrantly in another pan. He was not in sight.

She made a trip to the outdoor privy and when she returned, he was there, turning over the meat in the frying pan. Steak and fried potatoes were a far cry from her customary breakfast of yogurt and juice, but she felt hollow inside. The food looked and smelled better than any meal she had ever eaten.

His gaze traveled from her tousled hair to her feet lost in his socks.

"Hello."

"Good morning." She returned his smile. "Or is it afternoon? I feel like I've slept for a week." She approached the stove, bent over the skillet and breathed in gratefully. "This food smells awesome."

"Good!" He ran a quick, critical glance over her. "Your color is better, but you're still wan. And I believe you could do with a few good meals. Fill you out a little bit. How are you feeling this morning? Let me look at your wounds."

"I'm feeling much better, thank you," she said, as he

checked her cuts and bruises, gently feeling for heat or swelling. "And I won't argue with you over diet this morning. Shall I set the table?"

He smiled slightly and stepped back. "You're healing nicely. If you wish to set the table, go ahead, but there's not much to place on it." He dipped his head toward the cupboard where he kept cutlery and plates. "It's in there."

She opened the wooden doors to the cupboard.

"You're right when you said there isn't much to place. Two of everything and not a bit more. You don't entertain much, do you?" She gave him a teasing smile.

He jerked around to face her.

"What did you just say?"

Uh oh.

"I'm sorry. I was just joking with you. I should have been more tactful—" She broke off, somewhat alarmed by the look of utter astonishment on his face.

"Where did you get that?"

She frowned. "Get what? The table service? Out of the cupboard, of course. I thought you wanted me to."

He lifted his stunned gaze from the table to her.

"You brought the extra with you, didn't you?"

"What? I didn't bring anything with me."

"Then…where…how…?" His gaze returned to the plates and utensils on the table and clutched the back of a chair so hard his knuckles whitened. The sudden pallor of his face alarmed her.

"Andrew! Sit down. What's wrong?"

He remained where he was, his eyes fixed on the table.

"I've only ever had one of each." Slowly he lifted his gaze to her. "You brought them with you."

"You think I brought a *place setting*? You saw me yesterday. I had nothing but the clothes on my back."

"And I'm telling you that in all the time I've been in this house, I've never had more than one plate, one cup, one knife, fork, and spoon. Where did that extra come from?"

"I don't know. Maybe you overlooked them or—"

"No! I did not overlook anything! I have been over every square inch of this house a multitude of times. There has never been more than *one* plate, *one* cup, and *one* knife, fork, and spoon!"

He stalked to the cupboard and yanked it open, glaring inside as if he expected to find stacks of plates and dozens of forks. She stared at his broad back, waiting to see what he would say or do, but he stood like granite.

"Is it such a terrible thing to find extras in your home?"

He turned his head slowly to meet her eyes.

"But where…" He looked back at the cupboard.

She said nothing as he processed whatever strange notions were going on in his mind. After a bit, he turned to her. Bewilderment still colored his expression, but his gaze softened and warmed as he regarded her.

" 'Extras in my home,' " he repeated softly. "*You* are an extra in my home, and that's not a terrible thing at all."

He touched her cheek, traced her lips with his fingertips. She felt lost in his gaze, her skin tingling. She leaned toward him, waiting for him to take her into his arms.

He dropped his hands and turned from her to glance at the table.

"Please sit. I know you're famished. Tealround tea

often has that side effect."

She stood a moment longer, blood thrumming, body limp with disappointment. At last she sat.

"I'm starving," she admitted.

He smiled and brought her a plate heaped with steak and potatoes. It smelled warm and heavenly. She cut steak so tender that it hardly needed the knife's blade.

"How long did I sleep?" She put the meat between her eager lips, nearly burning her tongue. "Mmm. This is delicious."

He stood near the stove, looking at her from eyes that seemed as hungry as her appetite for food. He blinked and turned away to fill his own plate.

"I don't know. Many hours. Perhaps an entire day."

She paused with a crispy chunk of fried potato on her fork. "What time is it now? What day?"

He seemed to weigh the question as if it were a mathematical puzzle then slowly replied, "I have no timepiece or calendar."

"Well, at least you know if a day and night have passed and have a reasonable idea if this is morning or afternoon. I mean, I know it's cloudy outside, but..." Once again, her voice trailed.

He settled across from her but refused to meet her eyes. Why was he acting as if she'd asked him for his bank balance?

She put down her knife and fork. "Well, if you don't know the day or the time, then you just don't know it." She offered a smile. "But could you hazard a ballpark?"

He raised an eyebrow. "A what?"

"A guess."

"Oh." He shook his head. "I really have no idea."

She frowned. Was he playing games, or did he really

have no notion, no remote inkling of time?

He got up, took her plate, and added more food.

"Eat more." He set the plate in front of her again. "You need it."

She caught his arm, looked up at him until he met her gaze. His eyes, deep brown, and dark as rich earth, stayed on her steadfastly. She could lose herself in that hypnotic gaze. Her heart yearned for him, but suddenly her mind resurrected the memory of David, Robert, and Michael, each with his own selfish wants that had tortured her tender feelings and left her emotionally devastated. Refusing to get caught up in that "saving the lone wolf" in which some foolish, romantically starved women lost themselves and their dignity, she forced herself to take her gaze off him.

She refused to play the bumble-headed female again, but not falling for Andrew Wade was going to be tough. Real tough.

She picked up her fork and gazed absently at it. "Remember our agreement yesterday? I drank the tea you gave me. I ate, I slept, and now I'm eating again. I have kept my half of the bargain. You said you'd help me, so now it's your turn."

He took a deep breath, let it out slowly. "When you've finished your meal, go into that room there." He pointed to a small, closed door. "I have a tub of warm water for you. You need to soak those injuries and limber up your muscles. You'll feel even better. After that, come into the front room. I'll answer all your questions as best I can."

She knew he would never relent without her cooperation. She nodded and finished eating.

Later, she went through the door he had indicated

and found herself in a small, candlelit room. He had prepared a bath for her in a wooden tub. Steam rose from the water. A fresh towel, a washcloth, a bar of plain, clean-smelling white soap and a comb lay in a neat stack on a stool next to the tub. On the floor beside the stool, he had provided a container of salve with which she could dress her cuts and scrapes.

She skinned out of her clothes and got into the warm water. As eager as she was to learn what he had to tell her, she did as he instructed, soaking her battered body until the water began to cool. She toweled herself dry, treated her wounds, and dressed quickly. Combing out her long, wet hair, she walked into the warm parlor where he waited.

Fire burned cheerfully in the grate, adding its brightness to the room. He had drawn both chairs even closer to the hearth. He stood when she entered. His gaze took in every inch of her, returning to linger on her long, wet hair. He adjusted one of the chairs a few inches.

"Sit here and dry your hair. I'd hate for you to catch a chill."

His offer was so gallantly old-fashioned that she smiled as she settled where he suggested.

"Thank you." She turned her head so the drying warmth of the fire could reach her hair as she gently worked out any snarls. "And thank you for that wonderful meal, and for preparing my bath. I feel much better today. You have been so kind to me, far above the norm."

He returned her smile. "You're more than welcome."

For a while, neither one spoke as she continued to comb and dry her hair and he watched. The companionable crackling of the fire added an intimacy to their silence. After a minute or two, he cleared his throat. When she looked at him, he gave her an embarrassed smile.

"I apologize for the boorish way I acted when you first arrived. Perhaps you'll understand and forgive me after I tell you some things."

She stopped combing, reached out, and laid her hand on top of his.

"I understand that you are a very kind and decent man. You've taken wonderful care of a woman who barged into your home, unannounced and uninvited, demanding your assistance. There is nothing to forgive. *I* should be apologizing to *you*, and I do."

He turned his hand over, catching her fingers with his own. He looked at her hand as though it were a precious curiosity to be studied and cherished, then raised her fingers to his lips. The kiss he planted was warm and gentle and hesitant. His lips lingered a moment before he let go, the invisible imprint of that kiss a burning reminder.

Her heart beat fast, much faster than a tender touch of lips to hand warranted. She wanted him to kiss her, his strong arms holding her close. She closed her eyes, lost in the longing. When she opened them, she found him gazing at her, his yearning open and vulnerable on his face. Was her own expression so easily read?

"Andrew?"

He drew his gaze away, focusing on the fire at the hearth.

"You make my home as lovely and warm and welcoming as that fire. It was never that before, and. although those flames always burn, this room has remained drab and chilly, darkly depressing. Until you entered my home, I had no brightness, except for books, and I am weary of them."

His words soaked into her mind, touching each point of her soul.

I cannot, will not, fall in love again. Nor would she encourage him. In fact, she must discourage any tendency toward love he might show. Resolutely, she banished her burgeoning desire and pulled her hand free of his. Sitting back, she focused on the immediate challenge.

"Tell me about this place. Tell me why you're here, and why you live this way, shut off from the world. And I want to know why you can't help me leave."

She watched as the longing in his eyes faded. The smile he offered was intensely unhappy. Incredible despair filled his expression. She felt sick to her stomach, witnessing such sadness.

She dropped her gaze to blink back tears.

"Tell me," she whispered, looking up again. "Please."

Chapter 12

Andrew sighed, long and deep, shifting his gaze to the flames that crackled in front of them.

"Telling you my story. That *was* our bargain, wasn't it? But I cannot tell you what you want to know."

"But you said—"

"I said I'd tell you what I could, and I shall." He ran one hand through his hair. "Will it disturb you overmuch, I wonder?"

"Whether it disturbs me or not is irrelevant. I'm here, and you must tell me. Please."

He shifted restlessly, refusing to meet her eyes.

"I guess I should start at the beginning."

"Yes. Do that."

For another moment, a silence lay between them as Andrew seemed to gather his thoughts.

"I was born on Sumac Ridge, in the Arkansas Ozarks." He glanced at her. "Do you know of Sumac Ridge?"

She shook her head. "I'm from Ohio. Dayton."

"I see. Then you've never heard of our little mountain community. Close-knit, with big families and strong ties to the land. But Sumac Ridge is small, a poor place, quite isolated. The mountains are rugged enough to discourage visitors and deter homefolks from leaving. Professional people such as doctors, teachers, and ministers are scarce, even though folks there need healing, learning, and spiritual guidance just like everyone else."

"Of course," she agreed. "And most professionals seem to go where the population is. Where the *money* is," she added with some bitterness and self-recrimination.

He raised an eyebrow and waited for her to say more, but she shook her head, unwilling to distract him with her own story.

"Please continue."

"I was born on the Ridge to parents who valued their children above everything in the world. I loved them, the Ridge, and the people who live there. Even as a young boy, I knew I wanted to do something to help the folks on Sumac Ridge. Make their lives easier in some way."

He leaned forward, stirred the fire, and watched sparks snap and fly before settling back in his chair. Still watching the flames, he continued, "I enjoyed learning but really didn't want to teach. That takes a special talent, I think. Likewise, I couldn't be a preacher. My temperament isn't suited for a life of Godly pursuits, though I believe I was, at that time, a deeply spiritual man."

He glanced at her as though he thought his confession might have offended her. She met his eyes and waited patiently for him to continue.

"When someone on the Ridge became ill or was injured, there was no one there to help them except for Granny Hodge. She was as old as the hills but still got around to treat folks." He paused again. "Do they have granny women in Dayton, Ohio?"

"There are as many grandmothers in Dayton as any other town, I suppose."

He made a dismissive gesture with one hand.

"That's not what I mean. A 'granny woman' is an herbalist, a midwife, a nurse. Sometimes she's the only doctor some people know. For Sumac Ridge, it's Granny Hodge. Folks said Granny took her vocation one step further and practiced the black arts as well as the healing arts." He shrugged. "I don't know about that. For as long as I can remember, she took care of everyone up and down the Ridge, even the people in the town of Smith. When I decided to be a doctor, she was kind and patient with me, let me tag along when she made her rounds to the sick folks. Granny was good at teaching me herbal medicine and folk remedies. Much of what I learned from her was scoffed at by my professors. Still, her poultices and teas helped the sick and ailing." Here he paused and smiled. "Granny taught me those remedies I gave you."

"And did she teach you any of her 'black arts'?"

He chuckled a little, shook his head. "No. She knew I had no interest in it. We rarely discussed it, although she did tell me once that there were times when it's the only way to deal with some people."

"Some people swear by spells and curses and black cats and the like."

"Yes, and I suppose superstitious folks are the ones she used her sorcery on. But as I said, I wasn't interested in it, and she understood. In fact, I think she was relieved. It was tough, getting my education. My folks had six more mouths to feed at home, so I worked with single-minded purpose for several years until I had saved enough to study medicine. I was one year away from graduating. And then this —" he made a broad gesture with one hand and looked around the room as though seeing it for the first time. "—this happened."

Silence settled around him like a heavy cloak.

"What?" she prodded gently. "What happened? What is—" she made the same broad gesture he did. "—this?"

He turned his head slowly and regarded her from a stranger's eyes. His gaze chilled and frightened her with its bleakness, but she did not turn away.

"I don't know," he said at last. "As long as I have lived here, I've been unable to understand this place. All I can tell you is that I was walking the two miles between our house and the railroad depot. I had my valise and my books, ready to return to the university after the summer break. My memory's a little fuzzy, but I seem to recall hearing someone in the woods calling for help. I followed the voice and after that, I don't know. Maybe no one was there. Maybe I blacked out from the heat. Whatever happened, when I woke up, I was here." He turned his head to face her. "You are the first living, sentient being I've seen since that time. And it's been such a long time that surely you can understand how I had mistaken you for a figment of my imagination."

She felt as though her air had been cut off. Could the ridiculous story he just related be true? And yet hadn't something very similar happened to her, one moment going about life and the next moment waking up in an alien existence?

She fought for breath, leaned forward eagerly and managed to croak, "Do you mean…how did you…? Andrew, how long have you been here?"

He shook his head. "Without a time piece, I don't know, but it's been many years. My stay here seems an eternity."

She swallowed hard, fighting for calm. "When did

you leave home to return to the university?"

"It was late August. About the end of the month, I think."

She licked dry lips. "What year?"

"Year? Why, 1913."

She sagged against the back of the chair, feeling the blood drain from her face.

"That's impossible," she managed to choke out. "You have to be mistaken."

Or delusional.

He was a young man, no older than his early thirties. There was simply no way he could have lived for more than a century. *No way.* Nor could he have traveled in time. Things like that happened only in books or in science fiction movies.

Again, she told herself he had to be mistaken. Because if he were right, she had done some weird cosmic traveling herself. But how else could she explain her own arrival here? She had been in Lefty's apartment, preparing for bed; then she had been in those cold dark woods outside this house. Just that quickly.

"These things do not happen!" she said aloud, jumping up from her chair and startling her companion. She paced the floor, every nerve twitching almost beyond endurance. "This is crazy. This is all some weird, fantastical dream, and I'm going to wake up soon." She stopped pacing, threw her arms wide open, looked heavenward, yelling, "I'm ready to wake up now!"

But nothing happened. She remained in the fire-warmed parlor while the soundless cold wind blew through the dark forest outside and he watched her from his chair.

"Abbie." He got to his feet and went to her. Resting

both hands on her shoulders, he looked into her eyes. "My dear, this is not a dream. You will not wake up. If that were possible, I would have awakened long ago."

"No!" She lashed at him with her fists, pounding his chest and his arms. "I don't believe you! This is a horrid, horrid nightmare, and you're a part of it just like the stormy sky and the cold and the snake and that ghastly silent wind outside. I will wake up. I will, I will!"

He tried to calm her, but she struggled against him. "Let go of me. I want to go home!" she screamed. "I want to wake up!"

"I know you do. So do I. So very, very much. But, my dear, we're awake right now." He held her loosely, and his quiet, reasonable tone infuriated her.

He said nothing more but let her shriek and flail, like a tantrum-throwing three-year-old until, at last, she spent her fear and anger, and wilted into his arms.

For a long space of time, she rested against him, clutching his shirt, absorbing his gentle strength. Finally, she raised her face with its stinging, swollen eyelids to him. He stood there, so strong and stalwart, patiently taking in her useless fit of temper.

"I'm sorry," she muttered, scrubbing her eyes with the heels of her hands. "I had no right to talk to you like that."

He smiled and wiped away remnants of her tears with his thumbs, then enfolded her in his safe embrace once more.

"Don't you think I've cursed and raved like a lunatic a thousand times? Do you think I accepted this fate easily? But my rage did absolutely nothing to change my circumstances."

"Oh, but listen to me. Do you know the last time I

was in the sunlight and warmth?"

He shook his head.

"August 2," she said, "but the year was 2013."

He looked at her wordlessly.

"Do you believe me?" she asked.

He let go of her and turned away. Standing before the hearth, he studied the fire then walked to the window. He stood with his hands clasped behind him. Looking at his stoic posture made her want to start screaming again.

"Andrew?"

"I find it completely logical that you came here a century after I did," he said at last. "In fact, it makes perfect sense. Why your speech is sometimes gibberish to me, for instance."

She stared at his back. "Then how can you be so unruffled? How can you just stand there? Doesn't it all just blow your mind?"

He turned to her, his eyes oddly flat.

"I can stand here calmly because of what I told you a moment ago. I've finished with all my ranting and raving and venting my spleen. It only served to increase my frustration. I've searched for an escape from this place so many times that I can't begin to count them. I used to go outside and search until I was so exhausted, I fell asleep in the forest. Then I'd wake up, get up, and search again. I must have spent decades seeking a way out of this existence. I'm sorry, but you need to know there is no escape. The way always ends here."

"No!" she cried. She wanted to throw something at him. "You didn't do it right! You forgot to mark your path, or you went in circles, or you quit too soon." She stomped one foot like a petulant child. "*You didn't do it right!*"

He pinned a steely gaze on her then moved from the window to the bookshelf. He idly picked up and reshelved a couple of volumes. He walked to the fireplace and stood before it, studying the flames as if trying to find the answer they both needed.

"If an entire century has passed in the time I've been here, don't you think that has been time enough for me to find a way out?"

"You didn't do it right," she repeated stubbornly.

He expelled a long, slow breath. "Then what do you suggest we do?"

"Look for a way out together." She rushed to him, grabbed both his hands in hers and squeezed hard. "There are two of us now. We can do it. It's called teamwork." She tried not to see the bleakness in his eyes. "You gave up before you found it, that's all. You quit too soon. But I'm here, and together, we're sure to discover what you overlooked."

He did not take his gaze from her.

"This place is not right. There's something here that's peculiar, maybe evil. Don't you feel it? The only time I don't feel creepy is when I'm with you. We must get out of here. We can do it—together."

Chapter 13

Andrew refused to watch this beautiful, vibrant woman waste away into a mere shell of what he saw before him.

"Please hear me. This futile searching will break your spirit."

She stared up at him, the expression in her lovely blue eyes mutinous and stubborn. "I'll go alone if I must. I will face down the forest, even the snake." Her voice trembled at this. "But I *will* find the way out of here."

He fully understood the consuming desire to cast off the dark and desolate place. He ached to bring forth the warmth and sunlight of a summer day, the absolute joy of living. He yearned to share it all with her. Such strength of mind exuded from her, that he felt a slow awakening of hope. Might there be a chance, as miniscule as a pinpoint, that a path existed leading back to the lost world of sunlight and springtime and a renewing of expectation? If one miracle occurred—the miracle of Abbie's presence—wasn't it possible a way to freedom really did exist?

He wondered if he could summon the strength to lower his defense. Hope had failed him more times than he could count. He decided to take the chance.

"You needn't go alone. I'll go with you. But on one condition."

"And that is?" Wariness flicked across her face, and

her watchful eyes never left his.

"I'm willing to cooperate with you fully, but I will not move an inch to help you until you give your body time to heal from the lacerations during your excursion into the forest."

A frown settled between her eyebrows, and he saw her prepare to protest. In the short time they had been together he had learned this woman would never give up or give in easily. He held up one hand to stop her before she spoke.

"Before you start to argue with me, let me explain. Many of the plants that grow around us have mild poisons in them, none as severe as the dementia rose, but enough to make you ill." He took her hand in his and lifted it to study the angry red tear across the knuckles. "Some of these wounds are severe. If you go out, get scratched by another plant and its toxins get in your bloodstream, or if this cut or any other becomes infected, very likely you will end up in bed with fever, delirium, even gangrene. Need I go on?"

She studied her injuries.

"No," she said finally, slowly, with obvious reluctance. "I understand. If I do as you say, do you solemnly promise to go with me and help me find our way out?"

He gently squeezed the fingers he held then let go.

"I vow to help you look until we find it—or until you are satisfied nothing is there for us to find."

"And if, no, make that *when*, we find our way from this place and back to civilization, will you abandon this sad, reclusive existence?"

What a foolish, futile, and beautiful dream she awakened in him—to live again as man was meant to live, with a purpose beyond mere survival, perhaps to be with Abbie in a life that held precious treasures. Dare he entertain the notion, even for a moment?

Experience was his, and he knew full well there was no liberation from this dark prison for either one of them. He told himself he must not let his heart and mind be duped by such recklessly desperate thinking. He feared for her brokenness when she finally grasped the truth of this situation.

"When all is said and done, will you continue to be my friend?"

"Are you kidding? Of course, I will!" She paused. "So you promise to help me find the way out?"

He needed to be there for her, as a comrade and as a support. After all, who knew better than he did how much the companionship of another could mean? He refused to turn her down.

"Yes. Right by your side the entire time."

Her bright smile brought his heart to its knees.

"All right. I'll let my cuts heal. But how long will it take?"

"I'm not sure. A few days, I imagine."

She sagged against his chest, her hands splayed, as though taking strength from the strong beat of his heart. He pressed his lips against her soft hair. He could lose himself in those shining gold tresses.

"It all seems unreal. I feel so…"

He held her loosely, rubbed his hands up and down her back, feeling the line of her ribs beneath his palms.

"Lost? Confused? Alone?" he prompted.

She looked up and offered a small smile. "Lost? Yes. Confused, certainly. But not alone, Andrew. Never alone when I'm with you."

His heart bounded at her words. To be with another living being, to be needed, to have his company desired and enjoyed! He gathered her hands and kissed them ardently. Lost in her eyes, he began to believe anything was possible, even leaving this place of exile.

She was warm and soft in his arms. Her sweet scent twisted tendrils of longing around his heart and soul, even as she entwined her arms around his neck. Breath from her slightly parted lips invited him. So close to her, he had no power to resist.

He lowered his head, his lips barely touching hers for only seconds, giving her every opportunity to pull away if she chose to do so. Instead she pressed closer, melding against him, branding his lips with her own. Soft and sweet, hesitant, but he sensed an underlying passion, as if she wanted more than a simple kiss.

The heat of her body charged his blood, spurring him on with urgent need. In fact, that need began to block out all reason. He wanted to tear off the shirt and britches that swallowed her small body, but something stopped him.

"Treat her special, son, that woman to whom you give your heart." His father's words echoed, as fresh as yesterday. "Don't make her feel second best or second rate."

The voice seemed so real that he broke away suddenly, looking for his father. Had the voice come to him through time and space because Abbie Matthews was that woman? They hardly knew each other, but she had somehow found her way to him after all this time. Surely that meant something in the eyes of destiny. And if so, intimacy needed to come after love, after commitment.

His body ached for this woman, and it was with his father's counsel in his mind and with enormous willpower, he stepped back. She raised her bright eyes to his, her face questioning.

"I'm sorry." He turned away.

"Sorry? For what? For kissing me?"

He was embarrassed that the kiss could easily have gone so much further than it had.

"I need to get us some fresh water," he said, lamely, the only thing he could think of to get him out of her presence. "Perhaps you'd like to wash up, or go lie down, or read something."

He glanced at her, saw a most singular expression settle on her face.

"Is something wrong with me?"

"Of course not. It's just that…" His face grew hot, and he could not meet her eyes.

She stared at him, eyes brimming with hurt, then gave a short, brittle laugh and shook her head as though fighting her own thoughts.

"Even out here in the middle of the woods with only one other living soul, a man still rejects me. Excuse me."

"Abbie!" he said, but her footsteps pounded up the stairs.

Helplessly, he watched her flee from him. What had he done? What had he said that made her feel rejected? He had only treated her like the sweet lady she seemed to be, with the respect she deserved.

****

She fled upstairs and dashed into the first room she saw. Slamming the door, she leaned against it, eyes closed. Her breath heaved in and out of her lungs and blood thundered in her ears. If he followed her, which she doubted, she could not hear him. He probably had perceived her willingness to kiss him as desperation. No man wants a needy woman. Her face burned at the memory.

What was wrong with her, acting as foolish as a lovesick schoolgirl, blurting out a pity party for herself in front of him? Didn't she have a shred of dignity?

She took a deep breath to calm herself and blew it out slowly. After a moment, she opened her eyes. The room in which she'd taken refuge was not his bedroom. This one was more softly appointed, with pale cabbage-roses and lilacs on the wallpaper, delicate lace-trimmed ecru curtains, pillows, and bedcoverings. The mahogany furniture gleamed as though it had been freshly polished. A full-length cheval mirror stood in the far corner, and a dressing table was nearby. On a table beside the bed, a crystal vase sat full of fresh lilacs. It was only then that she noticed the flowers' delicate fragrance. Where had lilacs come from? She had seen no flowering shrubs, or blossoms of any kind.

She pushed her way from the door, momentarily stunned by the room that contrasted so sharply with the rest of the house. Why hadn't he put her in this room rather than in his own the night before? Did this room belong to someone else, someone she had yet to meet?

But hadn't he told her no one or nothing else lived here but him?

She walked across the soft woven rug of deep purple and pale lavender as she explored the room. The finely woven fabric of the bedcovering was soft beneath her fingers. The thick, downy bed would make a snug place to sleep. She ran her fingers over the wood furniture, finding it silky smooth and dust-free. A silver- backed brush and comb lay in the dresser, and neither looked as if they'd ever been used. Beside them a long, shallow crystal dish held hairpins and decorative combs.

Feeling extremely curious, she opened the top dresser drawer. She pulled out old-fashioned undergarments, but each one looked brand new: corsets, chemises and slips of silk crepe de chine, embellished with fine lace and tiny beads. One drawer contained nothing but stockings, garters, and panties. She assumed they were panties, white, wide-legged, trimmed with lace, and gathered at the knee. Other drawers revealed flannel nightgowns, silk nightgowns, handkerchiefs, gloves, scarves, other clean, white sleeveless garments she was sure were more articles of underwear.

A narrow door across from the bed opened into a small closet full of beautiful dresses made of delicate silks and fragile layers of lace. She fingered the lovely pastel fabrics and the matching satin sashes. On the floor of the closet were soft kid leather shoes, with small heels and sweet pointed toes. Every article of clothing looked at least a hundred years old yet brand new at the same time. She closed the closet door quietly.

Wait a minute.

What did it mean, this room and everything in it? Why was it here?

"Abbie?" He was calling her from the hallway.

Had he been expecting her? Not her specifically, but any young woman lost and confused, someone he could lure with sweet eccentricities and hold hostage with a crazy story of exile. Had he stalked her, drugged her, and brought her into the forest, then left her alone in the woods to find him instead of carrying her to the house? For what reason? That was nutty.

She tried to dismiss the notion, and yet she couldn't. At least not completely.

Her gaze swept the room that was so obviously a woman's room with its soft colors and feminine fabrics. She caught sight of her reflection in the cheval mirror: a disheveled woman wrapped in men's clothing far too big for her.

With a closet and dresser full of clothes that would probably fit her, why had he given her his shirt and trousers? Why had he put her to sleep in his own bed yet made no move to share it with her? Was he a crazy eccentric who preyed on lost young women, or was he a hopeless recluse who needed someone in his life? Why had he—

"*Abbie!* Where are you?"

She snapped her head around to stare at the door. He was in the hallway and the tone of his voice was one of panic, as if afraid she had left him. She fought the urge to lock the door, to hide from him. If he intended to keep her a prisoner here, he went about it in a truly odd way. First ignoring her, then treating her wounds and taking care of her needs. When she had left him earlier, he had wanted her to stay, but he'd been willing to let her go.

If he wanted to imprison her, he would have barred her way, or tied her up, or locked her in.

She moved cautiously across the room, her feet making no sound on the floor. She rested one hand on the doorknob, the other against the door.

"*Abbie!*"

She could not bear the anguish in his voice, as if his soul was being torn from his body. Despite her misgivings and the confusion about her own needs, her soft heart stirred. Turning away from someone in need was impossible for her. If he needed comfort, she wanted to give it. But this time, she'd react only as a friend, not as a would-be lover.

She took a deep breath and turned the knob. He stood in the hallway, staring at the door, his face colorless, looking as if he might collapse. She forgot her fear and rushed to him.

"What's wrong?" She caught his arm in both her hands and stared at his waxen face.

"How…Where…" He continued to gape at the doorway from which she just emerged. "That door, that room has never been there before."

"What?" She turned to stare at the door, to see if there was something unusual about it. It matched the door of the room across the hall. "Surely you knew there was another room up here."

He shook his head. "It's like suddenly finding that extra cutlery at the table earlier." He grasped her hand. "It's you. You've done something. Who are you? Where did you come from?"

She reared back slightly and tried to free herself from his grip, but he held on.

"You think I've pulled out a hammer and nails and built a new room in the last five minutes?"

"I think you're bewitched. Magical."

"Bewitched. Magical. We're back to that?" She yanked her hand free of his and took a few steps away from him. "You are too intelligent a man to believe in nonsense. Or I thought you were."

"Before you came," he continued, his gaze intense, "nothing ever changed here. No daylight or dark, no passage of time. There was nothing beautiful here. But since you arrived, I've seen the clouds break apart outside, as if they will go away at last. We have tableware for two people. There is now an extra room where before there was nothing but a blank wall. Something has changed, *and it all started with you.*"

She was reasonably sure he was a good man who harbored neither malice nor deceit. The strange world around them ruled out delusions and hallucinations, unless she suffered from them too. Nothing since she woke up in the cold, silent woods had made sense to her, and that included this very moment in time. By trying to use logic in a world out of alignment merely added to an unsolvable puzzle. And yet she had to give reason one more attempt.

"Andrew," she said quietly, "are you sure there's never been another person in this house?"

"One hundred percent positive."

She believed him. What other option was open to her in a world of silent wind, rooms that appeared from nowhere, daylight that never changed into night, and fresh-cut flowers where no flowers blossomed?

"Come with me." She led him into the bedroom. He stood one step inside the doorway and looked around, bewildered.

"Look." She opened the closet. "These are women's clothes." She pulled out a soft green gown with three-quarter length sleeves and ribbons at the elbows. She held it against her. "This would fit me. A little long in the hem and way out of fashion but better than sporting your clothes."

He crossed the room to plunder through swishing silks and rustling laces.

"Where did these come from?" He directed his gaze over his shoulder and fixed it on her.

"The dresser is full of underwear and nightgowns." She pointed toward it. He glanced that way but made no move other than to shake his head.

His glance fell on the vase of fresh lilacs. "Where did you find those?"

"I didn't find them. They were there when I came in. This room has been recently cleaned. It's been outfitted for a woman."

He sagged against the wall, his face ashen, looking utterly lost. Something inside her broke open. The remnants of her doubts and speculations about him were washed away in a flood of empathy. Insecurities regarding her value as a romantic partner seemed insignificant when she was faced with a world where magic might be happening all around them. All she knew for certain was that she and Andrew had nothing or no one to trust but each other. He had helped her, and now she must offer some consolation in a realm gone mad.

"I don't understand it, either, but we both know this is a strange place in which we find ourselves. For now, let's accept what's here. At some point, when we've pooled our efforts and diligently worked together, perhaps we'll understand better where we are and why we're here." His expression told her his confusion would not be easily sorted and solved. She took his hand in hers. "Right now, let's go back downstairs and have some tea."

"But what if everything down there has changed? What if it's gone? What if—"

"Then we'll face it. Together." She smiled reassuringly into his eyes and wished she felt as strong and confident as she sounded. "Come on."

He touched the side of her face with the fingers of

one hand. "All right. Let's go."

They went downstairs and slipped into a life together.

Chapter 14

During the time it took her cuts and abrasions to heal, Abbie finally and fully accepted that Andrew had never experienced delusions. Day and night blended into continuing sameness with no dark or light delineation. Storm clouds hovered, a constant but unfulfilled threat. The silent wind blew without ceasing. As she helped him to prepare meals, the food stock remained as if untouched although they used the stores for every meal. An eternal fire burned in the fireplace.

She fit the clothing she'd found in the upstairs bedroom. She discarded the corsets but found the stockings and extra petticoats added warmth to her body in a house that always seemed chilly. The bedroom upstairs was comfortable and always clean, the bed as soft and welcoming as it looked.

Each night—as much as it could be measured as "night"—before they retired, he paused to eye that door again as though expecting it to dissolve before his eyes.

"It's okay to just accept it and stop puzzling over it."

He nodded, gave her a smile. "You're right. And it's good. Another room in this house, one that is so suited for you, full of clothes."

She returned his smile. "Yes. A good thing."

As she sliced potatoes for their breakfast, she glanced up and caught his gaze on her. It was not a look of indifference or speculation; it was a gaze full of desire.

The knife nearly slipped from her fingers.

"Andrew?"

He blinked as though clearing his thoughts.

"I was just thinking how beautiful your hair is. It catches the light so that it's almost a spot of sunlight in this gloomy house."

Her fingers went instantly to hair that hadn't seen conditioner or a flat iron in days. The natural waves were pretty enough, and the mere fact that he likened it to sunlight touched her. She blushed like a schoolgirl.

"Thank you."

They held each other's gaze for a long minute, then he turned away.

"I'll draw some fresh water and make tea."

She smiled as he went outside, thinking how nice it was to have a courteous, sweet-natured companion with whom to share these strange days. With his dark hair and eyes and strong physique, he was easy to look at. She remembered how it felt being in his arms, close enough that his heartbeat reverberated against her own. In the time since their agreement to look for a way back to civilization, opportunity after opportunity to explore a romantic relationship presented itself. But the memory of past betrayals dogged her more tender feelings until she shoved away those notions. He seemed to harbor as much ambivalence as she did. Maybe he, too, had been deceived in his other life.

Or maybe he saw her only as a friend and companion. Something about that idea stung her, deeply.

She had just put the potatoes in the skillet to brown for breakfast when the door burst open.

"Abbie!" he shouted. "Look at this!" He held up a tomato, plump and red, fully ripe and ready to eat. "Do you know the last time I had tomatoes? Since that morning I sat at my mother's breakfast table before leaving for the university. Biscuits, gravy, sausage, eggs, fresh tomatoes from the garden…" He set the red fruit down on the counter then holding out his hand to her, he smiled broadly. "And there's more. Come see them!"

The pure joy on his face caused her to laugh in delight. She wiped the potato starch from her fingers onto a damp cloth and took his hand.

"Show me!"

Outside, she detected something different, something softer in the air.

"Andrew, wait. What happened to the cold wind? It feels almost spring-like out here."

He stopped, his fingers strong around hers, his palm warm and firm against the soft skin of her hand. "Yes. Come with me."

He led her a few feet past the well, to a small garden patch free of weeds and scrub. Several lacy-leafed tomato plants grew. A few red ripening globes hung heavily on the vines, while smaller green ones grew in abundance.

"I didn't know you had a garden."

"I had only an herbal garden. Nothing like this. The last time I drew water from the well, there was nothing around but briars and thickets. That couldn't have been more than eight hours ago."

She reached down and cupped a tomato in her hand, gazing at it for a long moment.

"How could that be? What does this mean?"

"For nearly a century nothing changed, and nothing grew. But now, suddenly something happened when you arrived."

She straightened and tucked a stray lock of hair from her face. "I'm an ordinary woman, and you know that by now, surely. The only exceptional thing I've been able to do is convince a jury that a guilty man is innocent. I certainly don't have the power to change the weather or cause new life to sprout overnight."

He studied her, his head tipped to one side. "You are anything but ordinary. And whether you accept it, or dismiss it as unreasonable, the facts of change remain." His expression softened. "Your arrival has changed my life. At least believe that."

The warmth of his smile, the hunger in his eyes, and a raw need to be with her filled his expression. He moved, seemed about to reach out to her. Every nerve in her body quivered with anticipation.

He broke eye contact, though, and abruptly turned away.

"With the changes out here, I suspect I might actually be able to eradicate the dementia rose." His voice was strained, as if he was fighting to sound normal. He cleared his throat. "After I do, we can try to find our way out with no threat to our health."

Why had he turned away? Why couldn't he see she would have leaped into his arms if he'd only made the first move?

She reminded herself that she preferred no entanglements with a man, any man. No romance, nothing physical. Being a friend and companion was enough. She clenched her jaw, determined to be strong.

Her thoughts turned to the dementia rose, the dangers it presented. "But you told me the toxins can be devastating. What if it cuts you while you try to remove it?"

"Not to worry. I have dealt with it many times. I know how to treat the abrasions."

She thought of something else. Something far more terrifying than a noxious plant. Just the thought made her weak.

"What about the snake? What if…?"

He touched her arm in a caring, supportive gesture. "There is no snake. It was a hallucination brought from that rose. You know this. Put all thoughts of that creature aside. It does not exist."

His words comforted her, but try as she might, Abbie would probably never forget the terror the serpent brought. Although it wasn't real, she would forever be watchful for it.

"I'll go with you to clear the dementia rose. You show me what to do, and with the two of us working, we can—"

He frowned and shook his head vigorously. "Absolutely not. Your cuts are healing well, but if you were to get another round of the poison, I'm unsure what effect it might have."

"But you'll be there! You just said—"

"*No.* I refuse to risk your health. And you can take that pleading look out of your beautiful mutinous blue eyes. I'm not going to change my mind, so you may as well trust me on this."

Trust him. Trust him to leave her, trust him to return. Was it too much to ask herself to trust a man who'd been nothing but kind and solicitous?

"All right I'll stay here. But I'm not going to like it."

"Consider it doctor's orders."

She wrinkled her nose.

Later, after breakfast, he left to accomplish his task.

When the door closed behind him, an unexpected longing filled her. She wanted to be with him. Whatever happened in this strange world, she wanted them to be together, whether as friends or eventually something more. Separation seemed intolerable now, as if half her soul was missing. For a woman who'd built a wall around her heart while carving her way in an exhausting, soul-shattering career, this feeling was new and unfamiliar, and it troubled her no small amount.

As she watched for his safe return, she stopped fooling herself. She recognized that it was very possible, even probable, that despite her best efforts and internal lectures, she had fallen head over heels in love with Andrew Wade. She fully understood that not only were the circumstances of this relationship unlike anything she'd ever known could exist, but he was also unlike any of the men who'd taken her heart and abused it. Of all three love affairs, none had brought her to such an awakening. Never had she felt such an instinct to care and to nurture. Other than her friend Lefty, no one in her life had ever demonstrated the image of true kindness and compassion. He had roused all those qualities in her, and more.

She told herself that maybe she felt so giddy and eager because these feelings were all so newly discovered. Maybe her yearning for him would diminish as time went on. Perhaps nothing more existed in this episode than two lonely people in a bizarre environment reaching out for comfort and strength. Surely, this was much too soon to assume love could have had a hand in any of it. She would enjoy this experience while it lasted, but solemnly vowed to keep love under wraps. Once she and Andrew were out of this situation and back in the real world, who could predict what would happen?

She chose a book from his full shelves and settled down to read. But the silence of the house gave her the jitters and she couldn't lose herself in the story. She longed to hear another voice, the sound of someone else's movements. Just the presence of another person in this cold, desolate place was a comfort. She had only been here a short time, and during those hours, he had been with her. What must it have been like for him to be here, completely alone, these many years?

How was it he had not gone completely mad?

In fact, she marveled at the way he was a gracious, caring host to her after their initial meeting. And she understood now why he had treated her as an illusion. In fact, she would have reacted the same way, and more so, had the roles been reversed.

She needed something to do, something active that would keep her busy until he returned. She went into a small pantry just off the kitchen and eyed the assortment of food. To her, food had always been something she needed to keep her alive, but never a focus of her day. Cooking and baking were skills she'd neglected from sheer indifference, preferring take-out or sandwiches. She now regretted that she knew so little. One dish she recalled watching their cook prepare when she was young had been a favorite. Could she make it? She was willing to try.

She gathered several apples and a loaf of bread and carried them into the kitchen. She sliced the bread, placed it on the stove top to toast then peeled the apples and cut them into chunks. She put these in a pan of water on the stove to cook. When the apples were partly cooked, she drained the water and added torn pieces of toast. There was nothing to sweeten or spice the bread pudding, but she remembered the sweetness of the tealround tea. Perhaps the leaves would sweeten this treat. She opened the cupboard where he kept his teas and other remedies. On the shelf below she saw butter, sugar, and cinnamon. For a long moment she stared in surprise because she knew none had been there before.

No point in questioning where they came from. By now, she knew this place was like no other on earth.

She added butter, measured sugar into the apples, spooned in the cinnamon, and stirred everything. When the mixture looked right, she put it into a pan and set it in the oven to bake.

Upon his return some time later, she greeted him as eagerly as wives greeted husbands at the end of the day on those old 1950s sitcoms.

"Did you have much success?" She handed him a cup of fresh hot tea.

"Thank you." He sipped the tea. "Actually, no. I searched the woods and saw not a single rose thicket." He sniffed appreciatively. "What smells so good? And why aren't you resting?"

"I'm not tired. I think this dish could be called bread pudding." She made a wry face. "I'm sure it won't taste as good as what Mrs. Cline used to make for me, but I thought it might be a nice change from the usual fare. And if you'll wash up, I'll dish some of this for you."

From the warming oven, she pulled out the pan. The result of her efforts was a sweetly fragrant dessert, brown and bubbling. He gazed at it speechlessly then looked up at her, a grin breaking across his features. While he scrubbed his face and hands in the basin, she served a generous mound of her creation onto his plate.

"So you couldn't find any of the dementia rose? You were gone a long time, it seemed."

"I searched extensively for it, but it's gone," he said through the fabric of the towel as he dried his face. He lowered it, revealing tousled hair and cheeks red from being rubbed dry. She could not resist reaching up and smoothing his hair. He smiled and held her gaze. For a moment, she was sure he was about to kiss her but, as before, he turned his gaze to the food on the table.

"I haven't had bread pudding in…well, since my mother made it for me." They sat down, and he tasted it. "It's sweet, but we have no sugar. Or cinnamon."

"I opened the cupboard door, and there they were. Plus butter."

His eyebrows went up, then his face relaxed, and he smiled. "I suppose I should stop being surprised. Good things are happening because of you."

"That's a sweet thing to say."

He shook his head. "I speak the truth. I hope our good fortune will continue."

His words, spoken so simply without foolish come-on lines stirred her, made her feel cherished, but her foolish heart longed for something more.

"Let's move into the front room to finish our tea," he suggested. They settled before the fireplace and sat in companionable silence.

"You were scratched by the dementia rose so severely," he said after a bit, "that the toxin got deep into your skin and other tissue." He lifted his gaze to meet hers. "Your hallucinations were powerful, violent. And yet I found no sign of it growing anywhere. I don't understand it. Unless it is your presence that, along with all the good changes, has also helped to eradicate the dementia rose."

Something in the way he spoke, the underlying tone of doubt, told her he did not fully believe this theory.

"There's another possibility, isn't there?"

Slowly he nodded. When he seemed hesitant to share his concerns with her, she said it for him. "It's possible that other types of thorns scratched me severely, and I was not delusional."

"I hate even to think it but, yes, that's a possibility."

She studied his face, noted lines of concern around his eyes and mouth.

"I know what that means. It means if I didn't have delusions, and if what I saw was real…" She fought rising nausea. "It means there actually is that huge snake out there."

He set aside his tea, got up and pulled her to her feet. He cupped her face in both of his hands, looked into her eyes.

"Shhh." He rubbed the balls of his thumbs over her lips. "If there's one thing I'm sure of, it's that there is no snake. If one existed, I would have seen it by now."

"But—"

He bent his head and placed a sweet, lingering kiss on her lips.

"Not to worry, dear one. Nothing here will ever hurt you because I will never allow that to happen. If there is a snake, I'll search until I find it, and I *will* destroy it. I swear on my life, nothing here will ever hurt you. *Ever.*"

He searched her eyes and smiled with such reassurance that her anxiety ebbed. Her trust in his honesty and compassion were given to him. She had no reason to doubt or fear this man.

He kissed her again.

"All right?" he whispered against her lips.

She leaned into him, allowing herself to feel what she'd so long repressed. She melded against him, feeling every part of his warm body against every part of her own. She wrapped her arms around his neck.

"Yes. All right."

"My dearest one." He gathered her to him, his breath warm against her neck.

He lifted his head to look in her eyes. She touched the side of his face with her fingertip then traced his features: the small, permanent furrow between his brows, the strong line of his jaw, lips she sensed had rarely lifted in a smile until recently.

"It is you who are the dear one, Andrew."

Raw hunger glittered in his dark eyes. Her heart leaped in response. As blood thrummed through her veins, caution screamed not to lose her heart to this man. And yet she willingly gave over to him, once more lifting her face to his. As though he sensed her need to be wary, His lips barely touched hers. He raised his head and started to pull away, but she caught him and would not let go. He stared into her eyes, seeming to ask silently if she truly wanted this.

"Yes," she whispered. "Yes!"

He hesitated for the length of two heartbeats, then bent his head, and found her mouth once more. His lips were hot and greedy against hers, moving, pressing, parting. She devoured his kiss as eagerly and passionately as he offered it. Sliding her hands to caress his head, she thrust her fingers into the rich thickness of his dark hair. He wrapped his arms around her and crushed her body against his. She molded herself to him while the kiss deepened, then deepened again. She joyously lost all caution and drowned in that kiss.

He dragged his lips from hers to taste her cheek, her neck, her throat, his breath hot and ragged against her skin. He lifted his head, staring down at her, his breath stilled for the moment, as if he could not believe the beauty of what he saw and the promise of what she offered.

She took his hand and led him to her bed.

"Abbie!"

She smiled and drew him closer.

"Abbie," Andrew whispered against her tangled, pale hair. "Abbie, Abbie, Abbie!"

She laughed softly in delight.

He raised his head and looked into her eyes.

"Your eyes seem to shine from an inner light," he said with wonder. "What a magnificent change you have brought into my life!" He cupped her cheek with one hand. "You are a sprite. Or maybe an angel. Are you my angel?"

She smiled again. "If it pleases you to think so, then that's what I am."

He lowered his head to hers, kissed her ardently, lingeringly.

"Yes," he whispered in her ear. "My own dear angel."

He kissed her again, more sweetly and tenderly than she'd ever been kissed. His lips lingered on hers, kissing each corner then fully.

He lifted his head, then suddenly turned and looked toward the window. He sat up, drawing her up with him.

"Look!" he shouted. "Look! The sun is shining!"

Indeed the sunlight poured in through the windows of that room.

The pair gazed in awe at the light until the waned and the gloom returned. But for a moment, a new bright warmth had filled the world around them.

Chapter 15

They settled comfortably into what became a pattern of days and nights. They marked that passage of time with living life fully, openly, joyously as a man and woman who are destined to be together forever.

As a team, they shared in the chores of housekeeping and cooking, of harvesting herbs and drying them. Andrew taught her which herbs served which purpose and showed her how to measure and crush the leaves and roots. Sunlight made its appearance from time to time, never lingering, but always returning.

He coaxed her out of the house and away from it toward the forest. The first few times, she looked around warily, expecting to see the huge snake at any moment, but he reassured and comforted her. She trusted him and did her best to release her crippling fear.

Along the front of the drab old house, scarlet roses and golden marigolds began to bloom, along with willowy lavender and snowy hydrangeas.

"You have brought life into this place and to me," he reminded her joyously and often.

Frequently, as they sat in the cozy parlor before the hearth, they discussed their vastly different lifestyles and generations.

One day, he seemed especially pensive, gazing into the fire, speaking little.

"Is something on your mind?"

He glanced at her, nodded slightly.

"I've been thinking about my family, wondering how they fared after I left. Then for some reason, I started remembering my little sister, Hazel. I was ten years old when she died. Pneumonia." He closed his eyes and shook his head. "That was an awful time. I stood at her bedside, watched her try to breathe and watched her die. I guess that's when I decided to become a doctor, maybe save some other little child. But I never got the chance." He opened his eyes, met her gaze. "Do people die of pneumonia in your time?"

"Sometimes. But I think it's because they don't get treatment soon enough, since there's treatment and medication that can take care of it in a few days. My friend, Lefty—er, I mean, Linda, got pneumonia a few years ago. She went to her doctor, got her meds, went home and recovered. She was back to work in a week."

He smiled, his eyes shining in wonder. "That is truly amazing."

"Kids are immunized against all those awful childhood diseases like measles and mumps and whooping cough. Smallpox and polio, too. Certain cancers can be stopped or slowed down. People who've had it can live years and years. The key there is a healthier lifestyle, early detection, and treatment."

He seemed to take all this in, then in an awe-filled voice, he said, "You know, that's a wondrous thing. A wondrous, blessed thing."

They lapsed into a companionable silence, which she broke a few minutes later.

"I believe I'll fix us some tea and cinnamon toast. Would you like that?"

He smiled at her, his eyes shining in the firelight.

"Very much."

She fixed their snack and brought it into the parlor. He helped her to arrange the food on a small table between their chairs.

"We're like an old married pair." He took his hot mug of tea off the table. Before she could react, he added, "Papa and Mama used to put us kids to bed, then they'd sit together for at least a few minutes each evening before going to bed. In the summer, they sat on the porch swing, and in the winter, they sat before the fire, like we're doing now. It was a comfort to me, hearing their voices, knowing they loved each other and all of us children and that we were safe."

"That sounds lovely. You must have had a wonderful family."

"Yes. I did. A large, boisterous, funny, lovable family."

"And you miss them."

He nodded. "Very much so. You know, you never talk about your own family."

"That's because I really have nothing to say about them. My mother gave birth, then she and my father spent as little time as possible with me while I grew up." She gave him a sad smile. "I suppose that's why I invested so much of myself into my career. But now I don't want that, either." She sighed. "All I want now is to be happy."

He gave her a warm smile, reached out and squeezed her hand.

"I want that, too." He paused, sobered. "I've told you about my brothers and sisters, my parents, our home and our town, what life was like. Won't you share with me?"

"Of course. But it's not very interesting, I'm afraid."

She told him about her law career, how she'd wanted to help others but had fallen into a trap she may or may not have set for herself.

"I was soul-searching when I found you. Maybe you were what I was searching for and didn't realize it."

"Ah, Abbie!" He reached out and brought her to his lap, settled her down in his arms. He kissed her tenderly and rested his head against hers. She snuggled down into his embrace. "My sweet darling, I'm so glad you found me. I waited so long."

They sat quietly for a while, content, the fire burning brightly in front of them.

"Tell me more about your world," he said.

So she told him of inventions and discoveries, advances in medicine, the World Wars and other conflicts, of space travel and modern communications. He listened without comment, his expression one of amazement, almost disbelief.

After a time, he said, "It seems to me that there is too much dependence on machines and not enough on humanity."

"I would have to agree with you. In my time, we probably would not be sitting together, talking this way, reading in the evenings, simply enjoying each other's company."

"No?" He frowned. "Why not? Don't lovers like each other?"

"We'd probably be watching television, or on the internet, using our smart phones, or our laptop computers. In fact, most people pursue solitary activities, even in a family unit."

His frowned deepened and he shifted beneath her. "I

doubt I'd like that. I'd likely never fit in your world."

An icy breath slithered down her back.

"Andrew." She shivered. "Andrew, don't you realize that when we find our way out of here, you will *be* in my world?"

He seemed speechless for a moment, then shook his head. "Maybe not."

"What do you mean? Of course you will," she said, almost shrilly. She did not want even to think of being anyplace where he was not. It had not occurred to her that he might choose to stay here rather than go into the modern world with her, not after they'd bonded such a close relationship. She gripped his shirt front in both her hands.

"When I left, there were cars and computers and smart phones, jets and television, microwave ovens and power tools. You'll see them all, and you'll get used to everything, and you'll realize the twenty-first century is actually a wonderful place to live."

"But when *I* came here, I left behind horses and wagons and threshing machines and steam locomotives. Automobiles were uncommon, as were telephones. In fact, they are almost unheard of in our community. Who's to say, if we get out of this place, we won't come out in my time instead of yours? For that matter, what if we find the world to be totally different than either of us has known?"

"Of course we won't return to a hundred years ago. How could we?"

He caught her chin gently and turned her face to his. "My own sweet angel, look at me. Do I look as though I'm a hundred and thirty years old? You must remember—something has happened to time as you and

I understand it. For me, it's as if minutes and hours have stopped. My hair neither grows nor grays. My face has not aged, my body is still vigorous. *Time does not move here*. But somewhere, beyond this place, it does. And we don't know at what pace it moves, or if it's going forward or backward. So if we get out of here, we don't know where we'll be."

She stared at him, a small hand of terror clutching her heart.

"If we get out of here, we must be prepared for anything."

She knew he was right, of course. What if they found their way out of this cold, dark site to step into a world foreign to them both? What if they entered some terrifying future environment as hideous and alien as something from one of those old *Twilight Zone* episodes?

She closed her eyes. Nausea churned in her belly. She opened her eyes and reached for his hand again. It was warm and strong and firm in her grip. *He* was not frightened, and she took comfort in that. She clutched his hand and let his strength flow into her.

"Whatever we face, my dearest friend, we'll face it together."

"Yes. Together."

They sat quietly, the only sound was of their breathing and the fire crackling in the grate.

"Andrew? I want to go to bed now." He met her eyes. "I really need to touch you and feel you and know you are real."

Without a word, he stood and carried her upstairs to the bed they now shared.

Chapter 16

"Abbie, you've done really well whenever we explore in the woods," he told her one day as they ate breakfast. "But we've not ventured very far away, and never out of sight of the house. I've wanted you to feel comfortable, to get accustomed to being in the forest."

She narrowed her eyes. "What are you saying, as if I couldn't guess?"

"It's time for us to take it a step further. Go farther into the trees. Today is a good day for that.

"Oh, but I—"

"That forest is out there. It is *not* going to go away. If we are to find our way out of here, you will need to be strong and courageous."

He was right, of course. Her fear of the woods, of living wild things, of being lost had crippled much enjoyment in her life. She remembered the time she had turned down an invitation to go with a friend to a lakeside resort in Minnesota last summer, and she had declined the opportunity to hike the Appalachian Trail a few years ago. In her heart of hearts, she had longed to go, but the thought of getting lost, of facing bears or snakes or even raccoons had forced her to stay safely in the city, away from natural beauty, away from new experiences.

It embarrassed her to remember how she had passed judgment on him earlier, declaring him to be afraid of new experiences, afraid to leave his house, when it was she who was the coward.

Hypocrite! she scoffed at herself.

"All right. But you must help me. And whatever you do, promise that you won't leave me there alone."

"Of course. When the time ever comes for you to face your demons on your own and venture out by yourself, you'll know it and you can tell me."

She swallowed hard, wondering if she could ever again go into those dark woods alone.

Although she did not enjoy the forest, she loved walking hand in hand with him on their daily forays into the woods. In fact, the forest floor was not nearly as overgrown and frightening as it had been when she first arrived. The wind offered a balmy whiff now and again, only blustering occasionally. For the first time, they could hear leaves rustle as the branches shifted in the breeze.

"It's foolish, I guess," he said one day, eyeing a patch of wild mint, "to continue harvesting fresh since none of the herbs lose their potency or flavor. It's just something I've done to keep myself busy." He looked at her with a grin, pulled her to him, and kissed her. "I have better ways to keep myself busy now."

****

One morning while he gathered tomatoes, squash, and string beans, she made sandwiches, wrapped them in clean cloths, got a couple of apples from the fragrant pantry and put everything into one of the buckets used to fetch water. She filled a jar with fresh water, capped it tightly, and wedged it in the bucket between the apples. Upstairs, she took one of the quilts off the bed and folded it neatly. She carried it down to the parlor where she picked up the book of poems he had been reading.

She turned to see him leaning against the doorjamb, watching her and smiling in curiosity.

"What are you doing, Miss Abigail Matthews?"

"Well, Doctor Wade, you and I are going on a picnic."

He raised one eyebrow. "Are we?"

She held out the quilt and book to him, then turned to pick up the pail which contained the meal she had prepared.

"Yes. And why are you looking at me like that?"

He took the quilt and book from her hand and looked at her quizzically. "I never thought of having a picnic in those woods. Are you sure you want to?"

"I'm not afraid when you're with me. Somehow, when we're together, everything feels right. You know? Safe."

"I *do* know. And everything is right and safe and good when we're together."

He brushed a lock of hair from her forehead and studied every aspect of her face as though memorizing each detail. His gaze bored deeply into hers.

"You have given me back my life. I don't know how I lived without you, here in this place or long ago on the Ridge. I love you so much."

He set aside the quilt and book and took her into his arms.

She let the handle of the bucket slide from her grasp. It clattered to the floor. She placed both hands on either side of his face and whispered near his lips, "And you have opened a new world for me, far from this place or the life I've always known." She kissed him. "You've shown me what true kindness is, and how it's possible to be pure in heart. I—" She almost slipped and said, *I love you,* but caught herself. Someday, maybe, she would utter those words again, but not yet, in case saying them jinxed everything good that was happening. "I care for you more than I can say."

He searched her eyes. She knew he sought the truth she was unwilling to speak.

"Can't you say the words, dearest? Or do you not love me?"

This was the first time he had asked her directly. She did not want to hurt him, but loving him and speaking it aloud would somehow commit her to him, and what if committing to him was not the right thing to do? What if she didn't really love him but only bonded with him because they were the only two people in their world? What if, when they found their way out, he discovered she wasn't his bright angel? What if she was unable to sustain a relationship?

"I don't know," she said. "How can I say it when I'm not sure what loving someone feels like? I thought I was in love before, and I was dead wrong every time. Even the love of my parents was nothing that made me happy. I guess I'm afraid of more than just the forest."

She bit her lower lip, looked up into his eyes. He smoothed her hair, fingertips brushing the sides of her face.

"Yes. You're afraid. But it's all right. When you're sure, and you know the time is right, I'll be waiting." Then as though banishing the moment, he kissed the tip of her nose and moved away to gather the quilt and book again. "A picnic, you say? Let's be off."

The day was lovely, with a soft breeze blowing. While the sun played hide-and-seek with the clouds, they walked hand-in-hand, going deeper into the heart of the forest than they had ever gone together.

"You're doing fine walking in these woods as if you aren't afraid."

"That's because I'm with you." She laughed self-consciously, dropping her gaze. "You know, after I met you and got to know you a little bit, my intention had been to help you overcome your fears. Instead, look at what you've done for me. Nothing in my life has ever felt so good and right as being with you."

He stopped walking to look into her eyes. "And you are happy here with me, yes? If we never find our way out, and I'm the only companion you'll ever see, will you be content in this place?"

The life she'd lived before, the life of cars and computers and convenience and a career which lined her pocketbook, all of it seemed nothing more than a distant memory. Her simple life here with him was real and solid. It fulfilled every dream to which she had aspired. Did this mean she loved him? And if she did, why, why, *why* was it so difficult just to admit it? He waited expectantly for her reply, his expression pensive and hopeful. All she could do at that moment was smile tenderly into his dark eyes.

"I want nothing more than what we have now. If you are my only companion, Andrew, it is enough."

A smile broke out across his face.

"Thank you," he said so humbly she nearly wept.

She hoped nothing ever happened that changed their lives. She'd live out her days in this place, with him.

"I'm getting hungry. There's a good place to have our picnic just over there." He dipped his head toward a small clearing flooded with sunlight. She thought she heard birds singing.

They spread out the quilt she'd brought, and he settled comfortably on it. She lifted her face to the sunlight. Near her, he stretched out on the quilt, hands linked under his head. She felt his gaze on her, but she did not move. Instead, she basked in his peaceful presence, knowing nothing bad would happen to her while he was nearby. Her anxiety let go until her body felt nearly disconnected with the world around them. She had no idea how much time had passed, but contentment and peace of mind filled her completely.

"Abbie?"

"Hmm?" She kept her eyes closed, feeling drowsy and far away.

His warm fingers circled her arm. That touch drew her from the ethereal disconnect and slowly back to him. She opened her eyes, turned her head, and smiled at him. He gently guided her down to the quilt, willing and pliable, in his arms. He undressed her, bit by bit, until she was naked and intwined in his embrace.

He kissed her sweetly, almost chastely, his lips barely touching hers then pulled away a tiny bit to look at her. For a time, they were suspended in each other's eyes. She touched his cheek, tracing the line of his jaw and down the strong column of his neck. She followed her fingertips with her lips, brushing kisses lightly against his skin. Returning to his mouth she teased him with tiny kisses until he resolutely took over the kiss, his mouth hard and demanding against hers. Weakness flooded her joints, turning her liquid and hot within his embrace.

He devoured her with a kiss so heated and so deep, she transcended her own body and soul to merge with his. A blinding flash of lightning seemed to set the world on fire, then thunder rolled angrily across the darkening sky above them. So lost in the consummation of love with him, she hardly heard the thunder's ominous threat. They clung to each other, cherishing the moment, guarding it as treasure.

The storm stopped, as suddenly as it started. Sunlight poured down on them once more. Passion ebbed and slowly settled into delicious comfort. He gazed at her as though burning each detail of her face and body into his mind. With his fingertips, he traced and explored every line and curve. As the dampness of their bodies began to evaporate, she shivered slightly. He reached for the clothes he had peeled from her body.

"Get dressed, dear one, so you don't get cold." Ever the caretaker, the watchmen of her heart, body, and health. No one had ever cared for her as he did.

This is what it feels like to be loved. She suddenly wanted to share her joy with him, this new certainty. She was ready to tell him how much she loved him.

"Andrew, I—" A sound came from the woods, a sound of movement, as though someone were walking toward them. He turned his head sharply, peering into the trees.

"Shh," he whispered, his gaze never leaving the woods.

"Dress quickly."

"What is it?" She stared into the forest as she slipped the dress over her head. "Is it the snake? Andrew, do you see the snake?" There was fear in her voice, and she despised it for the weakness it proved.

"Stay here," he said in hushed tones. "If it's that snake, it won't be with us long, I promise you."

"What are you—"

"Shhh!" he warned. "Stay here, dear one, and keep quiet. Everything will be all right."

She watched him move stealthily toward the trees, his muscular body taut and ready to spring into action. What did he plan to do? Drive it from the forest? He had no weapon with which to destroy it. Terror screamed in every cell of her body at the very notion of the giant serpent, but there was no way she would let this man face down that hideous creature alone.

"I'm coming with you."

"No!" He looked at her over his shoulder, a dark scowl on his face. "Stay back."

"I will not stay back!" she said as loudly as she dared.

"You will impede me."

"No, I won't."

He faced her, his frown deepening. "Having you with me will split my focus. I can't search for whatever is out there while worrying about your safety. Please, Abbie. If not for your sake, then for mine, stay here."

She huffed. "All right then." But she had no intention of doing so.

When he was a few yards away but still within eyesight, she crept forward. Every time he paused, she did. If he turned to look around, she ducked out of sight behind a tree. All was quiet, save for leaves rustling on tree branches and the sound of her own blood pumping in double-time.

She heard something to her left, a rumble, like wheels against a hard, hollow surface. Like the sound of a car passing over a bridge.

Could it be?

Was it possible they had found their way back to civilization, to a road or highway?

"Andrew!" she yelled as she hurried in the direction of the sound. "This way! I think I found—"

She tripped over a huge tree root. She staggered, groping for anything to break her fall, but grasped nothing.

She fell. And fell and fell and fell.

Chapter 17

She yelled for him, and Andrew turned in alarm. She was nowhere in sight.

"Abbie?"

When silence met him, he shouted. "Abbie! Are you all right?"

Still no reply. He rushed back to the abandoned picnic site. She would not deliberately wander off. Had she been following him after all? He peered through the trees in every direction and saw nothing unusual, nothing to mark her passage or his. The sky became overcast in a moment's time, darkening the world around him. Knowing her fear of the forest, he was sure the deep shadows would terrify her even more. The wind began to blow, cold and silent.

"Abbie! Where are you? Call out, and I'll hear you. Don't be afraid. Just stay where you are, and I'll find you."

Still she made no reply. Had she gone back to the house? It was unlikely. She would not trust herself to find it alone. Maybe she needed to relieve herself and had hidden from his sight. He stopped walking. Yes, of course. She merely needed to answer the call of nature and was protecting her privacy. She'd come out of hiding in a minute.

"Don't be embarrassed. Just let me know if you can hear me."

He listened, but only the silence of the forest responded to him.

"*Abbie, answer me!*"

The woods were soundless. The silent wind blowing its cold breath against him made Andrew want to curse, and he did so, uselessly.

"Abbie, you're scaring me."

He looked around in near panic, hoping to see her emerge. He would forgive her for frightening him like this, and he would apologize for swearing at her, but she never appeared. The dark, cold forest offered no sound to comfort him.

He crashed through the trees and thickets, calling for her. He ignored the thorns and briars clawing him as though trying to hold him back. Maybe he had irked her when he demanded she stay alone at the picnic site instead of going with him. She'd become more familiar with the woods, less fearful. Maybe in her irritation, she had flounced away and found her way back to the house. Once there, she probably would not come into the woods again, not alone. He cursed again, this time at himself for insisting she stay in the picnic area. He'd thought he was doing the right thing, protecting her from whatever creature crept or slithered around nearby, but obviously he had erred.

Fueled by the hope she was home safe, he raced to the house. He leaped up the steps and flinging the front door wide open, shouted, "Answer me, sweetheart!"

Silence greeted him. He sought every room, every nook, moved the chairs and looked under the bed, in the closets and cupboards. He went outside to the privy and looked inside.

"Where are you?" His voice was hoarse, his throat

burning and raw. "*Abbie!*"

His gaze landed on the well. In an instant, his mind conjured the image of her returning to the house for a drink and tumbling into the well. Reason told him this was a foolish notion because she had carried a jar of water in the pail with their food. Right then, though, he could not, *would not* listen to reason. He peered down into the depths of the well and saw nothing but his own murky reflection.

Quickly he lowered the bucket and watched it sink out of sight. He hefted himself to the edge of the well, grasped the pull-rope with both hands, and lowered himself along its length and into the cold water. His feet touched soft ground and gravel where the water was about waist high. Letting go of the rope, he dunked beneath the surface of the water and sought the area with his hands. His open eyes saw nothing in the darkness, and he knew she was not there.

Gasping from the cold, he shot out of the water and clutching the rope, pulled himself up, hand over hand, the length of the well and clambered out of it and onto dry ground.

By that time, his wet skin and clothes, the wind and his fear had chilled him to his very marrow. But he did not go inside to the comfort of the fire. Instead, he plunged once more into the forest, calling for her. At their picnic site, he grabbed up the quilt and her shoes, telling himself she would be blue with cold wearing only that thin silk dress.

He covered the familiar territory of the forest twice, shouting for her until his voice was nothing but a weak rasp. At the edge of the small clearing, exhausted, he looked across at the house once more.

"Please be home," he pleaded, willing her to be there. But inside himself, in the depths of his very soul, he knew she was not. Whatever mystical, magical event had occurred to bring her to him must have swept her away again.

He managed to call one last time. "Abbie."

He tried to run toward the house, but the cold, the damp and the despair had drained the last of his strength. He stumbled and fell hard on his knees, unable to go forward.

"Come back to me. Dear God in Heaven, let her come back to me."

****

She tried to wake up. The hideously slow process terrified her, as if she were awakening from the sleep of the drugged.

Someone spoke. The voice seemed far away, much too distant for her to understand the words or recognize the speaker. She tried to open her eyes, but the heavy lids refused. Her body remained inert in spite of her best effort to move. Within the fog of her mind, her thoughts grappled with reality. What was the last thing she remembered? A storm? Not exactly, but there had been a brilliant light and a crash of thunder.

She tried to turn her head on the pillow to see if he slept soundly beside her.

"She moved!" The voice was familiar, but not recognizable. Not the voice she wanted to hear. "Get the doctor."

"Andrew?" she managed to whisper.

"She's trying to speak. *Get the doctor!* Abbie! Abbie, can you hear me?"

Movements by the side of her bed, rustling,

someone grasping her hand. An unfamiliar voice, an unfriendly one, spoke.

"He's gone for the day."

Something brushed her arm, then it squeezed, squeezed, kept squeezing until her arm ached. She groaned. A rhythmic huff-huff then a soft hiss and the force eased.

"Her pressure's good, one-oh-two over seventy-eight."

Where am I?

"She's trying to speak and open her eyes. I saw her lips move!"

That voice. It was as familiar as her own, but she couldn't remember.

"She's done that off and on since she's been here. It means nothing."

"It means *something*! And I'm telling you, Fran, she's waking up. If you're not going to get Doctor Rhys in here right now, I will."

The tight grip on her hand loosened, and she sensed movement from the owner of the voice.

"I'm telling you, he's gone for the day," said the other one, snappish and unfriendly. "Doctor Stuart's on call and I can get him if you insist. But you're a nurse, Linda, and you know as well as I do all this mumbling and twitching is normal in a coma patient. It means *nothing*."

"I'm not listening to you." The voice was near her once more. "I'm going to believe the best. Abbie, can you hear me? Honey, it's Lefty. If you wake up now, I'll let you call me Lefty in front of the administrator, and every doctor, nurse, and patient in this entire hospital. But you must wake up. Let us know you're all right."

Someone clasped her hand gently and lifted it to a soft, warm cheek. She heard a sob, felt tears wet her fingers.

With extreme effort and more willpower than she knew she possessed, Abbie forced her eyelids to part. Only a slit, but she saw a fuzzy image peering into her face.

"*Abbie!*"

"Where..." Her voice came out a mere papery rasp. She tried again. "Where's Andrew?"

"I can't understand you, honey. Let me get you some water."

Her heavy lids closed without permission. She gathered her strength and tried once more. She saw a plastic cup with a flexible straw near her face.

"Take a sip, real slow."

She drank just enough to moisten her lips and tongue. Anything more would have taken more strength than she could muster. She closed her eyes again and felt herself slipping close to unconsciousness.

"Andrew," she managed to say.

"Someone has gone to get the doctor for you. He'll be here in a jiffy."

The doctor. Good. Someone had gone to get Andrew. She managed a weak smile and let sleep overtake her again. He would be there when she woke up, so everything was fine.

The effort to awaken and open her eyes the second time was much easier. Blearily she glanced around, found herself in a dark, cool room. Good. She was home with Andrew, in his bedroom, and all that hospital nonsense had been nothing more than a dream. She must have been scratched by the briars of the dementia rose again. She wondered how long she had been asleep.

She turned her head to look at Andrew in the bed beside her. He was not there. In fact, she was not lying in his bed. She was not even in his bedroom. Instead of Andrew's sleeping face, she encountered the soft, blinking lights of a machine and the awkward profile of an IV pole. She tracked the length of the tube and saw it connected to her arm.

A modern hospital. Why was she here? And where was he? Her stunned gaze probed the shadows of the room. She saw someone in the chair in the corner.

"Andrew?"

The person sat up suddenly then leaped out of the chair and hurried to her side. A soft light next to her bed flickered on. Lefty smiled down at her.

"You're finally awake! *Thank God!* How are you feeling, hon?"

She stared at her friend. How did Lefty get here? How did *Abbie* get here? And where was Andrew? She looked beyond her friend, around the room, toward the open door, seeking him but not finding him.

"Where is he? Is he all right?"

"Who are you looking for?"

"Andrew. Where is he?"

Lefty gave her an odd look. "Andrew? Who's that?"

"Andrew Wade. Is he in another room? Is he all right?" She reached for Lefty's hand and clutched it weakly. "Tell me he's all right!"

Lefty gave her a bewildered look. She turned, picked up the plastic cup from the rolling bed tray. "Have a little water."

"I don't want a drink. I want Andrew!" She tried to sit up, but the effort drew darkness around her vision.

Slowly, Lefty set the cup back on the tray. She picked up a folded white washcloth and wet it from water in the gray plastic pitcher. She gently patted its coolness against Abbie's forehead. Abbie weakly batted it away.

"Where's Andrew? I need to know if he's all right." Once again, she tried and failed to sit up. "Has something happened to him? Tell me, Lefty!"

Lefty carefully shook out the moist cloth and just as carefully refolded it. Her studied movements frightened Abbie.

"*What has happened to him?*"

"Abbie," she said slowly, quietly, "who is Andrew? I don't know him."

"But he was with me! We've been together all this time, weeks, months. In that house, in those woods. He said there was no way out, but...but there must have been because here I am, and he was with me, and I would *never* have left without him." She reached out and grabbed the other woman's hand. "*Where is he?*"

Lefty took a deep breath. In the shadowy room, worry etched lines into her face. She seemed to ponder her words before she spoke.

"You've been here in the hospital, comatose, for several weeks."

The words seemed to come from some far planet.

"That's impossible. I was with Andrew, in a strange place. I was there with him."

Lefty said nothing but Abbie saw clearly her friend did not believe her. She felt betrayed by the woman, angry that Lefty chose to doubt the truth. Maybe Lefty was jealous.

"We were together. Inseparable, except when he went into the forest to look for the dementia rose. We talked and laughed, and we loved each other…" She broke off, realizing that nothing she said would penetrate Lefty's skepticism. "We were together, and I want him with me now. Something must have happened to him."

She burst into tears.

Lefty sat on the edge of the bed and put an arm around her. "I don't know what to tell you. Where did you meet Andrew? Is he someone from Dayton you never mentioned? Or did you go into Tomville while I was gone and meet him? Please don't carry on like this. You're going to make yourself sick."

"His name is Andrew Wade. He lives in an old house in the woods…" She looked at Lefty, digging her fingers into the woman's hand. "Find him for me. Please!" She began crying again, head turned against the pillow, her body shaking.

"I'm getting the nurse."

A short time later, a short gray-haired nurse with a face like a dried walnut hull entered the room. Without a word, she grimly gouged something into the IV. When it invaded Abbie's bloodstream, deep sleep swallowed her effortlessly.

The next time she woke up, daylight streamed through the window. She was alone in the hospital room. The memory of Lefty's words trickled back into her mind. Had she really been lying in this room, comatose, for weeks? Had she been separated from Andrew for that long? Had they found their way out of that imprisoning world but somehow been separated, he into his world and she into hers? Surely, God would not be cruel enough to let that happen! She closed her eyes, struggling to recollect anything more, but try as she might, she could not remember leaving him. She would never have left him of her own free will. *Never*. Something must have happened.

A short man with curly salt-and-pepper hair, round glasses, and heavy dark eyebrows came into her room.

"Good morning." The greeting seemed perfunctory, as if he was far busier than he wanted to be. "I'm Doctor Rhys." He checked her pulse, her heart and breathing, took her temperature and looked into her eyes. He made notations on the tablet computer in his hands. "So how are you feeling? Mind fuzzy, any anxiety, odd dreams?"

She gave him a sharp look. "Did Lefty say something to you?"

He raised his eyebrows. "Lefty?"

She winced inwardly, remembering her promise never to reveal her friend's nickname. "Linda Richardson."

A small smile played across his stern features.

"Ah. *That* Lefty."

"Yes. And please don't tell her I let that old nickname slip."

"It'll be our little secret. Now, tell me about these dreams you've been having."

"So she *did* say something to you. You may rest assured, Doctor, that I've not been having dreams. Andrew and his world are as real as you and I."

"Um hmm." He entered the data in his small computer then looked up. "Tell me about 'Andrew and his world.'"

As she told the man about Andrew, the old house, and the creepy forest surrounding him, she knew how foolish it sounded. If she'd overheard another patient tell such a story, she'd have thought it preposterous. That very notion reflected in the doctor's eyes.

"I see. And tell me again how you arrived in that strange place."

"I…I don't know. I just woke up with no memory of how I got there."

"I see. And you don't think it's a little strange that you don't remember arriving in those dark woods?"

Doctor Rhys's blunt bedside manner left a lot to be desired, and she resisted his words.

"There are a lot of reasons I might have wandered off and woke up in the woods. I had just walked out on a highly stressful job. I'd been living on little more than coffee and toast for weeks. I was far from home. I was exhausted. I was alone, I was scared—" She broke off, knowing she sounded foolish and thinking she'd probably said too much, but added, "Stress causes a person to sleepwalk. I read that somewhere."

Surely, a smirk hadn't just flickered across his expression, had it? She bristled even more.

"Yes, I'm sure there are many articles online, but no amount of stress, or sleepwalking, is going to lead you into an…well, an alternate world where someone has lived for a century and where things 'magically' appear. These are called 'dreams,' or 'delusions' if you continue to believe in them when you're awake and lucid."

"So you're saying I'm delusional."

"Let's just say you're not lucid, right now."

She gave him a hard stare. "Doctor Rhys, I assure you am fully awake, perfectly lucid, and completely without delusions. What I experienced really happened, and I will find him again, whether he lives in the woods here in Arkansas, or in some 'alternate world' as you suggest."

He kept his face impassive and tapped something

into his computer.

"All right, then. Your blood pressure is good, temperature normal, eyes clear." He glanced up. "A nurse will be in shortly to draw blood." And with that, he went out of the room.

Later, a plump young woman with rosy cheeks and snug pencil skirt trotted into the room in three-inch heels. Her dark hair escaped whatever attempt had been made to give her a professional updo. She looked like a teenager playing at being an adult. With a bright smile, she effusively announced herself as Doctor Kirk from "upstairs." Abbie soon learned "upstairs" was Psychiatric Services.

The woman read questions from her computer tablet, smiling merrily the entire time. When Abbie gave her the same information she'd given Doctor Rhys, the woman nodded, made notes, acted as if she believed every word, though something told Abbie this young doctor believed nothing.

"I'm going to put you on a regime of meds. We'll start with—"

Abbie sat straight up in the bed. She felt a little light-headed but didn't care.

"You most certainly are not putting me on *any* medication! There is nothing wrong with me."

The smile never slid from her face, but it did take on a frozen quality. She met Abbie's eyes.

"But the meds will help control the—"

"If you say delusions or hallucinations, I'm going to scream. Andrew is not a delusion. He is real!" She swung her legs off the side of the bed. "I'm feeling just fine, and I see no reason to stay here. I want to go home."

"Where is home?" Doctor Kirk scanned through the

screen, eyes darting back and forth in their sockets as if she were the one needing medication. "Ah. Dayton. Dayton? *Ohio?*"

Abbie said nothing.

"How did you get to Arkansas from Dayton, Ohio?"

"I drove."

"And you plan to drive back there?"

"I plan to find Andrew Wade, and the sooner I get out of here, the sooner I can find him."

"Actually, we need to keep you here for a few days—"

Abbie shook her head as she got out of bed and began looking around for her clothes. "I'm leaving."

"Mrs. Matthews, I must advise you that you are in no condition—"

"It's *Miss* Matthews. And I must advise you, Doctor, that I am an attorney, so I'm well-schooled about my rights. I'm neither a danger to myself nor anyone else. I have the right to refuse medical treatment—and that includes whatever medication you want to use on me. I have the right to leave this hospital against medical advice, and that's what I intend to do."

She picked up the telephone, punched number nine to get to an outside line, then called Lefty to come pick her up.

Chapter 18

As Abbie waited for Lefty to arrive, her agitation gradually gave way to something darker, something far grimmer. What if the doctors were right? What if the entire time she'd been with Andrew truly had been a sometimes frightening but magnificent dream as she recovered from stress-related exhaustion in a sterile hospital bed? What if he did not exist?

It made more sense than waking up in a forest on a cold day in August and finding a young man who had lived alone for over one hundred years. It made more sense than a cold, silent, ceaseless wind, or a perpetually full pantry, or a fire that never burned out. There was a sudden deep sickness in her heart.

As she stared out at the parking lot in the brittle sunlight, truth seemed to settle in heavy, relentless strokes.

Andrew Wade, who had yearned for sunlight for decades, could not possibly exist. Everything she thought she had found—honest love, an honorable purpose, a fulfilled life— none of it was real. It had been a dream. Every minute detail of it.

Her heart bled out its life with every slow, painful beat.

Behind her, a man cleared his throat. She turned, saw Doctor Rhys. His face was as stony as ever.

"I understand you're leaving?"

"A M A."

A small upward tilt of his lips seemed less of a smile than a sneer.

"Against medical advice, yes, so Doctor Kirk informed me. Physically, you're still very weak. We don't know what happened to you, whether you fell or if you passed out and hit your head. Or if you went on a sleepwalking jaunt, as you cleverly surmised. It could happen again. Will you not reconsider staying a few more days, let us keep an eye on you?"

"I want to go." She feared she might break down in front of this man who had been instrumental in stripping away the loveliest moments of her life.

"Then I'll sign off on your case, and you're free to leave as soon as your ride gets here."

She nodded once, and he left.

****

Lefty seemed to think Abbie was made of glass, so she drove toward home accordingly. Her friend's constant stream of inane chatter pounded against her depressed mood and fell hopelessly unheeded. She stared out the side window, noting the sun, the dancing heat waves ahead on the highway, listening to the sound of hissing tires on the hot pavement.

Through the buzz of Lefty's cheerful voice, Abbie spoke her thoughts aloud.

"There was a time, not long ago, Andrew and I yearned for the heat and the light and the sound."

Lefty stopped talking abruptly. "What did you say?"

"It was cold when I got there. Dark and cold and windy. He said it was always like that. But inside the parlor, the fire in the fireplace burned bright and warm. Andrew's bed was warm, too, and being in his arms…"

Her voice broke.

Lefty shot a quick look at her then directed her attention back to the road. She slowed the car to a crawl.

"Are you feeling all right? Do I need to stop?"

Abbie rose from her grief long enough to say, "I suppose I'm fine."

Lefty stared hard at her.

"Really," Abbie muttered. "I'm fine. Please just drive. You're holding up traffic."

Lefty glanced in the rearview mirror. "There's not a single car behind me."

"Well, there will be if you don't drive. Please, just go. I'm fine."

The other woman kept transferring her attention between Abbie and the road, but finally settled her gaze ahead and increased their speed.

Abbie closed her eyes against the brightness of the sun, loving it and hating it at the same time. She would have loved it thoroughly if Andrew were with her to enjoy it; she loathed it now because he was not here. She gladly would embrace the dim chill of his world if she could be with him once again.

"How about a root beer float?" Lefty's voice cut into her thoughts. "I remember how you used to love 'em."

"No, thanks."

"C'mon. You've had nothing but a feeding tube, then the hospital's bland diet. *I'm* losing weight just watching you. Let's have a root beer float."

The underlying worry in her friend's usually cheerful tone pricked her conscience. She made an attempt at courtesy. "If you want."

"I want."

They stopped at a drive-through on the main drag in

Tomville. Lefty ordered two extra-large floats. Abbie drank about a fourth of hers, then put it in the cup holder. She felt nauseous.

"When we get to my house," Lefty said between sips as she drove home, "I want you to lie down."

"I will."

"And I'm going to fix some of my auntie's famous chicken soup. She swore it cured everything from pneumonia to prickly heat."

"That'll be nice."

Lefty hesitated a moment before continuing, "I have to be at the hospital tomorrow, so I got the new John Grisham novel for you to read, and a couple of magazines. Oh, and I have some DVDs and a player, if that's what you'd rather do. I'm sorry I don't have internet out here in the boonies."

Despite the dull ache in her middle, Abbie tried to respond with the gratitude her friend deserved.

"Thanks. I'll be fine."

Again, they rode in silence. Lefty turned off the secondary highway and onto the gravel road leading to her house.

"You didn't drink much of your float. Didn't you like it?"

Abbie picked up the big Styrofoam cup and took an obligatory sip.

"Yes. It's good."

"You all right? You hurt anywhere?"

How could she hurt anywhere when she was hollow inside? There was nothing left to feel but emptiness.

"I'm fine. Stop worrying and fussing."

They bounced along the gravel road.

"Well, I *do* worry about you. That's what friends

do."

Lefty steered the car into her driveway and stopped beneath the huge maple tree.

"I'm sorry," Abbie said.

She turned from her friend's probing gaze. The nearby woods trapped her attention. The memory of Andrew, of their last time together ascended into her mind with such swiftness and force that she reeled back in the seat. His touch still seemed to linger on her skin; his kiss still burned her lips.

She closed her eyelids and could see his dark eyes, full of love and passion and honor.

She clutched her hands to her chest to halt the shattering of her heart. She bent forward, keening inside herself like a lost child.

Lefty gasped in alarm and touched her shoulder. "Abbie! What's wrong?"

"I miss him," she sobbed. "I miss him so much!"

She knew she could never cry out all her grief and sobbing seemed only to underscore the wretchedly hopeless situation. Still, it took quite a while before she was able to sit upright, and longer until she could dry her tears.

"Are you all right?" Lefty asked.

She nodded, though she was most definitely not all right. She was in love with a delusion, an imaginary man. And yet, she refused to worry her good friend.

"I'm fine." She wiped her eyes with the heels of her hands. "I'm sorry. I'm sorry I'm such a crybaby."

"You have nothing to apologize for. I just wish there was something I could do for you."

Lefty got out of the car and opened Abbie's door.

"Come on, girl," She took her arm as if Abbie was

an invalid. "Let's go inside."

How many people would give their time and open their home to someone as foolishly sad as she was and expect nothing in return? Abbie knew how lucky she was to have such a friend.

"Thank you. For everything."

"I know if the shoe was on the other foot, you'd do the same thing for me."

She hugged Lefty hard then allowed herself to be steered toward the house. In the living room, the blue-checked sofa was ready with a soft, fat pillow and a cool sheet. A fan sat on an end table and the breeze it created fluttered the flounced edge of the crisp white pillowcase. The quiet, white noise it hummed was comforting.

"I thought you might prefer not being alone right now," Lefty said, "but if you'd rather lie down in the bed upstairs, I have it ready."

"No, this is fine. Thank you." She wearily laid down without coaxing and closed her eyes. She ached from head to foot, as if she had run a great distance.

The odor of cooking food awakened her. She heard and smelled everything with the same indifference that she watched daylight dwindle into dusk beyond the window. If she'd been lying in a stark room with no sound, sight, or scent, she would have felt the same way. She closed her eyes again. The fan stirred air across her face.

In the darkness behind her lids, she saw him. She noted his quirked brow and quizzical smile, smelled the clean, masculine scent of his skin, heard the soft rumble of his voice, felt the caress of his fingertips against her cheek.

"Here you go! Good for what ails you." Lefty's

voice broke into her thoughts, shattering them.

She opened her eyes just as Lefty settled a food tray on the coffee table in front of the sofa. The tray held a blue goblet of ice water and a bowl with a generous serving of fragrant chicken soup. She had no desire to eat, felt no thirst, but when she saw the deep concern that continued to fill her friend's expression, she tried to cast aside her despair.

She sat up and did her best to offer a cheery smile. "It looks wonderful. Thanks."

Lefty's worried expression relaxed a little. "Great. I'll get myself a bowl of it and join you."

Abbie nibbled a chunk of gently seasoned chicken and forced herself to swallow. The food was tasteless in her mouth. She sipped the water, took another bite. A minute later her friend returned, carrying her own soup bowl. Lefty's voice rose and fell as she chattered.

In spite of her best efforts, Abbie failed to focus on the smallest thread of conversation. She could only think of what she had lost by simply waking up. Why had her brain conjured such a futile dream? She told herself only weak or confused people indulged in tender emotions. Being tough and unbreakable enabled her to defend miscreants and predators without a second thought.

But that wasn't accurate, was it? She'd had qualms and tender feelings just like anyone. When that innocent child lost her life to one of Abbie's freed villains, Abbie had chosen to seek a new path. Somehow, in the wending way of destiny, the new path included love. What destiny failed to consider was reality. In all her life, she would love only Andrew Wade, and he wasn't real.

An unexpected mirthless laugh erupted from her.

"The day I met him, he staunchly declared that *I* was

unreal, a delusional vision, a product of 'brain fever.' He emphatically told me to vanish! I believe his exact words were 'You do not exist. Begone!'" Again she laughed bitterly. "And all that time it was he who was a product of my imagination." She met Lefty's somewhat bewildered gaze. "How ironic is that?"

"I don't know what to say. I wish I could do something. I feel so responsible for all this."

Abbie's spoon clattered into her bowl. "How could you be responsible for *any* of it, Lefty?"

"You came to me for help. You were a guest in my house. I should have been here for you instead of at the stupid conference in Savannah—"

"You had a commitment! And you'd scheduled it long before I came crying to you."

"But you're my best friend, and I saw how distraught you were when you first got here. I should've stayed, been a support and comfort the way friends are supposed to."

"So let's assume you cancelled your commitment. You stayed here and played mother hen to me. How could you have stopped whatever it was that happened?"

"I would have been here with you when you passed out instead of you lying there, alone, in a coma. I could have gotten you to the hospital as soon as it happened. You could have died!" She shuddered. "I'd asked you to call me if you needed anything and when you didn't, I assumed you were getting that much needed respite we had talked about. I didn't want to interrupt you with a call, especially as you had asked me not to." She looked up, eyes swimming, expression agonized. "I thought it was best to leave you alone. I never once imagined you might be sick or injured. My little home here is so safe and quiet and peaceful—I just never considered it." Her voice broke. "I'll never, ever forgive myself." She covered her face with her hands.

Something stirred inside Abbie, something living and viable and precious. Her friend's pain was so strong in the room she could feel its echo in herself. She put aside her nearly untouched bowl and knelt on the floor beside her friend's chair. She laid one hand on Lefty's arm.

"It's all right. I don't blame you. Not for a second! You didn't know. You *couldn't* have known."

"But I should have—"

Abbie squeezed the woman's hand. "No, you shouldn't have. It's all over now, and I'm fine."

"You're not fine!" Lefty's voice cracked. "I can see plain as day that you're in a worse place than you were when you arrived. Maybe if I'd been here and got you help sooner, you'd have not slipped into that world—"

"I'd never have met Andrew."

Lefty hesitated then nodded. "If you want to put it that way."

Abbie forced herself to smile. "I had the best... *dream* I've ever had while I was out. I'll carry it with me all my life."

She knew how foolish the words sounded, that no one, not even Lefty, whom she loved like a sister, could ever understand the love she'd felt for Andrew Wade, real or imaginary.

"I want you to let go of your guilt, Lefty. If nothing else, my dream was something beautiful. I don't regret a moment of that dream."

"Even the frightening parts?"

Abbie smiled. "Even those."

195

****

While she spent the next few days resting and recovering, she pondered her life. She meditated on the state of her heart and spirit. One thing the dream taught her was to forgive her foolish choices and grave errors in judgment. Learning from those mistakes helped a person move forward into a life that had meaning and hope. She discovered her capacity for tenderness and passion, two traits she never knew she possessed. Criminal law practice no longer lay in her future, and whatever path stretched before remained a mystery. Memories of her time with Andrew kept returning, but she resolutely shoved them back. She must move forward, not wallow in a dream.

One evening she and Lefty took a walk along the dirt road that cut through the nearby farms and neighborhoods.

"Exercise is good for the body and soul," Lefty said.

"It is. Even when the walk is more of a stroll than a brisk jaunt."

"It elevates the heart rate and brings the sweat. We need that."

It was nice to watch dusk gently sweep away daylight and feel the cool change night brought to the air.

"We must do this every day," Lefty declared when they returned.

"It was nice. But now I'm dusty and sweaty and need a shower."

"I'll fix us some sangria, and after we've gotten cleaned up, we can enjoy it on the front porch."

"Lovely," Abbie said, going up the stairs. Nice how her fear of night beyond the walls of the house no longer kept her indoors.

Refreshed from her shower, she slid into a thin, cotton nightdress, but the evening air was cooler now and she needed a wrap, something lightweight and comfy, something she had not brought with her from Ohio.

She rifled through the large closet, hoping to unearth a robe. The painting she had bought at the Lost Treasures Shop was leaning against the wall. Her blood quickened, and she took a step back.

That painting.

She had forgotten about it. Or had she? It tugged at her, called to her, in the same way it had drawn her into the junk shop's basement and the corner where it had been consigned, nearly out of sight.

She pulled it from the closet, needing to revisit all the shadowy details again, yearning to know what had drawn her in the first place. She laid it on top of the bed and looked down at it. She eyed the lowering, threatening storm clouds, the overgrown forest and tangle of bushes bent in the wind, the dark, bleak house.

She extended one trembling hand, tracing her fingertips across the painting's rough, cracked surface. There it was, all so very familiar, so dear that her heart nearly stopped beating. Andrew's home, the place where she had lived and loved him, the place she yearned to be.

No doubt remained. Her time with him had been nothing more than a fantasy woven from this grim painting. She fell across it, her despairing cry rising from the deepest place inside her. The dream, held at bay, came crashing back into her mind with a force that buckled her knees.

"I've lost him! I've really, really lost him."

Lefty's footsteps pounded up the stairs and down the hallway.

"Abbie!" She sat on the bed next to her. "What's wrong?"

"There really is no hope of it being real," Abbie said in a strangled voice. "It's all over."

She remained prostrate across the painting, sobbing until her throat was raw while Lefty sat helplessly nearby, rubbing her back.

"Is there anything I can do?"

But Abbie was powerless to respond right then. She lay, wilted and defeated, tears leaking silently onto the painting. At one point, she was certain she heard his voice calling her. She stiffened, listening hard, hoping, praying. Then, she realized what she was doing and cursed such a foolish imagination. Her ability to imagine things had created such an amazing man in the first place.

She began to gather her emotions and calm her heartbeat. How many more breakdowns must she endure before they went away? She sat up slowly and stared down at the painting, at her teardrops on the cracked paint, feeling as though her very soul had shattered.

"I know it's over," she repeated. "My brain conjured the whole things because of this…this painting." She shoved it away from her like something dead, and it thudded to the floor. "I had hoped that, maybe, somehow, somewhere, I'd be able to find that gloomy old house again. Find it was real, that he was an actual living, breathing man, and I had lived with him. But now, well, now I know for certain that horrible old house is nothing but an ugly painting. It's not real – and neither is Andrew."

She drew in a deep, shuddering breath "I must have made the whole thing up because—" she glared down at the painting and gave the frame a hard kick and the painting sailed under the bed, out of sight. She squeezed her eyes shut for a minute then opened them and looked at her friend still sitting quietly on the edge of the bed.

"I just had to *have* that horrible old painting," she muttered. "Then I dreamed about the blasted thing. Made it all up in the longest sleep of my life. I could've just as well watched something like it on the television and saved myself a lot of pain." Her voice cracked and she cleared her throat.

"I'll take it," Lefty got down on her hands and knees to pull it out from under the bed. "In fact, I'll throw it in the trash."

"No! I need to work through this, so I'll keep the painting for a while."

Chapter 19

A week later Abbie loaded her suitcases into the car just before sunrise. Lefty would be leaving for her shift at the hospital soon. The morning air was sweet with just the hint of the promise of autumn in a few weeks.

The two women stood in the green dimness of the front yard as daylight inched its way across the landscape. Lefty wore pink scrubs; she was working in the NICU that day. Abbie was in a pair of white cotton shorts and a blue tank top. No more designer dresses and heels for traveling. She decided she liked dressing down.

"I wish you'd stay longer. We spent so little time together."

Abbie closed the trunk. "I know. But I need to get back and start my job search."

"And you're sure you want to leave criminal law?"

"I already have, up here." She tapped her temple. "And here, where it counts." She placed her palm over her heart. "All I need to do when I get back is put it on paper and make it official. You and I both know I can't go back to what I was before. Life's too short and too precious to live in pursuit of disastrous decisions and the almighty dollar."

Lefty grinned. "It's good to hear you say that."

She smiled back. "I've learned what's important now, and I won't soon forget it. And I'll tell you something else. All this time I thought it was my job that gave me power. It didn't."

"Of course not. You're a strong woman. You always have been, no matter what work you decide to do."

Abbie took a deep breath and let it out slowly. The sun silently scooted above the horizon. A soft breeze lifted a tendril of her pale hair and tickled her face with it. She brushed it back.

"I have money set aside to help me restart. I'll get a less expensive apartment, and I have closets full of clothes, so no problem there. Who knows? Maybe I'll start my own practice. Or maybe I'll do something totally unrelated to law."

"What about that?" Lefty's gaze drifted to the painting Abbie had placed in the back seat. "Are you sure you're all right about it? Can you—"

"I'll be fine." This was not the time to think about the painting, Andrew, or her dream. She wanted to get on with reality.

"Don't let anything get you down."

Abbie smiled and hugged her friend. "How can anything get me down for long when I have a pal like you, huh? Thanks for listening to me, and for taking care of me. I appreciate you more than you know."

Lefty blinked back tears. "As Aunt Sally would have said, 'Pshaw, what are friends for?' "

Abbie got into her car. She slid on smoky sunglasses and looked at her friend through the open door. "You will come to visit me in Dayton, won't you?"

"Of course. And you better come here again, too. Three years is too long."

"It is, isn't it?"

"Email me. Text me. Promise me?"

"Yes, I will. I promise."

One final, hard hug, and she closed the car door. She waved as she pulled out of the driveway. As she drove along the dusty gravel road to the highway, she asked herself how many people were lucky enough to have a good friend like the one she just left.

She turned east onto the highway, lowered the sun visor against the glare and adjusted the rearview mirror. As she did so, her glance fell on the reflected image of the painting in the backseat. She'd get rid of it at the first opportunity.

Her first opportunity happened about two hours later when she detoured off the main highway into the small town of Gemstone to find a restroom. As she drove back to the highway, she spotted a red and white hand-painted sign in front of a large, red barn-like structure. The sign announced that the building was the Gemstone Thrift Store. Below, in small, uneven black letters that seemed to have been added as an afterthought, were the words "donations accepted." She hoped the request would include dark, depressing paintings.

Ten minutes later, she had persuaded a large, red-faced woman into taking the painting, although the woman had gruffly told her, "Ain't nobody in their right mind who'd want that thing."

Back on the main highway, she kept telling herself that getting rid of the painting was a good move. Keeping it would serve only to remind her of a time that didn't exist. Maybe its absence would bring her some relief.

But it did not. Within a few minutes, she felt worse than ever. A peculiar sense that she had left something crucial undone haunted her like a restless spirit. Three times she slowed the car and almost U-turned in the middle of the highway to go back and retrieve the painting. But why torment herself seeing it day after day, remembering what she would never have?

"It was just a dream, all in my head. There is no Santa Claus. There is no Easter Bunny, or Tooth Fairy. There is no Andrew Wade."

She turned on the radio and fiddled with the buttons in an unsuccessful search, trying to find a station that played anything other than country music. Blast it all, she needed something to listen to so she wouldn't have to think for a while, but she sure didn't want to hear anything to make her sadder than she was already. Sighing with resignation, she punched off the radio.

She knew the sooner she overcame her dream, the sooner she could get on with her life. After all, she was intelligent and resourceful. She had a sense of humor and playfulness. She thought she was reasonably attractive and tried to take good care of herself. It sounded like an ad for the personals: *SWF seeking love with the mysterious man of my dreams.*

As the morning progressed, sleepiness began to settle into her brain. Maybe she hadn't fully recovered from whatever had landed her in the hospital. When she spotted a small roadside café/convenience store, she pulled into the nearly empty parking lot. Inside the building, the air smelled of a poorly ventilated kitchen and stale air conditioning. Somewhere a radio pricked the air with bluegrass music. With a lively fiddle and banjo, at least it wasn't depressing.

She bought a cup of coffee and a bagel at the counter and sat down in a worn vinyl booth. She was one of three people in the store. The clerk behind the food counter paid scant attention to her and the tubby, dark-haired man behind the cash register near the door seemed intent on cleaning his fingernails with the blade of his pocketknife. She looked away, repressing a shudder.

She finished the coffee and bagel, and for a few minutes she sat where she was, allowing the resurgence of energy to hit her bloodstream. When she got up to leave, her glance fell on the display of hand-made candles and soaps. The simple white label read *Sumac Ridge Natural Products*.

Her heart leaped like a trout, and a shiver skimmed down her spine. Andrew said he came from Sumac Ridge. Until she met him, she had never heard of the place. Was it a weird coincidence that she conjured in her dream?

She turned to the girl at the food counter and dipped her head toward the soaps and candles. "Is Sumac Ridge a real place?"

The girl shrugged. "I dunno. I never heard of it."

She looked past Abbie at the fat man who still whittled cheerfully on his fingernails. "Hey, Leo, is there such a place as Sumac Ridge where these soaps are from?"

He looked up, scrunched his face in thought, and held the knife blade unmoving in his fingers.

"Not sure. Haven't lived here but a few years, but the candlemaker is a native. She could tell you."

A fire lit in Abbie's belly. "Does she live nearby?"

The man shook his big head and started shaving his thumbnail. "Lives back in the hills somewhere, but I don't know where exactly." He looked up, squinted his eyes at Abbie. "Whyn't you call her? Phone number's on the label."

She grabbed up a bar of lavender soap, paid for it, thanked him for his help, and hurried to her car. She punched in the numbers on her phone, mentally rushing the candlemaker to answer. She was so breathless that when the woman did answer, she practically gasped out her question.

"Is Sumac Ridge an actual place, or is it a name you made up for your company?"

The woman's laugh was sweet and soft. "Well, hello, to you, too," she said in a quiet drawl, then added. "And yes, Sumac Ridge is real. As real as Little Rock or Fort Smith."

"Would you please tell me where it is?"

"Of course, honey, but why do you want to know? There's not a blessed thing up here but me and Granny and my little factory."

"I...I've heard about Sumac Ridge. I need to...that is, I want to see it."

There was a brief pause.

"Well, you're more than welcome, of course. And I'll even give you a tour of my business." She laughed again. "I don't get many visitors, so it will be nice having you here. I'll give you some sweet tea, and we'll visit. Tell me where you're coming from, and I'll give you directions how to get here from there."

Abbie told her the name of the roadside store, and with a shaking hand, she wrote down directions the woman gave her.

****

Sumac Ridge Natural Products was run by Grace Ethridge. She lived on a rutted dirt lane that made Lefty's gravel road look like a superhighway. Grace's driveway climbed and curled up a steep hill then leveled as it reached her place on the summit.

An abundance of bright red zinnia, golden dahlias,

and orange marigolds surrounded an older, gray dwelling. Beyond the house sat another weathered building, shady and just as flower-banked as the house, but with a decidedly commercial air about it. Beside the door, a carved wooden sign read *Sumac Ridge Natural Products Welcome, Visitors!* It was to that building Abbie drove. She parked in a small, graveled space near the door.

A humid, warm breeze met her as she got out of the car. The welcome thrum of a noisy air conditioner promised coolness inside, but the brightly lit interior proved to be uncomfortably warm as she entered. And no wonder. Several vats, apparently full of hot wax and fat, sat on two industrial sized stainless steel stoves. The scents of cinnamon, patchouli, rose, and lavender mingled with the scent of wax and oil. Soap and candle making was not only a warm business but fragrant as well. She inhaled deeply.

"Welcome!" called the slender woman who approached from the back of the building. She wore a thin camisole of white eyelet, a flowing red skirt, and wide-strapped leather sandals. Her long, gray-streaked blonde hair was pulled back neatly into a low ponytail, and she did not wear a dot of makeup. Her understated appearance carried a beauty all its own.

The woman wiped her perspiring forehead with her arm and smiled at Abbie. "Welcome to Sumac Ridge Natural Products. I'm Grace Ethridge." She held out her right hand.

Abbie introduced herself and shook hands, charmed by the direct simplicity of this woman.

"Everything we make here is all natural." Grace swept her hand toward her little factory. "We use essential oils and vegetable fat, nothing animal. Would you like a tour of the place?"

Abbie glanced around.

"This is very unique. And I'd like to see it, but maybe you can show me around a little later. Right now, I need to ask you about Sumac Ridge."

Grace lifted one eyebrow, a gesture that clutched Abbie's heart with memory. How many times had she seen Andrew lift an eyebrow in just that way when he was curious or skeptical?

"All right. Ask me anything."

"Is Sumac Ridge really real?" The expression on the other woman's face caused her to rephrase her question. "I mean, is there an actual place, a town or something, called 'Sumac Ridge', or did you just make up the name for your company?"

Grace spread her arms, her expression still a mixture of curiosity and kindness.

"This is Sumac Ridge. That is, this range of hills through here. It's always been called Sumac Ridge—at least as far as I know. There's no town of Sumac Ridge. There used to be a little town down the road a piece called Smith, but the trains stopped running through there in the 1930s, so it's just a ghost town now."

"But Sumac Ridge had people living here a hundred years ago?"

"Oh, sure. Even longer ago than that. Listen, hon, it's so hot here. How about I get us some sweet tea? I have some in the back."

Without waiting for a reply, she took off toward the back of the building, the soles of her sandals hissing against the cement floor and her red skirt flowing around her calves as she walked. Abbie waited impatiently for the two minutes it took Grace Ethridge to bring the tea, but she gratefully accepted the tall, cold glass and swigged from its icy contents.

"That's wonderful! Thank you. You were saying that people lived on Sumac Ridge many years ago."

Grace nodded. She wiped the beads of tea off her upper lip with the tip of her index finger.

"It's not much of a community now, as you can see. Folks left the Ridge years and years ago, to find work in the towns or other parts of the country. We're remote and isolated, as you could tell just by driving up here. Industry never got this close, and I can't say that I'm sorry. I like it wild and untouched. There are lakes, resorts, and plenty of other tourist attractions around here, but if you want the real Ozarks, this is it."

Abbie nodded, but she wondered how anyone could prefer living as far away from civilization as Grace did. Unless, of course, that person had a companion like Andrew Wade. In which case, she could live on the moon, and happily.

"Have you been here long?"

Grace nodded and laughed. "You could say that. Six generations of my family were born on the Ridge. I left to do that popular thing in the 'seventies: 'find myself'. After about twenty-five years, I realized I'd left myself right here, so I came home."

Abbie stared at her. "You left, and came back?"

Grace offered a beatific smile. "So many people ask me that, and with that same I-can't-believe-it voice. But, yes, I came back home. And I started my own business."

"My goodness." She had thought Lefty lived in the back of beyond, but her friend lived in the middle of Times Square compared to Grace Ethridge. "Six generations, you said?"

"Yes. And unfortunately, I'm the only descendant of my family still living on the Ridge. Here, let me show you around the factory."

She put down her empty tea glass on a nearby table and took Abbie's arm, steering her toward the inner workings of her industry. "I do most of the work myself, but I have a couple of girls from Peace Valley to come in a day or two a week. Peace Valley is a little town about twenty miles from here."

Although she found the factory both unique and interesting, her mind was not on the tour Grace seemed intent on giving. She tagged along with her hostess. She had no choice, seeing that Grace kept a friendly arm linked through hers. The other woman clearly loved her work and loved to share it. Abbie forced herself to take an interest, but she waited for the right opportunity to ask the question that burned inside her.

Back at the table where the tour had started, Abbie held a fat, smooth sandalwood candle Grace had given her. Nervously stroking the smooth wax and feeling both foolish and hopeful, she cleared her throat.

"Have you ever heard of a man from Sumac Ridge named Andrew Wade?"

Grace, who had been lovingly but sadly examining a candle with a crack in it, laid it in a basket with other broken pieces. She glanced at Abbie in considerable surprise.

"Why, yes. He was my great-great uncle."

Chapter 20

The fragrant candle she held slipped from Abbie's clasp and hit the cement floor with a dull thud. She stared wordlessly at Grace who retrieved it and put it back in her nerveless hands.

"How did you hear about our mysterious ancestor? Granted his story was the talk of the Ridge a hundred years ago, but I didn't think anyone outside the family had ever even heard of him. Well, unless—" she grinned broadly, and clasped Abbie's upper arm in a friendly clutch. "—unless you're a cousin. Oh, what fun! I thought our clan had just about died out with only Susan Wade McLeod and me left, and both of us without a child."

Grace's words seemed to run together senselessly.

"I'm not a cousin."

The woman's forehead creased for a moment. "You aren't?"

Abbie shook her head. She licked dry lips and managed to say, "What can you tell me about him?"

"About Great-uncle Andrew?"

She nodded.

"Well, I suppose you know what happened to him, so what else do you want to know?"

Abbie closed her eyes and took a deep breath, trying to quiet her thrumming, pounding blood.

"All of it." She opened her eyes. "Everything you

know about him. What he looked like, the kind of person he was, did he have children…anything, everything."

"Since you know the name, surely you know the legend."

Abbie thought her heart might jump out of her chest and her brain might explode. She wanted to scream with the need to know, but she forced her voice to remain quiet and calm as she replied. "Tell me. Tell me everything."

"So you don't know the legend?" Grace asked.

She felt lightheaded. "No. Please. Tell me about him."

Grace's happy expression slipped a little and she sighed. "Too bad you aren't a relative. I would have loved to meet a long lost cousin." Her face took on a wistful expression. "We could have—"

Abbie had to bite the inside of both lips to keep from screaming.

"Grace, what is the legend? *I want to know all about Andrew.*"

"Are you a writer or journalist or something?" Grace narrowed her eyes slightly. "Because I don't want my family exploited for some story."

"No. I'm just a…" What could she say? *Just a friend, just a lover of a man who may have been your great-uncle?* "I'm just interested."

"A stranger who is more than just a little interested in an old family legend? Seems odd to me," Grace tilted her head, gazing at Abbie. "But," she said, after a moment and throwing her arms wide, "it's not a deep, dark, secret skeleton hidden away in the closet. Just a peculiar story. And it probably isn't true." She smiled. "By the way, would you like more iced tea? It's so hot today—"

"No!" Abbie barked. "I mean, please, just…that is…" She forced herself to take a deep breath. "No, thank you. No more tea. I just want to know the story." She offered a smile. "Please?"

Grace studied her a moment longer, as if she thought Abbie wasn't quite altogether in her right mind, but finally she shook her head slightly as if shaking off dusty thoughts.

"All right, then." She leaned her backside against the table and loosely folded her arms across her chest. "Well, the legend goes that my great-uncle was something of a paragon in the community. He was smart and kind, and he loved the people here on the Ridge. And people in these parts loved him. In those days, hardly anyone around here had money, but Andrew wanted to be a doctor." She leaned forward a little and lowered her voice as if betraying a confidence. "No one in this part of the world wanted to do more or be more than what they were. Country folks. Farmers. Not a lot of ambition to venture into the broader world."

She leaned back, took a drink of tea. "Apparently, my great-uncle worked from daybreak to dark for anyone who'd hire him, trying to earn enough money to study medicine. And he did. In fact, he had only a year or so left in his training when, one day in August, he left home, heading for the train station in Smith and never arrived. They looked for him for weeks, but he had vanished without a trace."

As Grace related the same facts Andrew once shared, Abbie felt the blood drain from her vitals. A high-pitched hum buzzed in her ears as the room shifted and dimmed. Grace, still happily chattering about the possibility of him simply going for pastures far greener than the Ridge offered, noticed Abbie's face and broke off in mid-word.

"You're white as a sheet, hon! Here, sit down quick."

She dragged an old wooden chair across the floor just as Abbie's legs buckled.

"Oh, my goodness!" Grace looked toward the back of the factory and called, "Granny! Quick, bring a glass of water and a cool cloth."

Her long, full skirt made a bright puddle of fabric against the gray floor as she sank to her knees beside Abbie. Genuine concern and watchfulness replaced her bright smile and chatter. She patted Abbie's wrists gently.

"Breathe deeply, darlin'. If you feel like you're going to faint, put your head between your knees."

Abbie took in air and blew it out noisily, just as she had learned in her stress management class a few months ago. She leaned back in the hard chair and took another deep breath. She knew, without a doubt, only Andrew had ever told her this family legend. Was it possible her dream had not been a dream at all but a very real encounter with the legend himself? More importantly, did Andrew Wade continue to exist somehow, somewhere, still young and vibrant and alive as when she had last seen him?

Grace had ceased to pat Abbie's wrists and now stroked her hands. She looked anxiously into her eyes.

"It's this awful humidity. And sometimes the smell of the essential oils can get so strong in the damp air. Granny, can you hurry with that water, please?" She half-stood and looked toward the back of the building then turned back to Abbie. "Are you feeling any better, hon?"

She tried to take slow, deep breaths, but her heart raced like a runaway train. She moistened her dry lips.

"Andrew is…was real?" She searched Grace's wide eyes. "Did you ever see him? I mean, a picture?"

Grace puckered her forehead, tilted her head slightly. "Real? Of course, he was real. The legend is just a story, after all. I fail to understand why you are so interested in him."

Abbie wanted to explain, yearned to share the truth with this woman, but words failed her. All she could do was plead with her eyes. She watched Grace battle with herself and finally come to a decision.

"Well, it's not my place to judge you or anyone else. I think there's a photograph of him in an album back at the house."

Abbie leaned forward and clutched Grace's hand. "Please. Will you get it?" She squeezed the other woman's fingers tightly. "Please."

Grace patted the hand that gripped hers. "All right. Don't get yourself all worked up again. I'll run to the house and get it." She stood up, glanced toward the back of the shop. "Here comes Granny with some cold water and a damp cloth. You sit right there, and I'll be back in a jiffy."

Abbie leaned back in the chair, closed her eyes.

She asked herself again if it could be true. And what would she do if the man in the picture turned out to be the Andrew Wade in her dream? Explore every inch of Sumac Ridge? Look on Tony's Buyers' List for a time machine? Check herself into an institution?

"Because I must be insane. Totally and completely

out of my mind."

Dimly she registered approaching footsteps, a dragging, shuffling sound of an old person. When the steps halted, she opened her eyes and saw a tall, icy glass of water being offered to her. The hand holding the glass was worn and gnarled with age. On it was a scarlet crescent-shaped birthmark, a mark she had seen before, and not so long ago.

She raised her eyes and met the rheumy gaze of the old woman from the Lost Treasures shop.

"*You!*" She stared at the old woman whom Grace had called Granny, probing those dim eyes for some unspoken knowledge. "You sold me the painting!"

Granny simply looked at her.

"You know about that house in the painting, don't you? You know where it is. You know where he is, don't you? Tell me!" She grabbed the old woman's forearm. "Please, tell me where he is!"

"Have this water," the old woman said, unconcerned that Abbie held her arm like a vise. "You're overheated. And I have a nice damp rag for your face." She held up a snowy white cloth. "You'll feel better."

The door to the shop opened and closed noisily, and Grace rushed to them.

"Thank you, Granny." She took the glass and held it nearer to Abbie. "Here, hon."

Abbie took it without shifting her gaze from Granny.

While both women watched, she sipped the cold water, felt the wetness refresh her parched lips and mouth. Granny offered the cloth, and she accepted it wordlessly. She told herself old people often bore striking resemblances to one another. Surely, this woman was not the same person from the junk store.

She patted the cloth against her cheeks, then buried her hot face in the cool, damp cleanness of it. It smelled of sweet fresh air.

"Thanks" She straightened and swabbed it across the back of her neck.

"Do you feel better now?"

"A little."

"Thank goodness. The heat in the factory can be overpowering sometimes." Grace glanced at Granny. "Thank you for helping." She turned to Abbie. "This is a photo album, full of pictures of my family." It was quite old and bound in dark green leather. "And here is the only photograph of Andrew Wade that I've ever seen." Grace released it to Abbie's eager hands. "This was taken the summer he disappeared." Grace rested her long index finger on a small, yellowed photograph.

With her heart nearly bursting from her ribcage, Abbie stared down at the familiar face of the man she loved. She pressed her fingers against her lips to keep from crying out. He had posed without smiling, but she saw the depth of compassion in his eyes, the underlying humor. There was his dear rumpled hair that always seemed in need of combing, his straight nose and firm chin, the finely chiseled lips that had caused her to burn for more than just his kisses.

She snapped her head around once more to face the old woman who held the answers.

"You sent me to him in the first place, and now you know where he is. Please, *please!* Take me to him!"

"What?" Grace squawked.

Abbie ignored her. "Please! You must take me to him."

"Now listen!" Anger replaced Grace's friendly tone.

"I won't allow anyone to come in here and scream at Granny. She's old, and she's fragile."

Granny did not give a moment's notice to Grace's protests. Instead, she spoke to Abbie.

"The painting holds the secret. You must go to the painting. You must hurry."

"But I can't go to the painting! I got rid of it!"

Alarm flickered across the aged features. "Then you must get it back, as quick as possible." Granny's eyes lost their dimness and seemed almost to glow as she stared at Abbie. "As quick as possible," she repeated. "Here is what you must remember:

Passion spurned;
hatred burned.
A curse of thirteen hundred moons must pass.
Then death will come,
unless love breaks the curse
to set the prisoner free."

Granny's gaze was steely, frightening in its intensity. "His time is almost gone."

"I don't understand. Where is he? Tell me how to find him."

"Go to the painting."

"I told you I don't have it!" She clutched the album to her chest, holding it so tightly her hands hurt. "Just tell me where that house is, that house in the painting. He's there, isn't he? Then tell me where it is!"

"You must hurry. His time is almost gone. I have done all I can, and I can do no more."

The old woman turned, her misshapen figure seemingly more bent than ever, exuding despair and pain. Abbie shot up from the chair, shoved the photograph album into Grace's hands, and grabbed

Granny's arm, stopping her retreat.

"Here now!" Grace shrieked, rushing to Granny's aid. "She's an old woman!" She tried to wedge herself between the two women and break Abbie's grasp. "Stop hurting her!"

"I'm not trying to hurt her. I'm sorry, Granny—"

"You leave her be, Grace," the old woman said, fastening her flinty glare on the candlemaker. "This is none of your concern."

"Well, Granny, if you think I'm going to let a strange young woman come in here, yelling and manhandling you—"

"She ain't hurting me, and this don't concern you. You leave us be." Granny pinned her with a look until Grace stood aside, helpless and jittery, her agitated gaze flitting from one woman to the other.

Granny turned to Abbie. Gone was the glow in her eyes, replaced by what seemed unbearable regret.

"I can't help you, child. I've—"

"I'll give you anything. All my money, my car, everything I have. Please, just tell me where he is."

Granny's mouth worked pitifully. Her eyes were full of desperation.

"Do you love him? Do you love him more than your own life?"

Merciful heavens, the very emotion she never wanted to feel, never wanted to acknowledge.

"*Yes!*" she said fiercely. "Yes, I love him! I would lay down my life for him."

A small beam of hope kindled in the old woman's dim eyes. She took both of Abbie's hands in hers and gripped them with gnarled fingers.

"I knew you were the one! I knew finding you was

the one good thing I've done. Now, you must rush, rush like the wind. Find that painting, and you will find your love."

"But—"

"I can't tell you more. Remember the words. Remember time. Remember love!"

Chapter 21

Abbie stared deeply into the old woman's eyes and in that moment knew she had one, and only one, chance to be with Andrew again. From that look she also knew failure to reunite with him would be devastating beyond belief. How would she find him? She had no idea, but anything was possible.

"I'll go," she told Granny. "I'll find the painting. And I will find him."

Granny said nothing, but Abbie read pleading, desperation, and hope in the old woman's eyes, as if finding him meant as much to her as it did to Abbie.

"Go. Go now!"

She rushed to the door and flung it open. She turned to look once more at the bent form of the old woman.

"Thank you."

Granny responded in neither word nor action. Grace spluttered and called to her, but Abbie obeyed Granny, wasting no time in explanations.

She drove recklessly over the rutted dirt road. She barely slowed when she reached the stop sign at the intersection. Spewing gravel from her squealing tires, she pulled onto the highway. The car skidded sideways. She knew a moment's panic, but controlled the skid then mashed the accelerator to the floor.

The narrow, twisting Ozark Mountain highway offered sharp curve after curve and steep hill after steep hill. Abbie, whose nerves were as tight as a guitar string, exhausted herself keeping the car under control. She entered the town of Gemstone at dusk and located the flea market. The parking lot was empty, and the door to the building was securely locked when she tried to enter.

She refused to accept defeat. She rattled the knob. Maybe someone was in the back or sweeping the floor. She pummeled the door with both fists.

"Hello!" she shouted. "Is anyone in there? Hello!"

She pounded the door, yelling until a woman came out of a house next door and hurried across the parking lot. A heavy-set woman with a deep frown etched on her broad forehead, she wore a flour-streaked red apron and carried a hefty rolling pin.

"Here now, stop that!" she hollered. "You want me to call the cops?"

Abbie turned to her in relief, recognizing the volunteer who had taken the painting from her that morning.

Ignoring the woman's thunderous expression and tense posture, she said, "Oh, thank goodness you're here! I need to have my painting back. You have to let me inside this place so I can get it."

The woman stood at the foot of the rickety steps, feet wide apart, arms crossed and rolling pin clutched menacingly to the forefront.

"I'll do no such of a thing!" she bellowed. "What in the world are you doing at this time of day, screaming and hollering like a fool and trying to break into the store?"

Abbie ran down the steps toward her. The woman tensed, drew herself up even larger and her glare deepened. Abbie halted.

"Don't you remember me? I was here this morning. I donated a big, dark painting. Don't you remember me?"

An expression of recognition crossed the woman's face, but she hung on to her defensive stance. She ran a critical gaze over Abbie's length.

"Now that you mention it, yes. What do you want?"

"I want the painting back."

The woman's eyes rounded. "Do what?"

"I'm sorry to bother you, but I made a mistake. I have to get my painting." In the dim evening light, she could not see the other woman well, but she was willing to bet the broad, florid face was three times redder than its usual color.

"You mean to tell me you're doing all that wild hollering and carrying on over that picture? Come back tomorrow in the morning 'bout ten o'clock. And for mercy's sake, stop all this racket. You got my mother-in-law ready to have a runaway."

She turned to leave. Abbie lunged and caught the fleshy arm, not caring if the rolling pin came down on her head.

"Please, ma'am! I must get that painting back. Right now. Tonight."

The woman looked down at her as if she really might offer a clout from her doughy weapon. She studied Abbie's face, and something flicked across her features. Her expression softened just that much.

"Can't you just come back in the morning like a normal person?"

"No." Sensing a weakening of resolve, she pressed her advantage. "Please, ma'am. I have to have that painting back as soon as possible. It was a mistake to give it away."

"And I reckon 'soon as possible' just can't be in the morning?"

"No, I'm sorry. Honestly, under normal circumstances, I wouldn't do this, but please, I'm begging you. Open the door and let me get my painting. I'll buy it back. I'll pay what you ask. But please, let me have my painting."

The big woman stared at her another minute, a bit like a scientist might examine a peculiar specimen under the microscope. Heaving a sigh that must have come from the very depths of her beleaguered soul, her animosity seemed to ebb as resignation took over. She lowered the rolling pin to her side.

"Well, I need to go get the key and make sure Mama Ida-Mae hasn't collapsed from nerves. You…now you just settle down and wait here. Set on them steps. I'll be back directly."

Abbie could not sit. She could not relax, and it had been foolish of the woman to recommend it. She paced the small area in front of the building, repeating Granny's words over and over—*His time grows short.*

What did that mean? It sounded so urgent, so ominous, as though his life was in danger. This thought, fully formed and recognized in her mind, brought such a rush of exigency she felt sick. She started across the parking lot toward the house when the woman stepped out her door and came toward the flea market, *sans* rolling pin. She held up a wad of keys on a heavy ring as she approached and shook them noisily. Abbie eagerly followed her up the steps to the door.

As the old door yielded to the woman's push, she muttered, "I sure as shootin' hope we don't get a gaggle of folks coming in here, thinking we're open in the middle of the night." She flipped on the lights, then closed and locked the door behind them.

It was hardly dark outside, but Abbie thought it best not to mention it. At this point, she didn't care if it was eight in the evening or two in the morning. She wanted the painting, and she would have it.

"Well, let us find that thing so's you can quit your faunching and fuming. If it was such an all-fired important painting why'd you leave it here in the first place?" The woman squinted her eyes. "I bet you talked to some hotshot dealer down in Little Rock, didn't you, and he offered you a wad of money for it, didn't he?" She shook her head. "People!"

Abbie said nothing. If she told the woman the truth, that the painting held the secret of a one-hundred-and thirty-year-old man with whom she was in love, she would probably be hauled off the premises by the aforementioned cops. She began searching the market, looking at every table and shelf, above and below them, in the corners and behind the counters.

After several minutes, she was close to tears. The woman gave half-hearted assistance by standing in the middle of the room and glancing around, muttering about her mother-in-law's nerves and voracious appetite.

"As you can see, it obviously ain't here," she finally announced, walking to the door.

"Wait!" Abbie said frantically. "Surely we haven't looked everywhere. Isn't there a room where you sort donations, or store them, or something?"

The woman, facing the door, sighed loudly, and turned around.

"Back yonder." She pointed. "But that picture was put on that table over there where all them books are."

Abbie glanced where she indicated, but of course she had already searched that area, as well as under the table on which the books sat. The painting was not there. She followed the woman into a windowless, airless backroom crammed to capacity with castoffs. She began riffling through piles of clothing, old shoes, threadbare sheets and curtains, dog-eared books, and worn-out magazines. The only pictures she found were two faded landscape prints in cheap, plain frames.

Rather than help her look, her reluctant companion weaved through the merchandise to a wall telephone with an old-fashioned rotary dial. She dialed a number.

"Edna Lou?" the woman said into the mouthpiece. "It's Rochelle. I've got some woman down here at the store looking for that picture she gave us earlier today...Yes, of course I'm with her. You think I'd let someone prowl and paw around in here alone? Well, she was yelling and banging on the door like she was here to get her baby outta jail, and Mama Ida-Mae was convinced it was the Second Coming and she'd missed it...Oh, you remember it, that ugly old picture of an old house and a storm...Yeah, that's the one, and we can't find it for love or money...*what?*...Oh for heaven's sake, no wonder we can't find it then."

Abbie froze and stared wild-eyed at the woman.

"What? What? Is it gone?"

The woman waved an impatient hand at her and kept talking to Edna Lou.

"Well, I know that, but what would *you* have done with all her carrying on? And what could Jimmy have done if I had called him?...Well, I'll tell you the honest truth, Edna Jean, I ain't gonna vote for him for sheriff again next time, and I don't care if he is your cousin. He don't know his head from a bucket of rocks… Well, just let me tell you something, if he put as much effort into being a sheriff as he did *running* for the *office* of sheriff—"

Abbie grabbed the woman's hand that held the telephone. "Is my painting gone?"

Rochelle tried to murder her with a look. "Let go of me! Yes, it's gone. It sold this afternoon."

"No!" Abbie sagged against the wall, feeling as though she might pass out. The painting held the key to finding Andrew, and it was gone.

"Oh, lordy, Edna Lou, she's going crazy again. You sell that painting to someone here in town?…Oh, her. I shoulda known. Listen, I gotta get off the phone before this gal starts foaming at the mouth. I'll talk to you in the mornin'."

She hung up the phone. For the moment she lost her annoyance and appeared genuinely concerned.

"You better set down, 'fore you fall down." She shoved a pile of yellowed underwear and stiff-looking shoes from a vinyl chair, and Abbie sank onto it, feeling as though her head was about to explode. "Now, you just calm down, missus. That picture is still in town, but it's been sold to Nancy Salem over on Parkview Drive. She might sell it back to you, though, if you was to ask her. She's a real nice woman, even if she is rich."

Abbie looked up, buoyed by new hope. She bounded out of the chair. "She lives here? In this town? How do I get there?"

"Well, now, you can't just go running off to folks's houses in the middle of the night and expect them to give you what you want. Someone a little less nice than me will sure enough call the law—"

"Ma'am, excuse me, I don't mean to be rude, but right now I don't give a gigantic flying fig what time of day it is. Tell me how to find Parkview Drive, and I'll find Nancy Salem if I have to knock on every door on that street."

Rochelle's mouth flew open. "Well, merciful heavens, after me opening up this store outta the goodness of my heart and you talking to me that way, why, I'm half-a-mind not to tell you Nancy's address or her phone number." She crimped her lips together as though she would never speak again for the rest of her life, then she said, "You know where the park is?"

"I've never been to this town before today. And I apologize for offending you. I just…" Her voice trailed, and she shook her head. There was no explanation she could give that would make sense to anyone. "I'm sorry."

Rochelle pinned her with that scientist's scrutiny again.

"Well, never you mind." Suddenly she was generous with compassion. "Let's close up the store, and I'll tell you how to find Nancy's house. It ain't hard, and you can't get lost in Gemstone, even if you was to try." She sounded almost pleasant. As she turned out the light in the storeroom and led the way back to the front door, she gave Abbie directions to Parkview Drive and concluded her instructions with, "You can't miss the Salems's house. It's the nicest one on the street."

She thanked Rochelle and ran down the steps to the car. She stopped and looked over her shoulder. The other woman turned the key and rattled the door to be sure it was locked and tight.

"Wait, please, before you go home…"

Rochelle puffed up. "Now, listen, I ain't gonna—"

"Just a minute."

Abbie got her purse out of the car and grabbed every bit of cash from her wallet. She offered it to the woman, saying, "I'm sorry I bothered you, and I'm sorry I was so boorish. I want you to take this for your trouble."

The woman looked at the wad of bills in her hand. This time, in spite of having very little light, Abbie saw a flush steal up Rochelle's ruddy cheeks. She shook her head.

"No. You keep your money. I didn't do anything, really."

"Yes, you did." But when Rochelle backed away a couple of steps, she added, "I see by your sign near the door that this thrift store helps to buy food for needy families. Take this for that fund."

Rochelle relented. "That's right kind of you, missus. And I'm sorry I was so rude, too. It's just that Mama Ida-Mae, well, she gets me all tense and then my tension slops out on everyone else. Well, good luck in finding your picture."

"Thank you. And thank you so much for your help."

Chapter 22

She had no difficulty finding the Salems' house.
From the brightness of the streetlights, it was easy to see
that the large Victorian house was indeed the loveliest
one on a street full of beautiful homes. Lamplight blazed
in the numerous mullioned windows, and walk-lights
illuminated the broad, curving brick sidewalk leading to
the front porch. She ran up the steps and to the front door.
She rang the bell, paused five seconds, and rang it again.

"Hurry, hurry, hurry."

The door opened by a pleasant-faced, chunky man
in his stocking feet. He wore dark slacks and a white shirt
with his tie loosened and top button open. In his hand, he
held a newspaper. He gave her a tired, mild smile.

"Mr. Salem?"

"The one and only. But I must tell you upfront I
don't take care of bank business at home after hours. I
learned that lesson the hard way. And we attend the
Presbyterian Church of Gemstone, so we aren't church
hunting."

"I'm not here on bank or church business, Mr.
Salem. My name is Abigail Matthews." She stuck out her
right hand. Gazing at her curiously, he shook her hand as
she continued, "I understand you bought a painting today
from the Gemstone Flea Market. It was donated by
mistake, and I need to retrieve it."

Mr. Salem drew in the corners of his mouth, either

in humor or annoyance, she wasn't sure which. He stood back, holding open the door with one hand and gestured an invitation with the hand that held the paper.

"Come in, Miss…Matthews, was it?"

"Abigail Matthews. Abbie. Thank you."

She stepped inside the air conditioned, well-lit interior of a home that smelled of lemon oil and beeswax. An eclectic mix of refurbished antiques with some pieces in a state of natural distress created an appealing, homey atmosphere.

"If I could just buy back the painting, please."

He shook his head. "I don't know what to tell you other than come in and sit down."

"You *did* buy a painting today at the flea market, didn't you? Rochelle at the thrift store said—"

"*I* didn't buy a thing, but my wife undoubtedly did. Have a seat, Ms. Matthews. Would you like something cold to drink? Or maybe some coffee?"

"No, thank you. Could I please speak to your wife?"

"Surely. I'll just go get her. But are you sure you wouldn't want something to drink?" He walked to the liquor cabinet on the other side of the room. "Maybe a glass of wine?"

"Not just now, thank you."

She tried to give him a patient smile, but she felt as stretched as a well-used rubber band around a too-large bundle. At this point, she had already lost precious hours backtracking, searching, and talking. Now she was so close, so close. The last thing she wanted to do was sip wine and make pleasant, inane chitchat with this very nice man. He poured himself a generous shot of whiskey.

"I really, really need to see your wife right away, please," she pressed as graciously as possible.

Mr. Salem nodded. "I'll get her."

He padded silently from the room and climbed the stairs to the second floor. She did not want to roam the room like an investigator looking for clues, but she had no capacity to sit and wait. She paced the tiled foyer, back and forth, the soles of her sneakers screaking on the hard surface.

"Well, I have to tell you, Ms. Matthews," Mr. Salem drawled as he descended the stairs, "my wife is a doll. Don't know what I'd do without her. As you can see, she's made us a nice home here. She entertains friends and family as if she were poured from Miss Emily Post's mold. She's a wonderful mother and my best friend." He stepped off the last stair and smiled at her. "But I don't understand her. She likes flea market finds, God knows why. She can buy whatever she wants, brand-new, and not have to clean it and fumigate it and strip it and restore it, but there you are, that's Nancy for you." He stretched out his arm toward the living room. "Please, come in and sit down."

She glanced up the stairs.

"Is your wife coming down soon? I really need to speak to her."

"Oh, sure. Please, have a seat." He ushered her into the other room, dipped his head toward a soft, inviting armchair.

She remained standing, clenching and unclenching one hand while fiddling with her purse strap with the other.

"God bless you, Ms. Matthews, I was born and raised Southern. Good manners are instilled in us, and I can't, in good conscience, sit until you do, and I'm very, very tired. Please, have a seat. Nancy will be down directly."

"Oh, I'm so sorry." She quickly sank onto the edge of the nearest chair. "I'm just so nervous, you see, and when I'm tense, I can't sit still."

"Ahhh." He settled into a recliner and elevated the footrest. He drank his whiskey and sighed. "That's better. Well, you know, I'm not as young as I used to be, and there's a great deal more of me resting on these two feet nowadays. I just have to sit down in the evenings. If you need to, please fidget all you want."

"Your wife will be down soon?" she asked again, as if the first twelve times had been inadequate.

"Well, 'soon' is a relative word in this house. She's taking a bath, one of those bubbly, candle-lit aromatic adventures with New Age music and a glass of wine. Say, you want something to drink now?"

He thunked down the footrest, picked up his empty shot glass as he got up and went to the liquor cabinet.

"Scotch?" He held up the bottle. "Steady your nerves a bit."

Maybe a stiffener would do her some good.

"Yes. Thank you. But not much. I'm driving."

After several minutes, in which she surprised herself by being able to converse intelligently with Mr. Salem without shrieking from frustration and impatience, a plump, pretty woman in a silky pink robe came down the stairs. Damp curls from the careless pile of dark hair on her head framed a face rosy from her warm bath. Abbie detected the subtle fragrance of lavender.

"Hi, I'm Nancy Salem." She held out a hand and shook Abbie's gently. "You must be Abigail?"

"Yes. But please, it's Abbie."

"Of course. Abbie, it is." She turned to her husband,

comfortably situated on his recliner. "A nice brandy, Mark. And you might want to freshen her drink."

Abbie looked at her empty shot glass. "No, thanks. Actually, I'm not here on a social call."

Nancy settled onto the sofa and curled her legs under her like a child. She accepted the drink her husband offered and smiled her thanks.

"That's too bad. You'll have to come back when you can stay and visit." She took a sip of her brandy but before Abbie could speak, she continued, "How long have you been in Gemstone? Are you settled yet?"

Abbie shoved aside the peculiarities of these friendly strangers and fought the irritation of participating in niceties, but it was obvious that these people lived and behaved by a certain code. No amount of trying to breach it would succeed. She stifled the urge to wail for her painting like a spoiled kid.

"I've never been to Gemstone before today. Just passing through, which brings me—"

"I know who you are!" Nancy said suddenly, leaning forward and laughing. "You are one of the Greenbrier Matthews, aren't you? I went to the University with Alice Ann. Are you related? You know, you do look a lot like her!"

"Umm, no. I doubt we're related. I'm from Ohio, actually."

"A Yankee!" Nancy laughed again, with obvious delight. "I should have known from your accent." She turned to her husband. "Mark-honey, when *was* the last time we had a Yankee in our living room?"

Mark looked thoughtful, but only for about five seconds because Nancy answered her own question.

"Oh, I remember! Two years ago last

Christmas. Danielle Ramsey's fiancée was from New Jersey. Remember him, Mark?" She turned a merry expression to Abbie. "That was *not* a match made in heaven, believe me. You'd have to know Danielle." She sipped her brandy and gazed at her. "Sweetie, you are just fit to be tied, aren't you, hon? What's wrong?"

Her question was so unexpected that Abbie was momentarily wordless. She had been casting about in her mind for a way to short circuit all this talk when Nancy pulled the plug on her own chatter.

"The painting," she blurted. "I want to buy back the painting."

Nancy blinked. "What painting is that, sugar?"

"The one you bought at the flea market this morning. You see, I foolishly donated it, and I desperately need it back."

Nancy stared at her. "You don't mean that hideous picture of the storm and old house?"

"Yes," Abbie twitched on the edge of her seat. "I want to buy it back from you."

Nancy drained her brandy before she answered. "Why, honey, I'd be more than happy just to give it to you—"

"Oh, thank you." She went limp with relief. "You don't know how much this means."

Nancy winced. "Let me finish, sweetie. I'd be more than happy just to give it to you, but I don't have it."

Abbie's breath left her. "But you just said...but you...where is it?"

Nancy set the snifter down on the old trunk she used as a coffee table and sat forward.

"Well, it just never occurred to me that anyone would want the picture. I bought it for the frame. That frame is at least a hundred years old."

"I don't care about the frame. You are more than welcome to that." The threat of tears burned her eyes; her voice shook. *"But where is the painting?"*

"Why, I'm afraid it's gone for good, honey. Destroyed. I put it in the incinerator this afternoon."

"The incinerator?"

"Yes." Nancy bit her lower lip, an apology etched deeply on her features. "I never dreamed someone would want that painting. It was so dark and disturbing, almost as if it was alive. It really gave me the willies. Oh, honey, don't cry. I'll buy you another painting or give you one of mine. Oh, dear. Mark, what'll we do?"

Mark had a strange smile on his face.

"Mark?" His wife stared at him. "You *did* burn the trash after dinner, didn't you? There was that awful thing from the refrigerator that Marie pitched in the garbage this morning."

He looked both happy and abashed. "Well, actually, I thought I'd just burn the trash tomorrow."

"You didn't burn it?" Abbie shrieked, ready to cover his face with kisses then bow at his feet.

"If Nancy threw your picture in the incinerator, it's still there."

"Oh! Oh, my goodness. Thank you, *thank you!*" She rushed to the man who had his recliner upright by now. She hugged him hard as he stood. "Tell me where the incinerator is, and I'll go get the painting."

"Why, it's liable to be covered with that gooey, fuzzy, gray-green stuff from the fridge."

"That's okay. I don't care about gooey green stuff if I can have my painting."

"Let me find my slippers." He shot a vague glance

around the room.

"Upstairs in your closet, where they should be when not on your feet, sugar."

"Oh. Well. Just a minute, then, and let me go put them on."

She thought she would burst out of her skin waiting for him to return, but he did come back, about five minutes later. He wore a pair of tattered sneakers and had changed from his dress slacks and white shirt to a pair of sweatpants and a T-shirt.

"Well, Mark-honey, what an outfit to wear in front of our guest!" Nancy laughed.

"I'm just going to the incinerator. Not likely to see anyone I know between there and here." He gave a wry grin to Abbie. "I'll be back directly with your painting."

No way was she going to sit around and wait while he strolled to the incinerator and sifted leisurely through garbage. Who knew how long that would take?

"I'll come with you."

"You'll get dirty."

"I can wash."

"Well."

She followed him down the marble-tiled hallway, through a large kitchen and out the back door.

"The incinerator is at the back of the property," he said as they crossed the considerable back lawn. "Now, normally, Marie burns the garbage, but she was in a snit today because Nancy had her clean out the fridge." He chuckled. "You don't want to cross Marie when she's in a snit. Just lucky this isn't Tuesday. Tuesday is the garbage pick-up day. But Nancy has a real sensitive nose. She can smell a fire before you light a match; so when she says take out the garbage and burn it, I take it out." In a whisper, he added, "But I don't always burn it."

"I'm glad you didn't burn it today."

"Me, too, since your picture is in it. Did you paint that picture your own self?"

"No, but I treasure it, and I need it back."

"Well, here we are. Now you just stand there and let me poke around in here and find it. Phew! That does reek! I think it was something with broccoli in it. Things with broccoli always stink, have you ever noticed? And Brussels sprouts. Why God ever created either one of them is beyond me."

Gingerly he plucked the top layer off the trash. She could not stand by and watch. She plunged both hands into the offal, ignoring the wetness and the odor. Once she thought she had the painting and pulled it out of the rubbish only to find a thick clump of damp paper towels. She thrust her hands in again, clutching and feeling, rejecting what must have been eggshells and peelings.

"Here now!" Mark said. "You're getting right dirty."

"I think I found it. Help me, please. Clear away the stuff on top."

Mark pushed away the rubbish, and she pulled out something large, slightly stiff and crushed, made of fabric. She squatted and smoothed the canvas out on the ground. By the illumination of the backyard security light, she saw Andrew's house.

"Oh, thank God, thank God." She gathered the painting to her chest. "*Thank God.*"

Tears flooded her eyes and flowed freely down her face.

"God bless you. I know those are tears of joy. But,

look, you're getting nasty stuff all over you. Come back inside and clean up. We'll try to clean off that picture, too."

Now that she had retrieved the painting, she did not know the next step, but one thing was certain–she needed to be alone so she could think. She doubted her reasoning power could work very well with this wonderfully kind but far too chatty couple hovering around her.

"Thank you, no. I'll take care of it." She got to her feet, the crushed painting still pressed against her bosom. "I can't thank you enough. I'll never forget you for your kindness."

"You're sure you won't stay a bit longer? Have you had dinner?"

"It's nice of you to ask, but I really have to go now." She was already walking, almost running across the back yard. "Thank you, Mr. Salem. Thank you both so much!"

Once inside her car, she put the painting on the seat beside her, started the motor, and backed out of the driveway. She recalled seeing a small, nondescript motel on the edge of town. She mashed down on the accelerator, driving as fast as she thought she could without getting pulled over in that small Southern town.

Chapter 23

Inside the dingy, beige room she had rented, she switched on both lamps and the overhead light. Beneath their blaze, she lovingly smoothed the battered painting on the bed.

She recognized every aspect of it—the ominous dark sky, tree branches bent in the wind, the tangled growth of brush and briars, the dismal house where she had found Andrew. Somehow, it seemed even darker and bleaker now. The tree branches seemed to droop from more than the wind, almost as if they were dying. The house seemed more run down, as though it was long abandoned. And hadn't there once been a light in the upstairs window? That would have been his bedroom window, she realized as she brushed her hand gently across it. Beneath her fingertips, the paint was stiff and cracked. Tiny bits flecked off.

She stared down at her fingers, then at the painting. She had obeyed the old woman's admonition to find the painting. Here, at last, it lay before her, bringing bittersweet memories into her mind. Having made the breakneck trip back to Gemstone, nearly having had the police called on her, disrupting a couple's quiet evening and plunging her arms elbow deep in garbage to retrieve this painting, she again wondered what next step she should take. There lay the painting, abused, cracked, filthy, and she was not an iota closer to reaching him than she had been when she woke up in the hospital. What good was the painting if she could not find the actual house?

A part of her mind not overcome with raw frustration and sheer nerves told her there might be a map on the back.

Gingerly she turned over the precious, fragile canvas. Her heart leaped when she saw writing through the stains. The writing was dim, almost illegible. She held the table lamp over it as she bent and examined what she saw.

"Passion spurned; hatred burned," she read aloud. It was the same words the old woman had told her in the junk shop when she bought the painting, and the same words she had quoted earlier today as she urged Abbie to find the picture.

She frowned, read the poem, examined it line by line, word by word, but it scarcely made sense.

A curse of thirteen hundred moons. Moons as in months? Thirteen hundred moons more or less equaled one hundred years.

She read the poem again, substituting one hundred years for thirteen hundred moons.

A curse of one hundred years must pass.

A century had passed from the time Andrew found himself lost in that awful place to the time Abbie had arrived.

One hundred years. A curse. Could it be possible? Did such things as spells and curses really exist? In a world where a man could live without aging for a century, where she had awakened in an alien setting, anything was possible—time travel, curses or spells, magic, or witchcraft.

She put the lamp back on the bedside table and sat on the edge of the bed next to the painting.

She recalled him speaking of Granny Hodge who had lived on Sumac Ridge and practiced black arts. Had she put a curse on him, maybe because he was going to be an actual doctor and the people would turn to him instead of her? But that seemed foolish. Andrew spoke highly of the old woman and how eager she had been to teach him her ways. Considering a curse was nonsense.

As she thought about it, though, Abbie realized she couldn't dismiss any notion as being too irrational or impossible–not when she had been with a man from a previous century, in a place neither he nor she could understand nor escape. She stared down at the bleak painting, at the dismal house and stormy skies.

Slowly a notion formed in her mind, and she allowed it to grow. Day and night did not exist in Andrew's world. Storm clouds had hung over his home without breaking. Silent wind ceaselessly whipped the trees and bent their branches. Until she showed up, nothing ever grew, or ever changed, or died. It was almost as if he lived…in a painting.

Could it be possible that someone had cursed Andrew into a painting? Cursed him into an exile of one hundred years?

She grabbed the lamp and read the words on the back of the canvas once more: *A curse of thirteen hundred moons must pass, then death will come, unless love breaks the curse and sets the prisoner free.*

"That means if one hundred years pass and the curse is not broken, he will die." She looked down at the painting. "He will die, alone, in that awful, awful place."

Unless love breaks the curse to set the prisoner free.

She pressed her palms to her face, staring at the place she now knew imprisoned Andrew.

"No! He will *not* die. I will go to him again, and this time he will leave with me."

But how? How could she return to him and bring him back with her? She jumped up, pacing, clenching and unclenching her hands, feeling as though she would fly into a thousand pieces any moment if she did not find the answer.

She had been there with him. Somehow, she had entered his world, and somehow, she had made her escape.

"If I did it once, I can do it again." She chewed on the knuckles of her bent thumbs as she paced. She pivoted and returned to gaze at the painting.

How had she traveled there? What had she done, what words had she spoken? What port of entry had she found?

She sank to her knees by the side of the bed, once again moved the lamp and held it steady so that every aspect of the painting was illuminated. She studied the house, the windows, and doors. She examined the porch, the lawn, the trees, and bushes. As she examined each point, her skin prickled with the familiarity of what she saw. There, just beyond that point of the house, but out of sight, was the well that never went dry. And there, that tiny brown dot on the door was the tarnished doorknocker shaped like a gargoyle.

Eagerly she looked at the windows. She was sure she could make out the shape of the two chairs before the hearth, though she saw no infinitesimal cheery glow. Upstairs, the bedroom windows were bleak and dim. He had drawn the draperies to help darken the room so she could sleep. Were they drawn now, limiting her view?

She examined the forest. Somewhere, in there among all those trees she had made love to him. That was the last time she saw him. They'd heard something moving, even thrashing in the forest. She'd thought it was that horrible, huge snake with evil, intelligent eyes. Andrew had gone to search. She'd heard the sounds, sounds like wheels against a road, coming from another place in the forest. She had called out to him, taken a few steps toward what she was sure was civilization and…and she had awakened in a hospital room, torn from him in the blink of an eye.

If she had stumbled upon a way inside once, she could find it again and once inside the painting, she now knew a way out existed. But where was that doorway? She had to hurry before the curse was fulfilled.

The impossible task slammed full force into her. Deep inside, she felt as though her heart bled, draining her life. She pressed her face against the cracked, painted surface as tears slid from her eyes and onto the canvas.

"Andrew," she murmured into the stained fabric, "be strong. I love you, and I'm coming for you."

She closed her eyes, fighting the sense of futility that surged from the center of her body.

"I'm coming for you. I will never give up."

An elusive memory returned, and she lifted her head. That night at Lefty's house, she had taken a shower and dressed for bed. She couldn't sleep and had brought the painting inside to clean it. She'd wiped off the dust. A tiny piece of paint had fallen away. She found where she thought it would fit and when she placed it there, in that right spot…

She sat straight up and looked at the lower left corner of the painting. There! It was there that the chip of paint was missing. The paint was still gone, but something, perhaps a bit of Marie's spoiled food from the Salems' refrigerator had soiled it.

She scrambled to her feet, ran into the bathroom, and dampened a washcloth. She dabbed away the dirt and uncovered what she had seen before: a swirling, dizzying blue. How could she have forgotten something so unusual, so significant?

There lay her threshold to Andrew.

She tossed aside the cloth, placed her fingertips on the blue, watched them disappear then felt her hand, her arm, her whole self, slide, slipping gently back into his world.

Chapter 24

This time her journey did not end with a violent landing. She seemed to float, ethereally in the gauzy blueness. As she looked around, she saw nothing, heard nothing.

Serenity enfolded her. Her very being was filled with a light and hope as she had never known. In this strange crossing, she knew all things were possible. Andrew's exile would soon pass away. His liberation was at hand.

The blue darkened, turned gray and dull. Her body took its weight again. Cold seeped into her pores and all light slipped away. She sensed something solid nearby, prepared herself, and a moment later felt ground beneath her feet. She stood, strong and unharmed, a cold silent wind whipping against her, shaking and bending branches of the surrounding thick forest. The tranquility that had been her companion as she entered this world now slid away completely as urgency took its place.

"A curse of thirteen hundred moons," echoed in her brain.

"Please God," she prayed and left the rest of her petition unspoken as she took her bearings. She had studied the painting closely and now understood exactly where she was in relationship to other portions of it. She would not get lost again.

She set out for the house, taking note as she went

that the flora was not as lush as it had been. In fact, parts of it were brown, as though it were dying. Her trek through the forest was easier because vegetation had diminished and crushed easily beneath her feet. Nearby she heard the distinct, sharp report as a tree branch cracked. It broke free and crashed to the ground. Leaves, edged in brown, swirled from the trees as if in the throes of an autumn wind.

The painting was changing, and she knew she had to move fast.

Reaching the tangled clearing in front of the house, she staggered and jerked to a halt when she saw that much of the roof had blown away. Urgency shook her out of her shock and spurred her onward.

As she ran toward the house, she saw numerous broken windows. The steps leading up to the porch sagged, and so did the porch roof. One of its supports had buckled and looked ready to give way completely.

"Andrew!" she cried. "Andrew, I'm here!"

Heedless of danger from the ruined environment, she rushed up the broken steps and across the deteriorating porch floor, fully expecting him to joyously fling open the door and welcome her into his arms.

"I'll never leave you again, because I'm taking you with me!"

She opened the door and froze on the threshold. Inside, the house was dark and cold, submerged in an aura of emptiness and neglect.

Although the house had been dismal and chilly before, it had carried within it the heartbeat of life—a fire always burned in the grate, the fragrance of a simmering stew or sizzling meat that whetted their appetites. The sense that someone lived and moved within had always lingered in the air.

She now felt nothing of his presence. She looked in the parlor, hoping to see him in his favorite chair before the fire. The parlor was vacant, the fabric of the chairs rotting. The hearth stood empty and cold.

"Andrew! Where are you?"

She dashed across the small passage and ran upstairs into the bedroom they had shared. It, too, was deserted. The lovely room across the hall that had been hers was gone as if it had never existed.

"Andrew!" she screamed as panic rose. "Where are you?"

Was she too late? Had the hundred years of the curse passed? Was he gone, was he…dead?

Not yet, not yet. One hundred years cannot be over yet.

"Andrew!" She ran back downstairs and into the kitchen.

He sat, slumped over the table, head turned from her and resting on his arms He was silent, cold, and unmoving.

"Please God, don't let me be too late!" She approached him. "Andrew? Can you hear me? It's Abbie."

He groaned then, a weak sound, barely audible.

"Oh, my love!" she cried. "I'm here, and I'll never ever leave you again."

She dropped to her knees beside him, brushed back his hair from his face, and stifled a gasp at what she saw. He was thin, almost emaciated, gray-faced. His eyes burned bright with fever. He looked at her, but it was as if he did not see her.

With obvious effort, he turned his head from her.

"Go away. Do not do this to me again."

"I'm not going away. Andrew, look at me."

"Let me die in peace."

She shook him. "I will not! You come with me now."

He roused himself enough to peer at her through eyes that seemed to grow dimmer with each passing moment.

"A witch, a fairy tale," he mumbled.

"No. I'm real." She cupped his face and forced him to look in her eyes. "Listen to me. I know where we are and how to get out."

"There is no getting out of Hell."

"Andrew, *listen to me*. I know what happened. A hundred years ago, someone cursed you into a painting. *This* is a painting you've been living in. That is why you've not been able to leave. But I know how to get out."

He stared at her, eyes dark with hopelessness. His cheek burned beneath her touch. Whether he heard, understood, or believed her, she had no time to ponder. She knew she must get him to safety. She had to do it *now*.

"Andrew, *I* got out. That time in the woods, our last time together, I stumbled through a portal, a passage we never found because the picture frame had all but hidden it in darkness. But the important thing at this moment is that I found my way back to you, and now you must come with me."

He gazed at her, blinked slowly. "I don't believe you. You agent of the devil. Go away."

"Andrew! We've been through this before! How can I make you understand that I'm real?"

Then she remembered what had happened that first time. If it worked once, maybe it would work again. She placed both hands on either side of his head and kissed him. She kissed him with all the passion and yearning she possessed, just as he had first kissed her. For a moment he seemed apathetic to the touch, but after bit, he wrapped his arms about her. As weak as he was, her lips against his awakened a response. He returned the desperate kiss.

He pulled away, looked into her eyes.

"Is it really you?" he whispered, lifting one hand to her cheek. "Have you really come back to me?"

"Yes. *Yes!* Not only come back to you but come back *for* you."

"And do you love me?"

"More than anything. More than life."

"Truly?"

She smiled gently, kissed his feverish brow.

"Truly, passionately, forever. And I refuse to be without you ever again."

His gaze caressed her face, memorizing every movement, every detail. "Then my prayer has been answered."

She kissed his lips again, lingering only a moment.

"We won't be parted again, I promise you." She stood, tugged on both his hands. "So now you must come with me."

He hardly moved. "I'm very sick. I fear I'm dying."

She tamped down the terror his words brought. In her sharpest, most demanding voice, she said, "I have traveled far to get you, so you come with me this minute."

He groaned. "I don't think I—"

"Andrew! Do you love me?"

"You know I do."

"Then enough of this nonsense. You must help me to help you. This world, this painting is disintegrating and we must go while we still can. *Now*."

While every nerve in her body screamed with a frantic urgency that bordered hysteria, she stared at him. Still, he did not move. She thought he might never move or speak again.

She cupped his face and looked into his eyes again. "Sweetheart. If you want to live, if you want us to be together, *you must come with me*. You need to get up and walk out the door with me. We must get to the portal before it collapses and traps us here."

He blinked slowly, as though taking in her words.

"I'm not leaving you," she said. "If you don't come with me, then I'll die right here, with you."

"No…no," he whispered. "I will go with you." He stood up with some difficulty. His slow movements were weak yet determined.

She slipped her arm around his waist, pulled his arm across her shoulders.

"Lean on me as much as you need to."

They got to the front door, which she had left open in her haste to reach him. He halted in the doorway. His eyes moved across the landscape.

"There is no more water. The food has spoiled. I've been hearing the trees fall. And something happened to the house. It's all dying around us, isn't it?"

If only she had known about and understood the curse, she would have come back to him sooner, before everything had degenerated to this state. If only…

But who could have ever believed a cursed painting

existed? No one from the world Abbie Matthews had inhabited most of her life. She had done what she thought was right. She had truly believed he was no more than the memory of a most excellent dream. They had each other at this moment, right now, and she must concentrate all her efforts on their escape

"Don't think about it, sweetheart. We'll be all right. Just be careful where you step as we cross the porch and down the steps."

They moved cautiously but as quickly as he could maneuver.

"We are truly leaving, aren't we?" he asked as they crossed the clearing toward the forest.

"Truly and absolutely."

"I shall not miss this place, except for those days you were with me."

She looked up at him. He gave her a smile, his fingers pressing into her shoulder. She said nothing, intent on making good their escape while the possibility still existed.

Once they were in the woods, however, movement became hazardous. Tree limbs fell at an alarming rate. Many crashed dangerously close. A branch missed them by mere inches. The groundcover beneath their feet gave way to their steps so that they tripped and stumbled, over and over, slowing their movements even more. It was as if the painting itself was trying to impede their progress.

"You know where we're going?" His breath was quick and shallow.

She saw his unspoken need to rest for a moment, but there were no moments to spare. They could not afford to stop.

"We're almost there."

A thunderous crash almost deafened them as one of the largest trees in the forest upended itself across their path, bashing into other trees and breaking them, pulling them down in its wake. Forward motion ceased to be an option.

"We have to go around this," she said.

"Or climb over it."

She looked at him. He seemed weaker with each step.

"Can you?" she asked.

"Can you?"

"Yes."

"Then so can I."

She hesitated, and in that moment of indecision another tree crashed. There was no longer time for self-doubt or second guessing.

"We must move quickly."

"I understand. I can do it." The determination in his expression belied his deteriorating physical vigor, and her heart swelled with love.

Climbing over the fallen trees, fighting against the branches that snagged their arms, legs, and clothing, stumbling, falling, standing and continuing, all of it consumed much of their precious time. When they cleared the last of the fallen timber, she was breathless and soaked with sweat, even in the cold wind. He was white-faced and shaking from thirst, hunger, fatigue, and fever. But she knew exactly where they were, and the knowledge gave her strength.

"A few more steps, sweetheart. We're almost there. I can see it from here."

They were within three yards of their escape when Andrew collapsed. She thought her own heart might stop, but she refused to give in to terror. His survival, their survival, depended solely on her strength and determination.

She knelt beside him, shook him.

"A few more steps, darling. We're almost there. You're almost free."

He did not move, and she realized he was unconscious. She must drag him out. To do so, she only needed to clear the path. She looked at his dear face, loving him and knew nothing was impossible.

"You will have your second chance at the good life you deserve, I swear it."

She set about clearing away the limbs and dead briars between them and the doorway out of this dark Eden. She worked methodically, stooping to pick up and toss the litter. When she finished, she straightened and turned to Andrew.

The snake, that huge black serpent who was the guardian of this cursed prison, lay coiled across the threshold between the painting and the world of freedom beyond. Coiled and alert, it was neither weakened nor diminished like the rest of the milieu. There was no way past that huge, hideous creature. It would kill them both before they had a chance to gain liberty.

The evil reptilian face seemed to gloat, knowing it had won. Andrew was cursed and would forever be cursed, dying in a barren, collapsing world.

In the distance another tree fell. Its reverberation shook the ground where she stood. In a few minutes, only desolation would remain. She must act now, this moment.

The snake never took its lidless gloating gaze off her as she picked up the heavy limb she had just pitched aside. She hefted it, got the feel of it in her hand, moved it a little to understand its weight. She thanked Lefty who long ago had taught her to swing a ball bat with power and purpose.

She fixed the snake with her own cold glare. It tensed as though probing her mind again then flexed its huge body, the tongue flicking and lashing.

Heaving the club, she approached the vile guardian of Andrew's world. It began to tighten itself into a hard coil, ready to strike. She looked directly into the glittering tiny eyes, knowing this serpent was not what it seemed.

She ignored the raging fear that threatened to take over and lay waste to everything she stood for, everything she tried to do. Her very insides shook with terror, but she would not fail to obliterate this final obstacle.

"Nothing, not you or this vile dying world will stop me from saving him. If it costs my life to save him, I gladly give it, because I love him more than myself, more than my own life. You will not have him!"

The serpent lunged at her, its mouth gaping like the entrance gate to Hell. She saw the fangs and leaped to one side. The snake missed its mark, hitting the ground with an ominous thud. It lashed its body sideways, curled back, ready to strike again.

She raised the club.

"I will fight you to the death." She prepared to bash in the sleek, triangular-shaped head. "Even if you kill me, I will still love him."

The snake froze in its place. She knew then this reptile was the embodiment of evil. It heard and understood her words. But no foolish notion, no restrictive prison, no hideous evil in the form of a serpent was enough to stop her from loving Andrew. Nor could it stop her from saving him.

"You have no power here," she said. "Fear was your authority, but I'm not afraid anymore."

As she spoke these words, her terror ebbed away.

The light in the reptilian eyes dimmed. The tight coil turned flaccid and weak. The huge body shrank, falling in on itself. Bit by bit, the serpent lost its power until nothing remained but dried skin. She prodded the desiccated membrane with the club, wanting to rid every vestige of the serpent from this place. It crumbled to dust and was blown away by the wind.

She stood only a moment, relishing her relief and her victory. But that moment was short-lived because the forest continued to fall around them, decimating itself. She knelt beside Andrew, feeling his pulse. It was weak. His chest barely rose and fell with each shallow breath.

With few trees to block her view, she could glimpse the house from where she stood. It appeared on the verge of total collapse. Another minute lost, and she would have to clear the path again. There was no time for that. Grabbing Andrew under his arms, she hefted his head and shoulders from the ground and pulled backward. Stumbling over the tree limbs, she had to stop long enough to toss them aside. At that moment, her greatest concern was that a limb would fall on him as she dragged him to freedom.

Please, please, God. Help me. Help me save the man I love.

She took a big step backward, and the ground beneath her feet gave way. The stormy dark sky steadily grew brighter and bluer. As before, tranquility quietly filled her mind, and she knew the struggle to free the man in her arms was over. In this ethereal blue that seemed to have no substance, she laid him down gently, and sat next to him, one hand over his heart. The beat was steady beneath her touch. She was weak from exertion and giddy with relief.

She no longer feared for Andrew's life or his well-being. This moment was what she had wanted for him from the first time she met him. To take him from the awful prison in which he lived and bring him into the light of a new day was her heart's pleasure and desire.

"Andrew," she said gently. "You will be fine. *We* will be fine. Wake up now. Open your eyes and see where you are."

When he did not respond, she knew another moment of fear. Had she been wrong? Was it too late for him to survive? Would traveling into the twenty-first century age him abruptly and snuff out his life?

She *had* broken the curse, hadn't she? Hadn't she?

"Andrew!" She shook him. "Please don't let it be too late for us!"

As she stared down at him, her eyes wide and swimming with tears, he stirred. Just a twitching of his eyes beneath their lids, then a frail flutter of eyelashes. Slowly, very slowly, he opened his eyes but immediately closed them against the unaccustomed light. Her heart began to beat again.

"Look, Andrew!" she encouraged softly. "Look, my love, and see where you are."

With studied and deliberate slowness, he again opened his eyes. Only slightly at first, then wider, then fully, gazing with awe into the gentle swirling blue light that surrounded them. After a long moment, his gaze searched until he found her next to him. He stared at her as one who had been handed a long-sought and elusive treasure. He took her hand in his, kissed it ardently, fingers tight around her own.

"I knew it was so!" he said in an excited whisper. "This is Heaven, isn't it?"

She clasped his hand to her heart and smiled down at him. "I don't know. It may be a part of Heaven."

"Yes." He looked around them. Color was beginning to return to his cheeks. The fever was gone, and his eyes grew bright with life.

"Yes," he repeated as he sat up and drew her into his arms. "This *is* Heaven. And you, Abbie, you are my own dear angel."

Epilogue

10 years later

On a cool afternoon in early May, Granny Hodge watched the family in their backyard. She blended into the dappled shade of an ancient maple tree, but even if she had not, they would be unable to see her. Granny still possessed the power to control some aspects of her life. Remaining unseen when she wished it was one of them.

Abbie knelt by a flowerbed, working the soil, preparing it for the rose bush she purchased the day before. There had been a time in her life when she never would have dreamed of working in dirt, planting flowers, pulling weeds. Never, in her wildest imagination, had she thought she would live in an old, refurbished Ozarks farmhouse, five miles from the closest town, sixty miles from the nearest city.

"Hey, my angel," Andrew said as he approached.

She glanced up, squinting in the bright sunlight of the spring morning. He smiled down at her, his dark eyes warmer and more loving than ever in a face that grew more handsome as it aged. The warm breeze tousled his unruly hair.

"Hey, sweetie." She grinned at him. "What brings you into the wilds of your backyard when you should be sleeping in?"

He held a glass of milk in one hand, and with the

other helped her to get to her feet.

"Drink this," he said as she brushed the dirt from her knees. "You know I'll plague you 'til you do."

She made a face at him, took the glass, and sipped.

"Cute as you look in shorts and T-shirt," he continued, "isn't it a mite chilly out here for you?"

"Nag, nag, nag." She quickly finished the milk. "Need I remind you, my dear sir, how pregnancy *always* affects my inner thermometer? I'm sure several of your expectant mothers have told you the same thing."

He grinned at her.

"Ah, but I'm not married to *them*. I just deliver their babies. They have their own husbands and significant others to nag them into taking care of themselves."

"Uh huh." Then twisting a bit on the balls of her feet, she batted her eyes and asked, "Am I really cute in my shorts?"

"Flirting with me again, are you?" He leered at her. "My dear young woman, this behavior is what got you in this condition." He patted her rounded tummy.

She threw her arms around his neck. "And don't you love it?"

He wrapped his arms around her, crushing her to him briefly and kissed her hard on the mouth.

"Don't I, though?" He cupped her face tenderly. "You *are* happy, aren't you?"

"Beyond measure. Beyond anything I ever hoped."

"And this life…do you ever regret—"

She placed her fingertips on his lips. "If I ever choose to return to law practice, I shall. But right now, this is all I could ever want."

"Cooking and cleaning and being wife and mother?"

"Yep." She kissed him slowly, loving the feel of his

lips, the warmth of his skin beneath her hand, the slight roughness of his unshaven cheek. "A dozen years ago I thought housewives and stay-at-home moms were fools. What did I know back then?" She smiled into his eyes. "*This* is living."

"Dad!"

The plaintive call broke their moment, and they watched the slender, long-legged ten-year-old run toward them. Born less than seven months after they had escaped the painting, their daughter had Abbie's silky blonde hair and Andrew's liquid, dark eyes.

She stopped and looked at them both, arms crossed on her chest.

"Dad. Will you *puh-leeze* tell Matthew and Levi to stop teasing Callie? Her whining is driving me crazy!"

He grimaced. Since when had "Dad" replaced "Daddy"? He supposed soon she'd be calling him "Father," in that bored adolescent tone girls seemed to adopt.

He let go of his wife and looked down at his daughter. Her silvery blonde hair shimmered in sunlight as she looked up at him expectantly.

"What's going on, Angela?"

She pointed across the yard at her seven-year-old twin brothers and four-year-old sister.

"They keep teasing Callie, the brats."

Andrew lifted his left eyebrow.

"So…you're suddenly concerned for your sister?"

"*Dad*. My birthday is *tomorrow*. Callie promised to leave my friends alone and not be a pest if I make Matthew and Levi give her back Victorian Heidi."

"Ah. And are the boys playing with her doll? Did they have it first?"

Angela rolled her eyes. "They are using her as an alien from the planet Badok. Victorian Heidi does *not* come from the planet Badok. I should know. I played with fashion dolls when I was a child."

Behind him, Abbie choked and turned her giggle into a cough. She patted Andrew's shoulder and in a somewhat strangled voice she said, "Go ahead and rescue Heidi, sweetie. I'll just return to my rose bush."

He shot her a look over his shoulder, grinning.

"Ah, Saturdays at home. I love it." Turning to Angela, he held out his hand to this beautiful child. "Let us reason with those boys. And if all else fails, let us brave the planet Badok and rescue Miss Victorian Heidi from their evil clutches."

"*Dad.*" She gave him a stern look of reproof that evaporated a moment later when she smiled. A smile like her mother's. A smile that melted his heart all over again. She took his hand. "Okay, Daddy. Let us go reason." A half-second later, she added, "You know what? You're the best dad in the whole world." She cast a look back to Abbie who was kneeling by the flowerbed again but watching them fondly. "And Mom's the best mom. I'm glad I was born."

****

Granny Hodge, hearing the child's words, let them soak into her tired old soul. Love had changed one deed done by her hand, a deed that had been too cruel. Out of that dark, desolate place in which she had cast Andrew Wade, in a momentary burst of light, a miracle had been conceived, and now it grew and flourished in the warmth of a sunlit world.

Maybe it was not too late for her. Maybe there were others she could help free from the fetters that bound them to unhappiness. Perhaps, one day, she could even redeem her own broken soul.

Clinging to that hope, Granny turned and walked away.

A word about the author…

A native of the Ozarks, K.D. primarily writes books set in the mountains of Missouri and Arkansas. Her stories are touching and often humorous, portraying ordinary people who keep the wheels of life turning. Her novel, In Front of God and Everybody, was in the top 12 finalists for the 2013-14 Mark Twain Readers Award, and she was the recipient of the Laura Ingalls Wilder Children's Literature Award in 2021.

With an unending love for books, McCrite worked for several years in public libraries in Missouri and Arkansas. She also worked in the field of mental health as a caseworker.

McCrite graduated from Drury University with a degree in psychology.

www.kdmccrite.com

Thank you for purchasing
this publication of The Wild Rose Press, Inc.

For questions or more information
contact us at
info@thewildrosepress.com.

The Wild Rose Press, Inc.
www.thewildrosepress.com